MW00561227

COMPASS

TO

VINLAND

Happy Reading!

Dani Resh

DANI RESH

This is a work of fiction. Names, characters, businesses, places, events, locales, and incidents are either the products of the author's imagination or used in a fictitious manner.

Copyright © 2021 by Dani Resh

All rights reserved. This book may not be reproduced or stored in whole or in part by any means without the written permission of the author except for brief quotations for the purpose of review.

ISBN: 978-1-954614-50-5 hard cover
      978-1-954614-51-2 soft cover
Resh. Dani.
Compass to Vinland.

Edited by: Melissa Long and Monika Dziamka

Published by Warren Publishing
Charlotte, NC
www.warrenpublishing.net
Printed in the United States

To my parents, love you guys forever and always!

CHAPTER 1
MORNING OF THE MIST

I woke up crabby as ever. I hated getting up, especially on mornings when it was still dark. As far as I was concerned, no one should get up before the sun. The darkness and the cold were irritating. My grandfather might have built an incredible house, but I was pretty sure he didn't know a thing about heating and cooling because it was always crazy cold in the winter and unbearably hot in the summer. Luckily, it was spring, so it was reassuring to know that the cold wouldn't last too much longer. But then again, I lived in Pennsylvania, and winter here had a way of holding on for as long as possible.

I pulled back the covers, and the cold air immediately hit me. I regretfully let my feet touch the arctic wood planks—I would have preferred to stay in the warmth and comfort of my bed—and quickly scurried over to my dresser. I yanked open the top drawer, which was a challenge because all the drawers tended to get stuck due to age and peeling paint. I pulled out the warmest hoodie I had and a pair of jeans that were way too short for me. I used to be embarrassed that most of my clothes were too small. I would beg my father to take me to the store to buy new ones, but he would simply nod and leave the room. I was never sure if he actually heard me. I tried to reassure myself that he was just forgetful, but as the years went on, I began to realize it wasn't just the clothes. He didn't seem to hear anything I said.

After I changed, I headed across the hall to the bathroom, brushed my teeth, and caught a glimpse of myself in the mirror. As usual, my hair was a mess. It always was. I had this thick, blond hair that grew like crazy. I tried to keep up with it and cut it myself, but it was a losing battle. And it wasn't just my hair; everything seemed to grow like crazy on me—my fingernails, my height. Maybe if I had a cool rock vibe, I could pull off my shaggy hair and grungy clothes, but my awkwardly tall, skinny physique wasn't doing me any favors. It wasn't like I was a freakish giant, but I was at least a head taller than everyone else in my class. Unfortunately, this gave me a bird's-eye view of all the crap that went on every day in the hallways of my school. Most days, I would keep my hoodie up and direct my gaze straight ahead, rarely looking at the harsh realities of middle school.

I grabbed a comb and tried to make my hair look as normal as possible. I failed. You could say there was just no rhyme or reason to it. A professional haircut would help, but somehow, I never seemed to find the time to get one, even though I never had any legit plans. I then headed back to my room to gather my stuff for school.

I threw my books and folders into my weathered backpack. Like everything else, I'd had this same backpack for forever. Lucky for me, it was just black. If my dad had bought the one with superheroes that I wanted when I was in elementary school, I probably would still be expected to carry that thing around. Fortunately, my dad had been extra cheap that day and bought me a plain black one that was on sale.

I slung my backpack onto my shoulder, left my room, and entered the dark, windowless hallway. I turned on the light switch, and a line of antique chandeliers that hung from the ceiling flickered and then eventually illuminated the space with a dull, amber glow. I was careful not to hit any of the tribal masks or shelves randomly hung throughout the tight space. Getting through the hallways of my house was a bit like getting through an obstacle course. There seemed to be little consideration for the fact that people would actually need to use them to get from room to room. Instead, the walls resembled an ancient artifact wing of a very cluttered, disorganized museum. At the end of the hall was a stairway that led to the roof. I climbed the squeaky stairs and reached the door that opened to the outside world.

The crisp morning air and dense fog greeted me. The rising sun was trying to break through, but the thick air prevented the rays from reaching their full potential. It was like a thick cloud had descended and engulfed my shoe house.

No joke. My house literally looked like a shoe.

More specifically, it looked like an old, worn-out work boot with peeling leather and shoelaces that were frayed at the ends. People used to say it reminded them of some old nursery rhyme about an old lady that lived in a shoe with a bazillion kids. At least, that's what I think it was about. I mean, really, who reads nursery rhymes anymore? But I have to admit, my house *did* look like something out of a fairy tale. I think that's why I dug the house so much.

When I was younger, I used to imagine that my house belonged to a giant. I know it sounds stupid, but let's be honest—little kids have crazy ideas about things. I just figured that a giant left his boot on my lawn, and my grandfather transformed it into our house. Of course, the older I got, the more I came to realize that there were no such things as giants, and the unique design of my house was simply the product of my grandfather's imagination. As far as I was concerned, no other house could rival it. There were winding staircases that led to oddly shaped rooms and floors that slanted every which way. My grandfather used colored glass bottles to fill the window openings, and when the sun hit the glass exactly right, brilliant cascades of color projected on the interior walls. It always made me feel as though I was living inside a kaleidoscope.

Even though I'd spent my entire life here, I was always discovering new, hidden rooms and crevices with odd objects in them. I had no idea what any of these things were. Most of them were strange instruments that I couldn't make heads or tails of—books written in languages with unrecognizable alphabets, tiny sculptures of some really bizarre-looking creatures. One of the weirdest things I found were three small jars with rocks in them. These rocks didn't look like they were anything special during the day, but at night, they glowed. Each a different color—red, green, and purple. In retrospect, I was a real idiot for not realizing how strange it was that these rocks could light up on their own. Then again, maybe it hadn't fazed me because I grew up with all this weird stuff, so in a way, it seemed normal.

Dark, racing objects began to emerge from the mist—a murder of crows, impatiently waiting for me to open the door to the roof of the shoe house. They began to fly in circles around the rooftop, dipping in and out of view as the fog concealed their presence.

When I had discovered the rooftop years ago, there were a handful of bird houses and feeders up there. I thought they were so cool and decided to make one myself. Well, that one led to another and another until, suddenly, I was running out of places to put them. None of the bird houses looked the same. Many were nailed together with various materials; some were painted; some were made of clay with stones that had been pushed into them before they'd hardened; some had pieces of tin for roofs or old car parts that I would find when I walked through the woods that surrounded my house. But my favorite birdhouse on the rooftop was the plainest one that looked like a simple cabin.

The reason I liked it so much was that my mother's name, Abigail, was etched into the wood on the bottom surface. She must have made it when she was young, way younger than I am now, because the handwriting looked primitive. I ran my finger across the letters like I did every morning when I came up here. My mother has been in a coma since I was four, so my memories of her are muddled. My dad and I used to go and visit her all the time, but eventually, he stopped wanting to go. Instead, Mr. Fitzgerald, my neighbor who lived across the street, started taking me to go see her. So even though it probably makes no sense, there was something about this bird feeder that made me feel connected to her. It was confirmation that she was once here, in this place, with this birdhouse. Moving, talking, creating.

I dumped my backpack on the roof floor and walked over to the bag of bird feed and poured seed into all the bird feeders. The crows pushed each other out of the way as they took their places around the railing that lined the edge of the rooftop, squawking angrily with puffed-out chests. They were glaring at me, waiting for me to acknowledge their gifts. Every morning, the crows would place an offering for me on the railing: pieces of fabric, bottle caps, beads, buttons, and even pieces of jewelry. If I didn't gather up their offerings quickly, they would get irritated at me and eventually try to place these objects in my hands or pockets. And let me tell you, it's a bit unnerving to have large-winged, black birds with claws and sharp beaks swooping down at you, even if they are just trying to show you gratitude. I gathered the random items—a broken watch face, a crumpled-up receipt, and a strange charm that looked like a foot—and shoved them in my pocket. I would put the gifts with the growing mound of offerings that were taking over my desk in my room later.

I grabbed my backpack and walked to the door and left the rooftop. I made my way down hallways and two more sets of winding stairs until I reached the ground floor. I navigated around the multiple pieces of mismatched furniture that were scattered throughout the family room and headed toward the back of the shoe house. There, protruding out of the back heel, was the greenhouse. It wasn't the prettiest space; it was slightly run-down, and many of the glass panes had cracks that were spreading outward like a jagged spider web. But the rich, green plants that dwelled there were full of life. They overshadowed the slanting ceiling and the tired-looking beams that struggled to keep the roof up. I walked over to an old, cast-iron sink that hung off the interior wall. Its lopsided position reminded me that I should tighten the screws before the sink came crashing to the ground and took out a chunk of the floor. I turned the handle of the sink several times before the water finally flowed out of the faucet, and I caught it in an ancient watering can I kept nearby. One by one, I watered my various specimens according to their specific needs.

The greenhouse was my special place. In here, I didn't think about how annoying school was or how my dad barely spoke to me. In here, the plants transported me to a thriving place, a place where I was successful, a place where I mattered. For some reason, I was really good at growing plants. I guess I was born with a green thumb or something because it's not like my dad ever showed me anything. My only education in horticulture came from a couple of books my neighbor, Mr. Fitzgerald, checked out of the library for me. I guess I could've checked them out myself, but I never felt the need. It was like I instinctively knew how to grow things and keep them alive. Mr. Fitzgerald took an interest in my gardening skills and was always stopping by to see the progress. It's not like he had much else to do since he was retired, and his wife had passed away a while ago. I didn't mind his visits; I just figured he was lonely and bored, and the plants made him happy, which made sense to me. I always felt better in the greenhouse too.

The plants grew and grew till the branches and leaves were pushing against the windowpanes, yearning to spread even farther than their glass boundaries. Once, I grew a pumpkin that was so big, I couldn't get it out the door. I had to cut it up, which was disappointing because it would've made a killer jack-o'-lantern.

After I left the greenhouse, I headed toward the kitchen, my least favorite room in the house. This room had been the setting for many uncomfortable interactions with my dad. I would walk in and was lucky if I'd get a grunt of acknowledgment. He was always hunched over his computer at the kitchen table, working on some elaborate plan to get himself out of Lewisberry. Of course, he never consulted with me about the plan or asked what I thought about moving. If he would've asked, I would've told him I couldn't imagine living anywhere other than the shoe house or being far away from my mother.

My dad had been trying to get out of town for as long as I can remember. He hated it here, and he hated the shoe house even more. I guess his parents and brothers disowned him when he married my mom, who was, in their opinion, the wild-haired woman who lived in the strange house that looked like a shoe, of all things. I always thought that sounded melodramatic and super outdated. It was like something you read about in some old book with ladies in corsets and men with top hats, but that's what happened.

My grandparents are a big deal in this town. They have the nicest house and, I guess you could say, the most money. I suppose they wouldn't be such a big deal somewhere else, but in this small town, if you got invited to the Larkin Estate for the Christmas Potluck, you were someone special. That is, unless you were my dad, Ben Larkin. Everyone thought my dad was the idiot for leaving his upstanding family for the crazies who lived in the shoe house, and I was a result of that bad decision. I even had a cousin in my grade, Emmett Larkin, whom everyone followed around like he was a god or something. I couldn't stand the guy—stupid superstar athlete with the perfect clothes, perfect hair, and gigantic ego. Emmett went out of his way to make sure that no one was too nice to me at school, like blocking me from sitting at a certain lunch table or making sure I didn't have a partner for group projects. I guess you could say there was no way I was going to be invited to any pool parties or Friday-night tailgates. That was fine by me. Hanging out with Emmett and his friends sounded like torture anyway. I wasn't interested in trying to win over the elites of the school with the slim hope of someday being accepted, especially since they could decide at any moment that I was no longer worthy. I saw one too many girls crying in the hallway after some popular kid decided they no longer made the cut. No thanks. I'd rather fly solo.

Anyway, that was why my dad had been obsessed with ditching this town for as long as I could remember. So far, none of his plans worked out, which made him even more upset and distant. Every time he got a rejection letter from a potential employer, he would barely say anything for days. During those times, I just fended for myself—found things to eat and even left him a couple of sandwiches outside his bedroom door. But today, when I walked into the kitchen, he looked excited about something. His face was all lit up, and I felt his eyes on me as I pulled a cereal box out of the cupboard.

"This is the one, Wren." Even his voice sounded different; it sounded hopeful. "I think I finally found our ticket out of here. They must have liked me in the phone interview because they want to interview me in person."

"Where's this one at?"

"It's outside of Pittsburgh," he said as he leaned back in his chair.

"Pittsburgh ... huh," I said as I poured the cereal into a bowl. "That's pretty far away."

"Not really. Only about three hours." He crossed his arms in front of his chest.

"What about Mom?" I asked without looking back at him.

I kept my focus on the opened cabinet door in front of me. The paint was peeling, and I could see the cedar wood grain beneath the peeling layer of pale blue paint.

He was quiet for a while. "She's not going to wake up, Wren. She would want us to move on with our lives."

I put the cereal back in the cabinet and slammed it shut. I wasn't hungry anymore. I wanted to scream at him. How could he say that? How could he give up on her? There was no way I was ever giving up on her. One day, she would open her eyes. Even if he didn't believe it, I did.

"I'm not saying this to hurt you," he said. "At some point, we need to face reality."

All I wanted to do was get out of that room. I wanted to get as far away from him as possible.

"Where are you going?" He seemed surprised by my reaction, which pissed me off even more.

How did he expect me to react? Did he really think for a second that I would be all geeked-up about leaving my home for some stupid job in Pittsburgh or being three hours away from my mother? More confirmation that he didn't have a clue about what mattered to me ... even worse, he didn't care.

I left without answering his question and headed for the door.

CHAPTER 2
GHOST HILL

Once outside, I was again engulfed in dense fog. The sun was high in the sky now, but it honestly didn't seem to make any difference. The fog was still so thick that you could barely see in front of you. Black, crooked branches poked out of the white mist and reached up toward the gray sky.

I got my bike out of the shed. I could take the bus in the mornings, but I preferred to ride my bike to school. I liked the freedom of leaving when I wanted and not having to deal with all the politics of school first thing in the morning. Anything to reduce the misery of school for as long as possible. Only when the roads were covered with snow and ice did I consider sitting in the back of the smelly bus.

I walked my bike down the uneven cobblestone driveway that led to the road. It was bumpy and full of spots where the tires could easily get lodged into the crevices. I learned the hard way that it was better to not start riding until I reached the smooth pavement. Once I was on the street, I realized it may not have been the smartest idea to ride to school that day. I could barely see the road ahead, which meant that people driving on the road would barely be able to see me.

"Hey there, Wren!"

I turned and saw Mr. Fitzgerald at his mailbox, putting some letters inside the metal container. Oh boy, could this man talk. He was always asking me about the books he checked out for me, about my greenhouse, about school, and if I needed anything.

"Hey," I said as I waved back at him. Seeing him brought to mind that I hadn't seen my mom in a while. "Hey, Mr. Fitzgerald, can we go see my mom this weekend?"

"Of course!" He moved the flag on the mailbox into an upward position. "How's Saturday morning sound?"

"That works," I answered him. "I just feel like I need to see her."

"Of course you do." He nodded at me as if he understood. Why did my neighbor understand me better than my own father? That seemed pretty messed up to me. "You sure you should be biking in this fog? Pretty thick. Someone might hit you."

I knew he had a point. I couldn't see crap. But I had already missed the bus, and I really didn't want to go back to my house and ask my dad for a ride. He was the last person I wanted to see right now.

"I'll be careful." I gave Mr. Fitzgerald a reassuring smile. "Got to go. Gonna be late."

I started to pedal up the road, but I could feel his concerned eyes on my back.

"Be careful, Wren!" his voice called from behind me. I lifted my hand in the air to acknowledge his concern and let the mist consume me.

It felt like I had entered a different world, one where you didn't know what was around the corner. After a little way, I reached the intersection of Pleasant View Road and Wyndamere, the notorious Gravity Hill, though some called it Ghost Hill. There were many stories about this place—some included ghost children who would push your car out of the way of danger. Others were about how it was the site of a Native American burial ground. Some people believed the place was now inhabited by dead Civil War soldiers who couldn't leave their post. I had no idea if any of the stories were true, but what I did know was that if a ball was placed at a specific spot at the bottom of the hill, it would roll up toward the top of the hill. Even more shocking, if you were to pour water on the ground in the same spot, it would defy gravity and flow upward instead of moving to the lowest point. People would come from all over to place their car in neutral at the bottom of the hill, and it would somehow roll upward. They would freak out and make YouTube videos. Local news crews had come and questioned the locals at one point. Some people got annoyed with the attention, but others thought we should market the hill to bring in more tourists. I didn't know if that was a good idea or not; I just thought this spot was cool. I liked that it made no sense in the real world because, as far as I was concerned, I didn't make much sense in the real world, either.

The hill already had an eerie quality about it, but the fog made it look downright spooky. That's why I almost fell off my bike when I saw a woman materialize out of the mist. As I peered down the hill toward her, I realized she looked familiar, too familiar. She looked like my Aunt Bryn ... who was supposed to be dead. I stood there for a second, holding my breath. Was I actually seeing a ghost on Ghost Hill? The woman put her hand up like she was waving at me. But then suddenly, it looked like someone grabbed her from behind and pulled her back into the mist.

I didn't move for a couple of seconds. I didn't know what to think. My dad had told me that she died in a car accident several years ago, so there was no way it could've been her. I got off my bike and started to walk it to the bottom of the hill. I stopped at the spot where the woman had been standing and slowly put my kickstand down. It made a squeaking sound, which stressed me out for some reason. My instincts were telling me to get back on my bike and get the heck out of there. But I couldn't help myself. I needed to see if there was really a woman in the woods. And as crazy as it sounded, I needed to see if it was my aunt.

I told myself repeatedly that there was no such thing as ghosts as I entered the woods. The fog wasn't helping to calm my nerves—it just made everything creepier—but I continued forward and tried to make as little noise as possible as I walked through the dried leaves and twigs. I scanned the woods that surrounded me, looking for movement. Nothing. I walked a bit farther and then stopped.

There was a sizzling sound like something was on a hot grill, but that didn't make any sense. I was in the middle of the woods, not in a park on a Saturday afternoon.

I trekked farther into the woods, pushing aside branches and stepping over fallen logs, but then I saw something I wasn't expecting. Before me was a small circle of earth that looked like it had been burned by something; it was charred and gray. The trees, vines, and grass within the circle were now blackened, fragile versions of what they once had been. I kneeled down and touched the dead grass, and it collapsed into ashes between my fingers. I brought my fingers up to my nose to see if it smelled like fire, but it didn't smell like anything.

I sat there for a while, trying to figure out what it all meant, but I couldn't come up with anything. I decided to head back to the road, but the dense fog was disorienting and left me with no sense of direction. I felt like I was in a fun house, but instead of being surrounded by mirrors, I was engulfed in a thick, murky mist. I wandered aimlessly, trying to get my bearings. Nothing looked familiar. In fact, with each step, the forest became more ominous, more threatening. I slowly rotated my body in a circle, hoping to catch a glimpse of the road through the thick foliage and mist. All I could see were trees that seemed to go on for an eternity.

How could I have gotten so lost? I spent countless hours in the woods around my house and never felt nervous or unsure of my surroundings. Why did it feel so different today? Something moved to my right. Without even thinking, I crouched down, taking cover behind a bush. I felt like an idiot once I realized it was just a deer who appeared to be even more startled than I was. I could hear its hooves hit the dried leaves as it gracefully darted off. Once it was gone, I unclenched my fists and took a couple of deep breaths to calm my nerves.

"Get a grip," I told myself, and I looked up into the sky and saw the position of the early-morning sun. I forced myself to focus and analyzed which direction the road should be in relation to the sun. Not sure if it was my stellar outdoor skills or pure luck, but I somehow made it back to the road. A rush of relief washed over me once my feet hit the pavement.

I could see my bike down the hill, parked on the side of the road. I ran toward it and saw my backpack on the ground next to it. I grabbed it and looked at the old watch I had attached to one of the straps. Even though it felt like I had only been lost in the woods for a couple of minutes, I had blown a good chunk of time in there. If I didn't hurry, I was going to be seriously late for school. I hoisted the backpack onto my shoulders and hopped on my bike. Once I pushed the kickstand back, I began to coast down the remainder of the hill. I turned the corner at the intersection and headed toward school, making sure I stayed close to the side of the road so I didn't get nailed by a car. I no longer thought the fog was cool. Now it was just annoying. I wanted the world to feel normal again. Clear.

As I rode, I couldn't stop thinking about my Aunt Bryn, my mother's only sibling. If I had to use one word to describe her, it would be "eccentric." Even if she was headed to the grocery store, she always looked like she was on her way to the Renaissance Festival. Her hair was crazy long and usually braided in some elaborate design, adorned with bits of ribbon or beads. Most days, she would have on a long, thick, wool jacket with brass buttons. It looked more like something a pirate would own than a woman in her midthirties living in the middle of Pennsylvania. I figured she must have found it in some old resale shop; it definitely looked old enough to be vintage. And she *loved* jewelry. I have never seen anyone wear so many rings or necklaces in my life. She used to come over all the time when I was little and tell me all these crazy stories. But she never acted like they were just stories; she acted like the stuff she told me was true.

She was hellbent on the idea that our family came from a place called Vinland. And let me tell you, this place sounded amazing, full of mythical creatures and magic. She even had a name for the people who came from there: Vins. When I asked why we were in the middle of Pennsylvania then, she said that many Vins were banished from Vinland, and once that happened, you could never find your way back. These people were stuck living with regular people, who were called Nullvins. One day, I asked her why we were banished, but I could never get a clear answer out of her. She would just say something about "true love," which made no sense to me. I don't believe in that crap. It's not like any of those Disney movies have an ounce of truth to them.

Of course, I totally got why she wanted this stuff to be real. Heck, I did too. A far-off land full of magic and outlandish creatures sure sounded a whole lot better than my daily existence. But as the years went on, there was no way I could go on believing this stuff. It didn't help that my dad made sure to crush any hope I had about it possibly being true. He would constantly tell me that my aunt was completely insane, always had been and always would be. Eventually, he came to the conclusion that just having her around wasn't good for me. When I was about eleven and he stopped letting her visit, well, let's just say the fights between my dad and my aunt got nasty. But my aunt wasn't going to let him stop her. She started to show up around town, at the bakery or the post office or right outside my school. It was easier that way. It kept my dad from getting all riled up.

Sure, she was a bit unhinged, but she was entertaining. And best of all, she would tell me all about my mom and my maternal grandparents. I loved listening to those old stories. I never really understood why my dad and I lived in the shoe house and she didn't. Technically, it seemed like it should've been her house. My mother was the oldest sibling, so you could say it was right that my dad and I lived there, especially since my mother was still technically living. But in my mind, my aunt was a legit Needlecoff—my mother's maiden name—and it just seemed like a Needlecoff should be living in the shoe house. Honestly, if anyone should've been called an intruder, it was my dad. I asked her about that once, and she told me we would one day all live there together again when my mom got better. Her, my mom, and me. She always left my dad out, which wasn't surprising. I would ask how my mom was going to get better, and she would always tell me I would heal her one day. Of course, that made no sense. It wasn't like I had a desire to become a doctor in order to save my mom. I just figured adults liked to tell kids crap like that to make them feel better. Or my dad was right and she really was crazy.

Then one day, I realized I hadn't seen her in a while. She wasn't randomly showing up around town in order to visit with me. I started to count the days until her next appearance. Days turned into weeks, and weeks turned into months. I was starting to get nervous that something had happened to her, so I eventually got up the nerve to ask my dad if he had heard from her.

He tilted his head a bit and squinted his eyes as me as if what I was asking him was strange. "Why?"

"Haven't seen her in a while." I tried to sound casual.

Then he told me to sit down and explained that Aunt Bryn had passed away in a car accident. I was messed up about it for a while. I felt like I was in a daze for weeks. I couldn't sleep, eat, or concentrate in school. Some teacher must have noticed something because I was called down to the counselor's office and was gently grilled about my well-being. After that, I got much better at faking my way through the day and hiding my feelings. A practice that, in retrospect, I don't recommend. But that was how I dealt with the murky death of my aunt. She was strange and quirky and didn't make a whole lot of sense most of the time, but I never questioned that she cared for me. She was family. At least, she was the only family member who felt *right*.

That was why the thought of seeing her on Ghost Hill bummed me out. I was so out of sorts after seeing her, I almost ran into a car pulling out of a driveway. And of course, it had to be my grandparents' house. That was just what I needed. Another reminder of how screwed up my life was. They were so snobby, they actually had a sign outside that said "The Larkin Estate," as if it were some important, historic landmark. It was pretty, I'll give them that—an old Victorian painted a pale mint green with a large wraparound porch. The estate was surrounded by a tall gate, and if you peered through the iron bars, you could see that the house was surrounded by carefully sculpted gardens. Not a branch or flower was out of place. But the gate was open now, and my grandfather was glaring at me because I had almost hit his car with my bike.

Once he realized it was me, his grandson, he looked away and waited for me to pass. My face burned with anger, and I thought that even though my aunt was most likely crazy, I'd take her any day over this elitist jerk. My dad and his family were horrible at ... well ... being a family.

As I sped past my sorry excuse for a grandfather, I checked the time again. I was going to be late, and my first-hour teacher was going to make a huge deal about it. Her name was something like Eloise Millie, but instead of calling her Mrs. Millie, all the kids called her Mad Millie. She had to be the worst teacher on the planet, always yelling and ridiculing her students. Even the kiss ups got yelled at in her classes. I had never met anyone as miserable as her. It seemed like nothing could make her happy. Even if she had won the lottery, I think she would still have a sour look on her face while she was holding up that huge check. She was the kind of person you didn't want to have on your bad side. And today, I was most definitely going to be on her bad side.

CHAPTER 3
MARIA TOVAR

I raced up the street toward the school, and to my dismay, I saw a trail of buses traveling in the opposite direction. Not good. I navigated my way through the empty parking lot and rode up to the bike rack, grabbed my lock from the exterior pocket of my backpack, and secured it to the metal bar. I headed to the front door and pulled it open—thank god it wasn't already locked—and ran down the hallway. After deciding there wasn't enough time to go to my locker, I turned and headed toward the stairs.

I jogged down the hallway until I reached Mad Millie's door. I reached out for the handle but hesitated. I knew it was going to be bad, but there was no avoiding it; it had to be done. I pushed the door in and entered the room. Everyone inside turned toward me. I was never one to crave attention, so I looked down and tried to pretend I was invisible. As I walked across the front of the room, I heard Mad Millie clear her throat and braced myself for her attack.

"Wren." Her high-pitched voice pierced my ear.

I stopped moving and slowly looked up. There she was, perched in front of her desk, her gray hair pulled back into a painfully tight bun. Her skeletal hand was extended toward me.

"Where is your pass?"

I shrugged my shoulders, even though it was hard to do with my heavy backpack. "I don't have one." I tried to speak as pleasantly as possible.

"Really?" A wicked smile spread across her face.

This teacher loved to get kids in trouble. Honestly, the woman needed a life if this was what brought her joy. She pushed herself off the front of her desk and briskly walked around to the back of it.

"Let me just make a note of your tardiness. Nothing disrupts the learning process more than rude interruption."

She opened her attendance book and started to write something down for what seemed like a long time. All she had to do was write the word "tardy" or even just the letter T next to my name, so I couldn't figure out what the heck she could possibly be writing.

Whatever. No point in standing at the front of the room. I began to walk toward my desk at the back of the room. I sat in the last seat in the last row. There was no one in front of me and no one next to me. That's how I liked it. A girl sat kitty-corner from me, but she very rarely turned my way. I yanked my backpack off my shoulder and tossed it on the ground and then slid into my desk. It was the old kind. The wooden top opened, and there was a space inside to keep your things in like back in elementary school. The wooden seat creaked so loud when I sat in it, I was always afraid it would fall apart under my weight, and I would be left sitting on the floor surrounded by desk parts.

Everything in the room was outdated. Mad Millie fought any new update the school tried to give her. She claimed she should have absolute control over her learning environment and had been teaching just fine for the past forty years without "all these new contraptions." In fact, that was one of her favorite topics, how technology was ruining everything, especially the younger generation. The school installed a smart board anyway, but she demanded they leave her a small portion of her precious chalkboard. They did, and that meant everything she wrote was on the tiny chalkboard since she refused to use the smart board. It was super annoying because she was always running out of room and would erase everything before we had a chance to copy it down.

As I started to take off my jacket, I heard Mad Millie say my name again and froze.

"What was the reason for your tardiness, Wren?"

Mad Millie was back in front of her desk. Her arms were crossed in front of her bony body, and she was glaring at me. I should've known she wasn't going to let me off that easily.

I wanted to say, "None of your business," or "What does it matter?" but I didn't. That was something Rusty Whitaker, our resident bad boy, would say before he got sent to the office. I glanced over to see if he was still sitting on the other side of the room, and surprisingly, he was. It had gotten to the point where he usually didn't make it past the first fifteen minutes of class. Mad Millie had it out for him, and everybody knew it. But Rusty never backed down; he always fought back. Part of me thought he was crazy for doing it, and part of me envied him. He was the exact opposite of me in every way. Shorter, stocky, dark hair, and tan all year round. He always wore this old, black leather jacket, even when it was way too hot for it.

Rusty caught me looking and grinned in my direction. There it was, the look that all the girls went crazy over. Even Kristy Phillips, the most popular girl in school, seemed to be enamored by him. She was always flirting with him, which really drove my cousin Emmett crazy. Emmett's had a thing for Kristy for as long as I could remember. I didn't know why he let it get under his skin. Kristy would never actually date Rusty. He was considered bad news in Lewisberry, and Kristy's parents would probably freak out if they saw how she acted around him.

I had no idea if he was as bad as people said since I never actually saw him do anything that bad. Sure, he was completely disrespectful to basically every adult he came into contact with, but I once saw him stick up for Matthew Callaghan. Emmett and his jerk friends were picking on Matthew for no reason, and Rusty just stepped in and told them to knock it off. I decided then and there that Rusty couldn't be as bad as everyone made him out to be. Especially since he often told Mad Millie everything I thought in my head but never had the guts to say out loud.

But that morning, he wasn't getting into trouble. I was.

"Wren, I'm waiting."

My attention went back to Mad Millie. She was staring at me, waiting for me to reply. My mind quickly ran through excuses. It's not like I could say, "Oh sorry, it's just that I thought I saw my dead aunt on Ghost Hill, and when I followed her into the woods, I saw a mysterious circle burned to a crisp for no apparent reason." I mean, maybe I could say that, but I wasn't going to.

"Overslept." There, that was simple enough. That would work.

"Are you telling me that school isn't a priority to you?"

Oh geez. She wasn't going to miss the opportunity to make a scene. But lucky for me, I didn't have to answer because just then, the principal, Mr. Schmidt, came in, followed by a girl I had never seen before. Unlike every other girl in school who dressed exactly the same, this chick was wearing some baggy overalls, clunky boots, and about a billion bracelets. But it was her hair that caught my attention. It was like an explosion. Endless curly shades of chestnut were pulled together in a messy knot on top of her head, but quite a few chunks of it couldn't be contained and had fallen to her shoulders.

She stood patiently by Mr. Schmidt as he introduced her to the classroom.

"Students, this is Maria Tovar. She's from Arizona. I expect you all to welcome her."

When the principal put his hand on her shoulder, she glanced at his hand and moved slightly to the side, making his hand fall away from her shoulder.

"It's Maria," she corrected. She rolled the letter *r*, making her name sound much more exotic.

"All right then." Mr. Schmidt laughed a little as if he were amused by her, and then he tried to say her name like she did but failed miserably.

Mad Millie, however, did not look amused. In her mind, children should never correct adults. In retrospect, Maria had sealed her fate with Mad Millie right there and then.

"Well, I'll leave you to it," Mr. Schmidt said and began to exit the room.

He turned back and looked briefly at Maria with Mad Millie hovering over her. If I had to guess, he was probably rethinking putting her in such a miserable classroom first hour. I mean, starting a new school is tough, but starting with Mad Millie is downright brutal. But he ended up just turning back around and leaving the room, which I thought was lame. If he were a good principal, he would've said there had been a mistake and whisked her out of there and given her someone else for first hour. But he wasn't, and he didn't. More confirmation that adults were generally disappointing.

"Once we get started, you'll have to let me know if we are too far ahead," Mad Millie said, glaring at Maria as if she were from another planet, one she never wanted to visit. "Where did he say you came from? Mexico?"

"Arizona. Not Mexico." Maria answered her without hesitation, gathering a chunk of her hair and placing it behind one ear, which seemed pretty pointless because it didn't stay behind her ear for very long. "And actually, my school was rather advanced, so I'll let you know if you're moving too slow. Now, where should I sit?"

And just like that, Maria Tovar put Mad Millie in her place. Sure, Rusty had always put up a fight, but this girl rendered Mad Millie speechless. That was something I had never seen before. She just wordlessly extended her arm in my direction and pointed to the chair in front of me.

I watched as Maria started to head down my aisle. She was looking at the floor as she made her way toward me, but she looked up as she got closer, and then the strangest thing happened. She *smiled* at me. And I don't mean a smirk or a nod; I'm talking the real deal. It caught me completely off guard. I even looked over my shoulder to make sure no one was there, even though I knew the answer. Then she did something even weirder as she approached her desk.

She leaned in toward me and whispered, "Thank god you're here."

What? Why would she say that? We didn't know each other.

She slid into the seat in front of me, and I stared at her bouncy strands of hair. I couldn't concentrate for the rest of the class. I sat there and tried to figure out why she had acted like she knew me. I racked my brain, trying to remember ever meeting a girl with dark eyes and wild hair, but I couldn't. Honestly, there was no way I would've forgotten her if I had met her. She was pretty unforgettable.

Mad Millie lectured us on something having to do with linear functions, but I honestly couldn't tell you a thing about it. Rusty must have said something to make her angry because I saw him leave the room, but I had no idea what he'd said. All I knew was that the bell rang way quicker than I expected it to. I sat perfectly still, waiting to see if Maria would turn around.

She gathered her things, stood up, and glanced my way. "See ya."

"Yeah," I answered, trying to sound cool. "I'll see you."

I felt stupid after I said it. I should've come up with something better than that.

I looked for her for the rest of the day. I even went into the bathroom and ran my fingers through my hair and tried to stretch out my hoodie sleeves so they would look longer and not end halfway up my arms. I paid more attention in the hallways than usual and waited anxiously in the next couple of classes, hoping she would walk into the room. But she didn't. At the end of the day, I was unlocking my bike from the rack when I felt someone tap my shoulder. I turned around, and she was right behind me.

"There you are," she said, smiling like we had been friends forever.

"Here I am." Again, not my most clever response.

"Where were you all day?" she asked.

I didn't know how to answer that. It's not like I was hiding from her. "Guess we don't have any other classes together."

"That sucks. Everyone here is really weird." Her gaze drifted to all the people scurrying to their buses or getting picked up.

"Really?" I asked her with raised eyebrows. Weird? As far as I was concerned, everyone in Lewisberry was about as average as could be. There was nothing weird about any of them. Honestly, I wished they were a bit weirder so I could fit in.

"Definitely. I was so relieved to see you this morning." She smiled at me. "At least you go here."

"Do we know each other?" I finally worked up my courage to ask her.

"Well ... not really." She looked down quickly. "It's just ... my grandmother told me about you. She said we would have a lot in common."

"Who's your grandmother?" I asked.

"Camilla Tovar," she answered.

"Mrs. Tovar? From the bakery?"

"Yep."

"Right. Same last name," I said. "Guess I should've put that together."

"I've come to live with her for a while," she explained. "Wasn't too happy about it. And I really didn't want to come to this weird school, but she told me it wasn't all bad. She said you'd be here and you were pretty cool."

Well, that's very flattering, I thought. I liked Mrs. Tovar. She was always waving me into the bakery and giving me free samples.

"Yeah, your grandmother's all right."

Her grandmother had this cool Spanish accent and always had on something that looked like it came from a faraway land—a scarf, a piece of jewelry, or a shawl. Now that I knew they were related, I could definitely see that they came from the same family. Maria's clothes had the same flair as her grandmother's, and there was something similar with their facial proportions.

"But how did you know what I look like?"

She paused for a second and looked down at the ground, then her head sprang up again. "She had a picture."

"Really?" I thought that was odd. Why would she have a picture of me?

"So I'll see you tomorrow. Better find my grandmother."

She repositioned her bag on her shoulder and turned briskly. Her unkempt hair bounced up and down as her feet hit the pavement.

I watched her get into a car and was struck by how odd the day had been. My life had always been predictable, but there was nothing about that day that I saw coming. Little did I know that this was just the beginning.

CHAPTER 4

A CURIOUS CONFRONTATION

I woke up early the next morning with a troubled mind. I couldn't stop thinking about seeing my aunt. Of course, I knew it wasn't *really* my aunt, but the whole thing made me realize how much I wished she were still alive. Thinking about her made me miss my mom all over again too.

As I passed my dad's room, I remembered that my mother's old chest was in there. My dad made it clear that his room was off-limits, which pissed me off. I hated it when adults gave kids such stupid rules. But that morning, seeing his door slightly ajar made me want to go in there and look through the chest. My dad had already left for the job interview in Pittsburgh, so it was the perfect time. I slowly nudged the door open with my foot and flipped the light switch. It had been a long time since I had been in his room. Where the rest of the house was buried under patterns and designs, my dad's room had no personality. It was simple, with plain, drab walls. His bed was neatly made, and next to it was a dresser and nightstand. Everything was put away. There were no books, no pictures, no nothing.

In the corner of the room, I could see something large was covered by a sheet. It was my mom's chest. My dad had covered it with a sheet, as if a thin piece of cloth would somehow keep all the pain away. I walked over to the chest and pulled the fabric off. A cloud of dust filled the air and made me cough. Once the dust settled, I was reminded of how beautiful the chest was. It was carved with vines and foliage, and every so often, a jewel or crystal could be found embedded into the design. Just like my favorite bird feeder on the roof, the name "Abigail" had been carved into the top of the chest.

I kneeled down to unlatch it, but what I found instead was a big, metal lock. Weird. I didn't remember there being a lock on it. I tugged at it a bit to see if it was really locked. It didn't budge. Why would my dad lock up the chest like that? I sat back on my heels and looked around the room. There had to be a key somewhere. Where would my dad put it? I walked over to his nightstand. Feeling determined to find that key, I went through the drawers, which wasn't hard to do because my dad was crazy organized. I could see there was no key inside, but I still took everything out and made sure to put everything back exactly where I found it. Same with the dresser—nothing but perfectly folded sweaters and T-shirts and a flashlight in the top drawer. No key.

Next was the closet. It was pretty dark in there, so I took the flashlight out of the dresser and searched the entire thing. The floor, the top shelves—I even went through the pockets of the clothing that was hanging in the closet. I looked for hidden drawers or secret compartments, but I found nothing. I did, however, find a small, wooden box that was under a pair of dress shoes. I pulled it out, hopeful that the key would be inside. I sat on the floor and opened it. Inside was a pile of old photographs.

The first one was a picture of a boy about ten or eleven on a horse. I turned the picture over; someone had written the words, "Ben Larkin with Blaze, 1994." I turned the picture back over again and gazed at it. Now that I knew it was him, I could definitely tell it was my dad. Even as a young boy, he had a long face and concerned eyes. The next one was a family portrait. It looked like one of those stupid photographs where everyone puts on their best clothes and pretends like they're the perfect family. It was the kind of picture rich people would blow up and hang in their houses. A younger version of my grandfather stood behind my seated grandmother, and there was my dad, standing next to his two brothers. No one was smiling. Their heads were slightly angled up like they thought they were better than everyone else.

But the next picture really threw me. It was another young version of my dad, but in this picture, my dad was smiling. His hair was all messed up, and his eyes looked alive. I had never seen my father like this, and there was a part of me that was relieved to know he had been capable of being happy at one point in his life. But then a feeling of sadness washed over me, and I suddenly felt cheated. Why couldn't I have *this* version for a father? Why did I have to live with the broken version?

Was it me? Did he hate being a father? Did he resent me? Did he blame me for some reason for my mom being in a coma? That might sound dramatic, but I sometimes got the feeling that was really how he felt.

I'd had this heart issue when I was a little kid, and they weren't sure I was going to make it. I guess my mom was really messed up about it and took me to every doctor she could find. My dad said she was obsessed with finding a cure. He told me she never left my side. Day in and day out, she tried to find a way to make me all better. And then something unexpected happened. One morning, my mom didn't wake up. My dad and I rushed her to the hospital, but the doctors had no idea what had caused her coma since she wasn't sick or anything, and they had no idea what to do to wake her up. So she'd been lying in a hospital now for almost ten years, with tubes and machines surrounding her. Honestly, it hurt every time I walked into that room. It never got any easier to see her like that.

But the craziest part is that shortly after my mom had fallen into a coma, they couldn't find anything wrong with my heart. My condition simply disappeared. The doctor said it was a miracle, which was great, except for the fact that the one person who wanted to hear those words more than anyone couldn't hear them. She was the one who had fought so hard for me to get better, researching everything, traveling all over the place, and meeting with doctors.

It wasn't fair. And if I thought about it for too long, I would get so angry that I couldn't even see straight.

I used to go to the hospital every day. At first, I would just stare at her, watching for a sign that she was coming around and waiting for her hand to move or her eyes to open. Once Mr. Fitzgerald started taking me, we would bring books and read them to her. We went through a lot of classics: the *Sherlock Holmes* series, the *Lord of the Rings* trilogy, *Alice's Adventures in Wonderland*, the *Harry Potter* series. Honestly, we read too many to name.

I put the pictures back in the wooden box and made sure to place it where I had found it. Still no key. I sat on the bed, trying to come up with a place where my dad would have hidden it. The kitchen. The living room. Or maybe it was just on his key chain. I looked at the clock on my dad's nightstand. It was getting late; it was already past seven. I had better get to school. I couldn't afford to be late two days in a row. Mad Millie would lose it. I went over to the sheet that was lying in a heap on the floor, draped it over my mother's chest, and left my dad's room. I then went into the kitchen to grab myself a breakfast bar and headed outside.

As I rode my bike to school, I was grateful that there wasn't any fog. I was half expecting to see my aunt again as I reached Ghost Hill, but thankfully, there was no sign of her. Once I reached school, I headed for Mad Millie's classroom. I wanted to be sitting down when Maria came in. I waited, tapping my pencil until I couldn't do that anymore and started tapping my foot instead. The girl who sat kitty-corner from me turned and gave me an annoyed look. I didn't really care if she was annoyed, but I stopped tapping my foot anyway. Then Maria entered the room. She looked like she was barely aware of her surroundings as she made her way to her desk.

She accidentally bumped into Emmett, and he turned briskly to see who had been stupid enough to run into him.

"Walk much?" He never failed at being a jerk.

But Maria didn't reply. She just stared at him.

"Guess you don't just look weird, huh?" Emmett laughed and glanced at his friends for reinforcement. They joined in, of course. No surprise there.

Maria didn't seem to notice that they were laughing at her. I decided I needed to save her from the humiliation that is middle school.

"Hey, Maria," I called out to her from my seat, "don't pay any attention to them. They're a bunch of idiots."

"Who? Them?" She glanced briefly toward them. "Yeah, I know."

She still looked slightly dazed, but she continued to walk down the aisle and eventually sat down in her seat. She bent down and pulled her notebook out of her backpack and plopped it on my desk, her bracelets jingling every time she moved her arm. "I seriously don't understand what's going to be on this test. Can you help me?"

"Sure." I leaned in to get a better look at the problem. "Which one are you having problems with?"

"Which one am I *not* having problems with?" she said with a huff.

Maria pointed to a problem that had a lot of erasure marks surrounding it. I explained everything I knew as quickly as I could. For some reason, math wasn't that hard for me, but I could tell it didn't come that easily for her. I had my doubts that she would ace the quiz.

After class, we parted ways, but she found me again at the end of school. I saw the popular girls point and giggle at her as she talked to me. It made me anxious that people were talking about her, but she seemed completely oblivious to their glares or their opinions of her.

Maria proved my theory the next day. It all started when Mad Millie came into the classroom and headed for her desk and sat down. After her endless endeavor of taking attendance, she grabbed her purse, and after shuffling through the contents, she began to look for something in her desk. She was clearly not finding what she was looking for because she pretty much went through the entire desk. Eventually, she stopped searching and walked to the front of the classroom. She stood there, turning her head from left to right as if she was waiting for everyone in the class to focus their attention on her. Mad Millie's body was leaning so far forward, I wondered how she kept her balance.

"My wallet is missing," she said. "Anyone know where it could be?"

Everyone was silent. No one said a word, except for Emmett: "I saw Rusty up there earlier. Maybe he did something with it."

"What?" Rusty exclaimed. "What the heck are you talking about, Emmett?"

Mad Millie loudly cleared her throat. "Mr. Whitaker, you wouldn't happen to know where my wallet has disappeared to, would you?"

"No. Why would I?" Rusty said defensively.

Mad Millie briskly walked toward Rusty as if she could no longer restrain herself. "Where did you put it?"

"I didn't touch it. I don't know what you're talking about!" He sat up taller, preparing for her attack.

Once Mad Millie reached his desk, she grabbed his canvas bag, unzipped it, and dumped the contents of it on the floor. There wasn't much in there—a couple of pencils, some crumpled pieces of paper, a sandwich, and, surprisingly, a copy of *The Catcher in the Rye*.

"Hey!" Rusty stood up, agitated.

"Take off your jacket and hand it to me," Mad Millie demanded with her arm outstretched toward him.

"No," Rusty said, holding onto his jacket as though she were going to rip it from his body. "Ya know what? You want me gone so bad? I'll just leave, and I won't come back this time."

"Well, that's a surprise." She let out a sinister-sounding laugh. "Wouldn't expect anything else from you. Dropping out of school seems to run in your family."

Mad Millie looked around the classroom nervously after she said that, as if she knew she had crossed the line. Everyone in the room was staring intensely in their direction, waiting for Rusty to respond with some sarcastic remark like he always did. But Rusty didn't say anything; he just bent down next to his bag that was now lying on the floor and started to shove his belongings back into it. I glanced over at Emmett, who seemed to think this whole situation was really entertaining. Rusty stood up and started to move toward the front of the classroom, but Mad Millie blocked his path.

"You're not leaving here with my wallet," Mad Millie spat at him.

"Listen." Rusty's voice was gruff. "I don't have your wallet."

He said each word slowly, as if Mad Millie was an idiot who couldn't understand him.

Mad Millie walked past him and opened the wooden top of Rusty's desk. Everyone leaned in toward the action, anxious to see what was inside. Mad Millie reached inside the desk, and then her hand went straight up in the air, her wallet clutched between her fingers.

"What is this then?" She was grinning from ear to ear with victory.

"Hey, I didn't take your wallet." Rusty backed away from her. "I have no idea how that got in there."

Mad Millie just laughed at him. "Of course you do." She opened it up, examining the contents.

"No, I don't. I never touched your stinking wallet, and I was never up by your desk." Rusty shot a look at Emmett, realizing he had been set up.

"Deny it all you want, but tell me, Mr. Whitaker, who's going to believe you?" she sneered at him.

"I believe him," someone said firmly.

It took me a second to realize who it was: Maria. She then stood up next to her desk.

"Maria," I whispered to her, "sit down. You don't want to get involved in this."

She just glanced back at me and shook her head, letting me know she wasn't going to sit down.

"Maria Tovar." Mad Millie turned her attention to our side of the classroom. "I don't know what you think you're doing, but unless you have some firsthand knowledge of this theft, I think you should take your seat."

"He didn't take your wallet," she said firmly.

"And you know this because …"

Maria didn't respond immediately. "I just know," she finally answered.

"Well, that is not good enough for me. Perhaps you helped him steal it," Mad Millie said as she glided toward the front of the classroom.

"Someone put it in there to frame him."

The entire class gasped at her statement, and Mad Millie stopped moving.

As if in slow motion, she turned back to Maria. "And who are you accusing?" she asked in a low voice.

It didn't make any sense. As far as I knew, Maria didn't even know Rusty. I had never seen them talk or anything. Why was she sticking up for him? Had she seen something? I watched helplessly from my seat as Mad Millie focused her attention on Maria. I knew this wasn't going to end well. I glanced over at Emmett and his pals; they were all glaring at her too. I knew they had something to do with the wallet, and they were going to be pissed if she screwed up their plan to frame Rusty. It was pretty clear that it drove Emmett crazy that Kristy Phillips had a thing for Rusty. As far as Emmett was concerned, it made no sense for Kristy to like Rusty instead of him. After all, he was the rich, popular kid, and Rusty was just "white trash." If I had to guess, Emmett wanted Kristy to think Rusty was as bad as everyone said, even if it meant framing him to get his point across.

I wanted to grab Maria's hand and pull her back down into her seat. "Maria," I said as quietly as possible, "you should sit down."

"No." Maria looked down at me. "I know he didn't do it."

Mad Millie was back at the front of the classroom. "I don't know what you think you saw, Miss Tovar, but if you can't provide additional information, I think you should sit down. Mr. Whitaker has a history of bad behavior and—"

"I have never stolen anything in my life," Rusty defended himself.

Mad Millie cleared her throat and acted as if she didn't hear Rusty. "As I was saying, being new here, I don't think you have the ability to judge the situation properly."

"Are you kidding me?" Rusty was still standing by his desk. "Her judgment is spot on. Bravo new girl!" Rusty began to clap loudly.

Mad Millie's shrill voice tried to overpower Rusty's clapping. "Get out of my classroom!" Her hand shot up and pointed toward the door. "Both of you—to the office!"

She looked wild with madness, which was perfect considering her name. "I will not tolerate this behavior in my classroom."

"All righty." Rusty slung his bag over his shoulder and walked to the door. Before leaving, he turned and looked back at Maria. "Come, my lady."

Rusty half bowed as if he were an English gentleman or something. "I shall escort you to the principal's office."

Maria looked a bit confused, but then she gathered all her things and walked up the aisle to the front of the classroom. Mad Millie watched her like a hawk the entire time. Rusty held the door open for Maria. They exited the room, and then Rusty made a point of closing the door with a loud thud.

After they left, I sat there in a state of confusion. None of it made sense. If I was being honest with myself, something about Maria leaving with Rusty really bothered me. It wasn't like I knew her that well or anything, but having someone to talk to at school felt pretty amazing. Maria actually made first hour bearable. By the look of it, I wasn't the only one who was troubled. Kristy Phillips didn't look so happy either; she was biting her lip and had a concerned look on her face. My bet was she wasn't too thrilled to see the new girl stick up for her crush, something she never would've had the guts to do herself. Emmett was giving one of his buddies a high five, and Mad Millie was locking her wallet in one of her desk drawers. I leaned back in my chair and tried to make sense of it all. I concluded that Maria must have seen something. It was the only explanation. But one thing was for sure: Maria Tovar had just left first hour with Rusty Whitaker. And for all I knew, she wasn't coming back.

CHAPTER 5
A BUMP IN THE ROAD

The next day, I got to Mad Millie's classroom early because I wanted to see if Maria would show up. She never did. Neither did Rusty. I knew that if Mad Millie had gotten her way, they both may have been suspended. I decided I would stop by Maria's house after school to find out what had happened, which was a pretty bold move for me.

Once the bell rang, I hightailed it out of there and headed for Mrs. Tovar's house. Once I was on the road, the sky turned dark like a storm was rolling in. The air felt heavy as I skidded to a stop in front of Maria's simple, white farmhouse. It's not like there was anything extraordinary about it, but it always looked super cozy. It looked even more inviting that day with the threatening skies as a backdrop. I parked my bike and walked up the concrete path to her house. I rang the doorbell and waited … but nothing happened.

I walked around the house and peered into the windows, looking for a sign that someone was home. No sign of life. I went back to my bike. I was disappointed, but I decided I had better not wait around. I would be lucky to make it home before the rain started. I jumped back onto my bike and started to head up the street, gusts of wind hit me so hard that it was difficult to steer my bike. The sky now had a rosy tint that made everything look strange. It reminded me of when you sometimes end up with a weird photo where the color is off and there are strange spots and splotches all over it, and you can't figure out why it looks so odd.

Once the rain started, I angled my head down and peddled faster, trying to see where I was going as cold rain pelted my face. I was peddling so quickly I almost didn't notice there was something on the side of the road. At first, I thought it was an unfortunate animal that got hit by a car, but as I got closer, I realized it was a person. And not just any person—it was Maria. I skidded to a stop and hopped off, letting my bike fall onto the wet earth. I ran over to the side of the road and kneeled beside her; she was lying motionless in the dirt. Had she gotten hit by a car? I quickly looked her up and down—no visible injuries, no blood, no scrapes.

I leaned in toward her. "Maria," I said as loud as I could while gently shaking her shoulders.

She didn't respond.

I watched her chest to see if she was breathing and was relieved to see it moving up and down. I sat back on my heels. I needed help. Someone would drive down the road eventually. I looked around to see exactly where I was. It really wasn't my lucky day because the only house I saw was Rusty's—the perks of small-town life. Everyone knows where everyone lives. Even in the harsh weather, the house looked uninviting. The paint had peeled so much that it was hard to tell what color it once had been, and the bushes surrounding the house had grown so high they covered most of the windows. Rusty's house wasn't my first choice to go for help, but I didn't really have another one.

I tried to lift Maria, but between her dead weight and the slickness of the rain, I was afraid she would slip right out of my hands. Instead, I dragged her to a nearby tree to shield her from the unrelenting rain. I looked back at the colorless house and hoped Rusty would be home. I had never met Rusty's parents, but I heard people in town talk about them, and I didn't think they would be much help. They didn't have the best reputation. Both of them spent most of their time at the local bar, loudly arguing with each other.

As I got closer, I noticed that items had been left on the lawn so long, weeds had grown through them. I walked up the steps that led to the porch and almost fell when I realized one of the steps wasn't fully attached. I grabbed the railing to catch my balance and carefully walked up the rest of the stairs. I reached the door, but I didn't see a doorbell. The screen door was ripped, so I reached my hand through the frayed mesh and knocked loudly on the door. No reply. I banged again and nervously looked back at Maria. What if no one was home? What would I do then?

Finally, I heard someone on the other side of the door. Locks turned back and forth, and someone pushed on the door from inside. It was as if the person didn't know how to open their own door. When the door finally opened, a strange woman stood in the doorway. She looked like a mess. She was wearing some sort of nightgown that was falling off her shoulder. Her hair was disheveled, and her eyes were glossy and unfocused.

"What do you want?" She leaned against the doorframe as if opening the door had taken too much effort, and she needed a moment to rest.

"There's a girl on the side of the road. I think she's hurt. Do you have a phone I could use?" I answered her.

She laughed. "Those idiots at the phone company turned off my phone … so, no."

She began to shut the door, so I quickly put my foot in the doorway. Did she not hear the part about a possibly injured girl? Was she really going to just shut the door on me?

"Wait!"

"Get lost, kid."

The door pushed harder against my foot. That was when Rusty came up behind her and grabbed the side of the door with his hand.

"Mom, I got this." Rusty positioned himself in front of her and gestured for her to go back inside the house.

"Whatever you say, son." She turned and walked back into the darkened room, swaying from one side to the other as if she were on a ship.

Rusty wouldn't look me as he spoke; he just kept his eyes down. "What are you doing here?"

"I found Maria on the side of the road. I think she's unconscious or something," I said.

"Maria? The new girl? Where is she?" His eyes no longer avoided mine. He looked right at me, waiting for me to respond.

"I dragged her under that tree." I turned and pointed toward where Maria was lying. "I was hoping I could bring—"

Before I could finish that sentence, Rusty moved past me, jumped over the porch railing, and ran toward the dark figure. I ran after him through the rain. His reaction irritated me. It wasn't like he had some kind of special relationship with her just because she stuck up for him at school.

Once he reached Maria, he kneeled next to her. "What the heck happened?" He looked up at me.

"I don't know," I answered him. "She was like this when I found her."

"You found her here?" he asked.

"No, by the road. I moved her." I was suddenly worried that maybe I shouldn't have done that. Weren't you not supposed to move people when they were hurt? "Do you think someone hit her?"

"It doesn't look like she was hit. Okay, you get her feet," Rusty said as he lifted her from under her arms.

I grabbed her by the ankles, and we carried her toward Rusty's house, carefully navigating through the rusty tractors and old toys that littered the yard. Luckily, the front door was still open, so I followed Rusty through the door and into the front room. Even though it was only late afternoon, it was dark inside the house from the storm. But not dark enough that I couldn't see how much the inside of the Whitaker house matched the outside. It looked as though nobody had cleaned the place in years; in fact, it was difficult to follow Rusty because I kept tripping on random items that had been left on the floor. I carefully navigated around piles of mail, clothes, and musty cardboard boxes.

Rusty's mother leaned against the opening that led into the kitchen, lazily holding a wine glass in her hand. Behind her, I could see the kitchen counter was covered with dirty dishes.

"You're getting the carpet all wet," his mom said, her words slightly slurred.

I couldn't believe she cared about the carpet considering what the house looked like. Rusty just ignored her, so I did too. Together, we carried Maria down the hallway.

"Come on, my room is on the right." Rusty led me to a door with a bright light pouring out of the opening.

Once inside, I had to stop for a second and look around. It wasn't what I was expecting. Rusty's room looked like it came from a different house. It was clean and organized, but the most shocking thing was that there were books everywhere. They were on his desk, his dresser, and even lined up on the floor. There were a couple of worn-out Stephen King paperbacks on his nightstand, and I wondered if he had actually read them over and over again or if they just looked so beat-up because he picked them up at some garage sale. Rusty certainly didn't give the impression that he was a big reader in school, so I was shocked. I gave him a confused look.

"Not a word," Rusty warned me as he gently began to lay Maria down on the bed. We worked together to remove her soaking wet jacket and shoes. There was a blanket folded up on the bottom of the bed, and Rusty carefully draped it over her body to keep her warm.

"What do you think happened?" I asked.

"I have no idea." Rusty looked down at her lying in his bed. "Why would she just be lying there like that?"

"Well, what do we do now?" I gestured toward her. "Do you think your mom would drive us to the clinic?"

"Dad took off with the only working car a couple of days ago." Rusty went to close the door to his bedroom. "Haven't heard from him since."

Once it was shut, I could see a whole bunch of locks on the interior of the door. I wanted to ask him about them, but I decided now wasn't the time.

"What about *your* dad?" he asked me.

"He's not home from work yet." I paused to think, and then I said, "I could bike into town. See if Mrs. Tovar is at the bakery."

"Yeah." Rusty was quiet for a second. "Why don't I go? Not really into the whole nursing-people-back-to-health thing."

"Okay," I said, even though I wasn't sure I wanted to be alone with his less-than-friendly mother. "You want me to wait here with Maria?"

"I'll be quick." Rusty was already zipping up his jacket.

"Is your mom going to be mad that you're leaving us here?" I asked.

"Doesn't matter." He walked over to the door and pointed toward the locks that lined the edge of the door. "She's not going to bother you."

"Why do you have all those locks on your door?" I asked.

"My parents are drunks. Sometimes, it's better if they can't get to me." He opened the door and started to leave the room, but then he stopped and looked back again. "Lock the door behind me."

"Really?" I asked, finding it so disheartening that Rusty had to lock his parents out. My father's indifference didn't seem so bad now.

"Really," he said firmly and walked out the door.

CHAPTER 6
FEELING FAINT

I closed the door once Rusty left and locked it as he instructed. I looked around the room to distract myself from thinking too much about why it was best to lock out his alcoholic parents. There was a big map on the wall with pins stuck in various places around the world, probably marking all the sites he wanted to visit, since I doubted he had ever been to any of them. I walked over to his desk, which had more books and notebooks stacked on the surface. There was a picture on the desk, so I picked it up to get a better look. It showed a soldier, probably around twenty years old. I wondered who it was, but then I remembered that Rusty had a couple of brothers, so I assumed it was one of them. I wasn't sure how many brothers he had, but I was pretty sure he was the youngest—at least, that was what I had heard around town. I put the picture back down and pulled the chair from the desk over to the bed so I could sit next to Maria and keep an eye on her. It made a loud, scratching noise on the wooden floor, so I quickly picked it up. I didn't want to draw any unwanted attention from Rusty's mom.

I placed the chair next to Maria and looked down at her. I wished I knew what to do. Honestly, I had never been in a situation like this. I reached out to touch her hand to see if she had warmed up at all. It still felt cold. I took her hand in both of mine to warm it up. What happened to her? I hoped it was nothing too serious. I felt so helpless. I just wanted her to wake up and be okay.

I had never prayed before because we didn't go to church, and I honestly had no idea how I felt about religion or God. I tried not to think about big, heavy topics like that. But at that moment, I thought I would give it a shot. I squeezed her hand and closed my eyes and asked whoever was in charge to wake Maria up. I wasn't expecting much, but suddenly, this heavy feeling took over my whole body. I couldn't open my eyes even if I wanted to. It was like they were glued shut. I almost felt like I was floating, and an image of my mother appeared before me. Not the version of her lying lifeless in a coma, but an open-eyes-and-smiling version. Her blond hair cascaded over her shoulders, and she was wearing a white dress that almost glowed in contrast to the gray forest that surrounded her. It was reminiscent of a lifeless autumn landscape before it was covered in a winter snow. She beckoned to me to follow her, and then she turned and began to run in the opposite direction. As she moved through the forest, it came to life. Brilliant green leaves sprung from the branches, and shoots of grass pierced the layer of brown, decaying leaves that covered the ground.

In my mind, I attempted to follow her, but I physically remained fixed in place. As she got farther away, her image faded, along with the scenery. I was now surrounded by a dark, empty space. The nothingness gave me an uneasy feeling. I looked around for a sign of something, anything. But my uneasiness was soon replaced by a tingling sensation in my chest. I wasn't sure what was happening. Slowly the tingling intensified and then spread down my arms until it finally reached my fingertips. I felt so out of control. It was like something was taking over my body, and I was defenseless against it. What freaked me out was that I had no idea what it was or what it would do to me.

I was panicking.

My heart was racing.

I was gasping for air.

Once I reached the point where I could barely breathe, I decided to calm myself down. I concentrated on forcing air in and out of my lungs, and thankfully, I started to feel the tingling subside a bit.

I heard a gasp and felt Maria's hand slip out of my grasp. Surprisingly, I was able to open my eyes. I immediately looked down at my hands. I expected to see—I didn't know what. Some evidence of what had transpired. But besides my vision being a little blurry, my hands looked completely normal. I turned to look at Maria.

There she was, awake and sitting up. "Wren," her eyes scanned the room as she spoke, "where are we?"

"Rusty's place," I answered, but my voice sounded weak. What was wrong with me?

"Why?" She leaned toward me, waiting for me to answer.

"I found you on the side of the road. You were passed out," I tried to explain.

"Passed out?" she asked. She was staring off into space as if trying to remember what had happened.

"Yeah. Do you remember anything?"

"I just remember walking to your house."

"You were coming to my house?" I didn't know why, but that made me really happy. I hoped that my inability to speak loudly clouded my enthusiasm. It would've been embarrassing if she knew how excited I was that she had been coming to visit me.

"Well, you *are* my only friend in this town. My abuela made me promise not to leave the house, but I was going stir-crazy. So when she left for the bakery, well … I figured I had a little time."

"Then what happened?" I asked her.

"I was just walking … I passed a guy with a dog … a really *big* dog." Her forehead was all scrunched up as she spoke. "Then nothing. I don't remember anything after that. Next thing I knew, I was waking up here."

She sat up taller and looked around the room. "Did you bring me here?"

"I found you on the side of the road on my way home from school." I tried to point out the window, but my arm felt weak, so I put it back down. "Rusty's house was the closest—"

"Where is he?" Maria asked.

"He went to get your grandmother." The room suddenly started spinning, and I felt incredibly dizzy.

"Oh no! He can't get her. She's going to kill me." Maria stood up and started pacing back and forth anxiously. "This isn't good, Wren. She told me not to leave her house under any circumstance. What am I going to tell her?"

When I didn't answer, I could feel her eyes on me. "Wren?"

Maria walked over to where I was sitting and leaned toward me. "You all right? You don't look so hot."

"I don't know what's wrong with me."

I could feel my cheeks grow hot with embarrassment. I was supposed to be taking care of her, but now I was the one who needed help. It was pathetic. I mean, this was my chance to be the hero. But I completely blew it. I swear I had the worse luck.

Maria pressed her palm onto my forehead to check my temperature. "You don't feel hot or anything. Are you sure you're telling me everything? Did anything happen before I woke up?"

"What do you mean?"

What was she fishing at? Could she tell something weird had happened?

Luckily, that's when a knock sounded at the door.

"Wren, it's Rusty."

I somehow managed to stand up and walk to the door. My sight was blurry, but I was able to turn the knobs, pull the chains, and unlock the door. I didn't even have a chance to open the door all the way before Mrs. Tovar whisked into the room. She threw her arms around Maria and held her tightly.

Rusty came in behind her and glanced at me. His eyes widened. "What happened to you?"

I didn't answer him. I just used the wall for support and made my way back to the chair I had been sitting in.

"Are you all right?" Mrs. Tovar asked Maria as she pulled back and scanned her eyes up and down her body as if looking for any possible injuries. "What happened to you? Rusty said that Wren found you on the side of the road."

"I don't know exactly," Maria said in a far-off voice. "I was walking to Wren's house—"

"And why were you doing that? I thought I told you to stay inside the house."

It sounded like Mrs. Tovar was getting pretty angry.

"I know." Maria looked down, most likely not wanting to meet her grandmother's piercing glare. "I'm sorry. I didn't think anything would happen."

"And yet something *did* happen," Mrs. Tovar said bluntly. "I thought we discussed that it is no longer safe."

"What's no longer safe?" Rusty butted in.

Mrs. Tovar just shook her head. "Nothing to concern yourself with, Rusty."

"Kind of sounds like it does. This happened outside of *my* house." Rusty clearly wasn't going to let it go.

Mrs. Tovar ignored him. She kept all her attention on Maria. "Let's get you home. Hopefully, you learned your lesson. From now on, when I tell you to stay indoors, you do it."

"All right." Maria nodded. "But I think we should give Wren a ride home. He looks sick or something."

Mrs. Tovar turned her attention toward me. Her eyebrows pinched together as she spoke. "What's going on with you, Wren?" she asked.

I tried to downplay how crappy I felt. "I'm sure it's nothing. Must be coming down with something."

Like how Maria did earlier, Mrs. Tovar reached her hand out and touched my forehead. "You don't feel hot." She paused for a second before asking, "Can you make it to the car?"

"Of course." I tried to sound as capable as possible, but I doubted I was very convincing.

Maria must've known I wasn't being entirely honest because she came to my side and helped me up, which made me feel really stupid.

"Come on, Wren," she said. "Let's get you home."

The rest of the night was a blur. I remembered sitting in the backseat while Mrs. Tovar drove to my house. She never stopped talking. She was going on and on about how irresponsible it was for Maria to leave her house. I thought I heard her say something about them having to leave town now, but I hoped that wasn't true and I misheard her. I decided that my brain was not taking things in correctly.

Once we got home, I saw my dad's car parked in the driveway. Maria and Mrs. Tovar came inside with me, and Mrs. Tovar disappeared into the kitchen. When Maria asked where my room was, I somehow lifted my hand high enough to point toward the stairs. We climbed up the narrow stairs to the third floor, which was tough and awkward, and I'd rather forget the whole experience. I hoped that the image of me needing her help up the stairs wouldn't be seared into her brain forever so I could eventually convince her I wasn't as wimpy as I seemed that day. Once we made it to my room, I went directly to my bed and hit the sheets. I was out in seconds, and it was the best sleep I'd ever had in my life.

CHAPTER 7
CIRCLE OF DEATH

I woke up the next day with the sun bright outside my window. I turned to look at the clock and realized it was almost noon. I couldn't believe I had slept that long. I sat up in bed, expecting the dizzy feeling to come back. Thankfully, it didn't. I wasn't sick anymore; I felt fine. Whatever was wrong with me the night before was gone.

I got up, ran up to the roof, and fed the birds. They were super irritated with me since it was way past the time when I usually showed up. Some crows graced me with their presence, but none of them brought me any gifts. After feeding them, I realized it was time for me to feed myself. I headed downstairs and went straight to the kitchen. I was so hungry, I didn't even care what I ate. Everything was fair game. I devoured what was left of an old pizza, a banana, a hunk of cheese, and some chips. I was peeling an orange as I glanced out the front window. Mr. Fitzgerald's house was barely visible from my vantage point since his house was surrounded by pine trees, and there were a bunch of trees in front of my lawn. I had almost forgotten that it was Saturday, the day we were supposed to go see my mother. It was a little weird that Mr. Fitzgerald hadn't come banging on my door earlier. He was always up at the crack of dawn, ready to go. Then again, if he had been banging on my door, I probably slept right through it.

I left my half-peeled orange on the counter and walked out of the kitchen. I grabbed my hoodie off the coat rack and slipped it on as I walked out the front door of the shoe house. I sprinted down the uneven cobblestone driveway, crossed the street, and headed toward my neighbor's house. I loved walking up his driveway because the pine trees towered above me on either side and made me feel like I was in an ancient forest. I always felt like a hoard of Vikings would come bursting through the trees at any moment with their axes held high in the air.

As I got closer to his house, I realized something wasn't right. One of the soaring trees looked dead and black, standing in complete contrast to all the trees that surrounded it. I left the driveway and walked over to the black tree. As I got closer, I could see there was a dark circle of burnt earth on the ground surrounding it. It was exactly like the section of the woods I had discovered by Ghost Hill the other day. The blackened area was large and symmetrical, about the size of a small car. As I moved closer to the scorched earth, I could see that everything inside the circle was dead—the grass, the weeds, and the towering pine tree.

A fire could never have done this. There was no way it would've created such a perfect circle; it would have been erratic and uncontrolled. I leaned into the burnt sphere to get a better look. The bark was shriveled and curling up on the edges, like little sheets of burnt paper. The blackened tree reached into the sky with bare, withered branches. It looked so broken and fragile. If I touched it, it would probably collapse into a pile of ash on the ground.

I turned toward the house. Where was Mr. Fitzgerald? Was he all right? I ran up to the front door and rang the doorbell, but no one answered. I banged on the door, and it opened from the impact of my fists. He must've left it unlocked.

"Mr. Fitzgerald?" I asked cautiously as I leaned my head inside the house.

No answer.

I crossed the threshold and walked into the kitchen. There was no sign of him. I walked down the hallway to his bedroom. There was an open suitcase on his bed. Various items were inside of it, but others were lying on the bed. It looked as though he was in the middle of packing, which was weird because he hadn't said anything about going out of town. There was a book next to the suitcase, and I picked it up to read the cover—*Those Banished from Vinland*. Well, that caught my attention. Automatically, my mind went straight to my aunt and her constant stories about the mythical place. Why would Mr. Fitzgerald have a book like that? My mind was reeling. First the tree in his yard and now this. As much as I wanted to deny it, it was becoming all too clear that I needed to start considering whether there was any truth to the things my aunt had told me. As I laid the book back on the bed, a handful of coins in a small pile on the bed jingled, catching my attention. I grabbed a bunch and took a closer look. They weren't American, that was for sure. They were all different sizes and had different letters on them. Some had pictures of waterfalls, mountains, and caves. Maybe he was going to a foreign country, and he just forgot to tell me.

Or maybe he was trying to get away from whatever did that to his tree on his front lawn.

If I felt uneasy before, now I was officially freaked out. The problem was that I didn't know what any of it meant. But one thing was for sure, Mr. Fitzgerald's house didn't feel safe. I walked back to the front door and cautiously looked around before leaving his house. I felt too exposed as I walked up his driveway, so I decided it would be better to walk among the trees where there was more cover. When a car came up the road, I hid behind a tree and waited for it to pass. Once it was gone, I sprinted across the street and was back in my front yard.

As I walked toward my house, I started to think about all the weird things that had happened in the last couple of days: the ghostly image of my aunt on Ghost Hill, the weird sensation I felt when I held Maria's hand, the dead-looking earth both in the woods and now on Mr. Fitzgerald's front lawn. My mind was racing. Was Mr. Fitzgerald all right? Was there a chance my aunt wasn't dead? Could ghosts be real? What could burn up grass like that?

My thoughts were interrupted by a noise on the gravel. It was Rusty. He was riding up my driveway on my bike. He must've quickly realized it wasn't worth trying to ride over the gaps in the cobblestone because he got off and started walking it toward my house.

"Hey," I called out to him.

"Geez, man!" Rusty grabbed his chest. "You scared me."

I was still a way away from my house and was partially hidden by trees, so I guess I should've given him a break for not seeing me, but I couldn't help but snicker, especially considering his tough-guy reputation. "Sorry," I said, trying to sound like I meant it, though I wasn't sure if it worked.

"Just bringing back your bike," he said. "Where you want it?"

"Thanks. You can just leave it there." I gestured to where he was standing.

He parked the bike and walked over to me. "You doing all right?"

"Yeah." I stood up taller, trying to emphasize that I wasn't as wimpy as I must have seemed the day before. "Why do you ask?"

"Why do you think? You looked really sick yesterday, Larkin," he said. "What exactly happened while I was gone?"

"I don't know. It just hit me fast. Maybe it was a twenty-four-hour bug or something. I'm fine now." I didn't want to talk about it with him. If I tried explaining it to him, he would no doubt think I was insane. So I changed the subject. "Hey, have you seen Maria?"

"Not today," Rusty said. "I stopped over at Mrs. Tovar's house, but no one was home. But, man, you should have heard her grandmother when I went to get her from the bakery yesterday. She was pissed. I'm guessing Maria's in some serious trouble. Probably on total lockdown."

I had to admit that Mrs. Tovar did seem very protective of Maria. But after everything that I had seen, maybe she had a reason to be so worried.

"Can I get your opinion on something?" I hesitantly asked him.

He gave me a strange look. "I ... guess," he said slowly.

"I saw something really strange this morning in my neighbor's yard." I pointed toward Mr. Fitzgerald's house.

Rusty's gaze followed my hand, and his eyes narrowed as if he was trying to see what I was talking about, which was impossible because there was a line of trees where my yard met the road, obscuring a clear view of Mr. Fitzgerald's house or even the road itself.

"What do you mean by 'strange'?" He turned back toward me, waiting for a response.

But before I could answer, I heard cars coming up the road, a lot more than usual. I shifted my position so I could get a better view of the road between a couple trees. The cars were parking on the road in front of my house! I didn't know why, but I suddenly had a really bad feeling in my gut. I turned around to look for a place to hide. My gaze fell upon the huge willow tree on the edge of our property. Beyond the tree were dense woods that continued for many miles. I had always loved that willow. It was easy to climb, and once up there, no one could see you when the leaves were in bloom.

"Can you climb trees?" I asked Rusty.

"When I was five," Rusty answered me with sarcasm.

"No, seriously." I pointed to the willow tree. "I think we should get up in that tree."

"What the heck is wrong with you, Larkin?" His eyebrows were drawn together as he spoke, obviously confused. "I mean, I knew you were a little weird, but now I'm beginning to think you're as crazy as everyone says."

"It's those cars." I pointed to the road.

"You're afraid of cars?" Rusty was still not following.

"Listen!" I tried to sound as serious as possible. "Weird things have been happening. A chunk of my neighbor's lawn is all burned up, and it looked like he was trying to get away. His suitcase was all packed on his bed, but there's no sign of him. I'm staying out of sight until I figure out what's going on. It's up to you if you want to follow me."

I ran for the willow.

Once I reached the tree, I glanced behind me and was surprised to see Rusty right behind me.

"Okay." He looked up at the interior of the giant willow tree. "How do I climb up this thing?"

I planted myself and bent my left leg to create a step for Rusty. "Here."

Rusty stepped onto my thigh, reached up to grab the lowest branch, and pulled himself up. I looked back toward the road; a long line of strange people was now on my front lawn. They moved with caution and determination, scanning their surroundings as they proceeded forward. I had no idea why they were at my house, but it didn't look like a casual visit.

Since I was taller than Rusty, I was able to jump up and grasp a thick branch and then swing my body until my legs were able to wrap around the branch. I scurried toward the center of the tree, where Rusty had found a secure place to sit. I moved slowly and with precision. I didn't want the branches to move and creak from my added weight. I was thankful that the drooping branches of the willow tree were already full of leaves, concealing us from view. I wanted to remain invisible.

CHAPTER 8
VISITORS

Between the leaves and branches of the willow, I could see the strange visitors walk up my cobblestone driveway. There were a lot of them—maybe six—and they were being led by a very tall man with auburn hair. Everything on him looked expensive, and he had a way of walking that made him stand out from the rest of the group. It was clear that he was the one in charge. The others walked silently behind him, no one moving ahead of him or saying a word. Once they passed us, I could see some of them had a symbol on the back of their jackets. It looked like the letter *w* with two half circles below it and a line running through the center.

"Are they from some kind of gang?" Rusty whispered to me.

"I don't know," I whispered back.

As they got closer to the shoe house, a swarm of crows flew away from the roof. Countless large, dark birds flew in unison, squawking loudly as they hovered above the strangers on the lawn. The tall man gazed at them with suspicion, but the birds eventually moved away from the strangers. It looked like they were flying our way.

"Why does it look like they're coming over here?" Rusty whispered loudly. His eyes were wide as he watched the birds get closer.

"Don't worry," I answered him. "They're friends of mine."

"You're friends with birds?" Rusty asked me as a few of them landed on some of the branches of the willow tree. "Well, I guess that makes sense."

I tried to downplay the weirdness. "It's just because I feed them."

Rusty's eyes dashed from one branch to another as the birds surrounded him. "Well, I don't feed them. Does that mean they're going to peck my eyes out?"

"No," I answered him. "You're fine." At least, I thought he was, but I had to admit that the crows were a bit unpredictable.

I watched as the group of strangers approached my front door. The tall man stepped up onto my small, concrete porch and knocked on my door. The knocking sounded particularly loud for some reason. He probably had really big hands. The crows had calmed down, and their black eyes stared down at the people below. Silence filled the air.

"Who are they?" Rusty whispered to me.

I just shook my head and mouthed that I didn't know. I looked back down at my house, anxious to see what they would do when no one answered the door. The tall man turned the handle to my front door as if he were going to walk right into my house. It didn't budge, which seemed really weird to me because I didn't remember locking it when I left.

The tall man stepped back and turned his attention to a shorter man whose thinning hair suggested he was older than the rest. He was wearing a black suit jacket, but unlike the tall guy, he couldn't pull it off. Instead, he looked like a cheap imitation of the man in charge. He took something from his pocket and approached the door. He leaned over and poured something from a container onto the porch directly in front of my door.

"What is he doing?" Rusty asked me.

"I have no idea," I answered him. Why did he keep asking me questions like I knew exactly what was happening? "It kind of looks like he's pouring sand or something, doesn't it?"

"Yeah," Rusty responded. "No, wait, it looks like he's drawing something."

He was right. It did look like he was drawing some kind of design. The balding man then stood up and placed a hand on my door. All of a sudden, his body went flying backward, and he landed hard on the ground. Some of the others gasped, and one of them bent down to help him get up.

"What was that?" the tall man roared. He turned so quickly, his jacket moved behind him like a cape.

"The house must be protected by a rebound spell," the less-refined man tried to explain as he stood up, brushing himself off. "All magic will be rebounded back on the aggressor!"

"Well, break it!" The tall man was clearly irritated with the old man.

"I'm sorry, Mr. Ashford. I'm sure if the others assist me, we will be able to penetrate the barrier." The balding man looked around and gestured for the others to approach. "All together."

He moved toward the door again with determination. The others followed and lined up behind him. One by one, they placed a hand on the person's shoulder in front of them. The balding man held up his hand to place it on my door again. He hesitated for a second, but then he reached out and placed his hand on the wood surface. Just like before, he was thrown backward by some powerful force, and the others were thrown back with him. They were all left lying on the ground, scattered on my lawn.

The tall man walked over to the balding man. He reached down, grabbed him by the collar, and pulled him to a standing position.

"Perhaps you are not all that you claim to be. We agreed to this alliance because you claimed that the Wrathful were invincible, the only ones capable of casting unbreakable spells. And yet, you can't even get into a Crafter's house!"

He released the failed trespasser and let him fall onto the ground in a heap.

"Pathetic."

The man tried to plead his case. "But ... but this is Bertram Needlecoff's house! He's not just any Crafter. He's considered the most powerful of his kind."

"Are you telling me that the Crafter's magic is superior to that of the Wrathful?"

"Well, n-no, of course not," the suited man stammered.

A young man stepped forward; he resembled the man in charge because he was almost as tall and even had the same shade of auburn hair. Yet, his frame was much thinner, and he looked like he could've been blown over by a gust of wind.

"It seems that we chose poorly, Father," he said. "We should have aligned ourselves with some potters and dressmakers. If only we knew how powerful the Crafters were."

The sarcasm was obvious, but I wasn't sure what he was talking about.

"We have been duped into believing that the Wrathful are a formidable ally. What a waste of our time!" Ashford turned away from the balding man and began to walk back to where his vehicle was parked on the street.

"Caterina! We'll message for her!" The fallen man had pulled himself back up and was chasing after the man in charge. "She'll be able to break it. She is the Mother of the Unbreakable, after all. We'll get in there and get the Vinland shoes. I'll come back with her straightaways."

The tall man stopped walking and turned his body back toward the man following him. The balding man backed away from the intensity of Ashford's stare. And then it happened. The grass surrounding Ashford's feet began to shrivel up and die. The burnt grass spread outward from where he stood, moving so quickly that the balding man and some of the others had to jump back to avoid the circle of dead radiating from him. That was how the earth had gotten all burned up! This man had been responsible for it. He burned up the woods at Ghost Hill and Mr. Fitzgerald's lawn. But how could he do that? What *was* he?

"Dude," Rusty whispered, "what is happening?"

I shook my head. "What makes you think I know?"

"You said to climb up this tree," Rusty continued. "You must know something."

"Will you shut up?" I hissed. "The last thing we need is for these people to hear us."

He nodded. Clearly, he agreed it was best to *not* be discovered by these crazy people.

The young, thin man stepped forward, careful not to venture inside the circle of death. "Father, calm down. We'll get in there. I mean, how hard can it be?"

Ashford glanced over at the young man, and the burnt grass stopped spreading. He sauntered over to the balding man and said, "Summon Caterina immediately."

"Of course." The balding man bowed his head as if he were in the presence of royalty. "I won't disappoint you, Mr. Ashford."

"You already did." Ashford turned away from him and walked toward the road. "We need those shoes. And we need to find them before my brother does."

The young man walked briskly until he was at his father's side. The others were silent as they followed their leader. From the way they hung their heads as they walked, I figured they were all in serious trouble.

Rusty and I remained hidden in the willow tree, watching as they reached the street. Car door shuts and engines started, and we waited until the rumble of the cars was no longer audible before we started to climb down the tree. One by one, the crows pushed themselves off the branches and flew into the sky above.

"Yeah, adios, creepy birds." Rusty waved his hand as if to shoo them away. Once they were all gone, Rusty turned his gaze back on me. "What the heck, Wren?"

I couldn't think of anything to say. Everything had happened so fast, and my thoughts raced. I couldn't seem to grasp what I just witnessed. The dead grass, the people being blown across my lawn, the things they said about my grandfather.

Then it hit me.

Everything my aunt had told me was true.

CHAPTER 9
HIDDEN FROM VIEW

Rusty was grilling me. "Wren, you gotta tell me what just happened!"

"I can't," I answered him. "I'm as freaked out as you are."

"Then why'd you say we should climb the tree?" he asked.

"I just had a bad feeling." I honestly didn't know what else to say.

Rusty gave me a skeptical look, but then he sighed. "Well, I guess you were right. I mean, that was insane! What were they doing? Why was he talking about freaking shoes?"

"I have no idea," I answered him, but I wasn't really paying attention. My mind was still racing. Why would they come to my house to look for a lousy pair of shoes? I tried to remember if I had seen any shoes that stood out. I knew everything in that house. I had been through every cupboard, every drawer. Actually, there was only one thing I hadn't gone through: my mother's chest. The chest that was locked. The one I still had no idea how to open because I couldn't find the dang key. I looked at Rusty. "How are you at picking locks?"

"Whoa, hold on," Rusty said as he raised his hands up in front of him. "What does that have to do with anything?"

"I just want to check something out," I answered him.

Rusty moved his hands to his hips in a defensive stance. "So why do you just assume that I know how to break into something?"

I didn't have time for this. "Get over yourself. It's a simple question: yes or no?"

"Maybe," he answered. "But seriously, what does that have to do with anything?"

"I know everything in my house, every inch of the place, except for this chest that my dad has locked up in his room. Maybe the shoes they're looking for are in there. The thing is, I haven't been able to find the key."

Rusty shrugged his shoulders. "I could give it a try. But why would they be looking for shoes? And what did they call them? Vinland? Is that a brand or something?"

"It's a place," I answered simply and hoped he wouldn't ask me to elaborate.

He shook his head in disbelief. "I've never heard of it, and I know a thing or two about maps."

I remembered that he had a big map in his room. Crap, he wasn't going to buy into my explanation. "It's a really small town."

"Okay, sure ... so they're looking for a pair of shoes that come from a really small town?"

"How should I know? Are you going to help me or not?"

"Geez! I said I would try," Rusty replied.

"Okay, then let's go."

I jumped down from the tree and scanned my yard to make sure there weren't any stragglers hanging around. I heard Rusty hit the ground behind me. We then sprinted across the yard to the front door of my shoe house, briefly stopping by the burnt grass.

"What the ...?" Rusty bent down to get a better look.

"Come on." I nudged him. "Let's get inside before they come back." I ran up to my front door and turned the handle. I opened the door and began to walk inside when Rusty suddenly grabbed my arm.

"What a minute," Rusty said. "They couldn't get that door open. How did you just open it?"

I paused and thought about it. He was right. They couldn't get in, but it wasn't locked. Why couldn't they get the door to open?

"I ... just opened it like usual," I said as I stared down at the door handle.

"Close the door and let me try."

"What's that going to prove?"

"That you're the only one who can open it. That something super weird is going on," he answered.

I decided it was worth a shot. I pulled the door shut and stepped away from it. Rusty reached for the knob, turned the handle, and pushed. The door didn't budge. He moved his body so he could use all his weight and pushed harder. Nothing.

"What the heck?" he said with labored breath. "It's not like you're stronger than me."

"Well—" I began.

"No, seriously." Rusty moved away from the door. "Are you the only one who can open the door?"

"My dad can."

"Just you and your dad then?"

"I have no idea. My aunt used to and my mom. But now ... I mean, no one really comes around. I never really thought about it."

What did all of this mean?

"Maybe it's a family thing," Rusty said with a shrug.

"You may be right."

I reached for the door again and opened it, pondering how crazy it was that I was able to open the door and others couldn't. I entered the living room with Rusty right behind me. I waited for him to get inside, and then I closed the door. It felt safer inside now that I knew the house wasn't going to let anyone in. I decided then and there that my grandfather was even cooler than I'd already thought he was.

"This way." I started to make my way to my father's room, weaving through furniture and statues.

"Well ... your house doesn't disappoint."

"What's that supposed to mean?"

"Let's just say it's as crazy looking on the inside as it is on the outside," he answered me with a grin.

I wasn't sure if that was a compliment or not, but I just let it go. I had more important things to think about. I walked up one set of stairs and was once again standing in front of my father's bedroom door, which was closed. I turned the handle and walked in. The chest was still in the corner, the sheet draped over it like before. I yanked the sheet off and pointed at the lock on the front of the chest.

"There it is," I said. "What do you think? Can you get in there?"

Rusty walked over and kneeled in front of the ornate container. He examined the lock and then peered up at me from the floor.

"This thing seems ancient. You sure there isn't a key?"

"If there is one, then my dad must have it because I've looked everywhere."

"And I guess asking him is off-limits?" he asked, his tone suggesting he already knew the answer.

I nodded. "Pretty much."

"Sounds like you get along with your dad about as good as I get along with mine."

Rusty stood up and took off his leather jacket, laying it on my father's bed. He then rolled up the sleeves on his shirt. He was getting down to business. He reached into his back pocket and pulled out a pocketknife. He bent back down and began to pry the lock.

"You got any bobby pins around here?"

"Bobby pins? Isn't that what girls put in their hair?" I asked.

Rusty moved into a crisscross position in front of the chest, insinuating that this could take a while.

"Yeah, ya know, those little metal things about this long." He held up his hand and created roughly a two-inch space between his thumb and his finger.

I shook my head. "Don't think we have any. It's not like any girls live here."

"Well, you have such pretty, girly hair, so I thought it was worth asking," Rusty laughed.

I rolled my eyes at him and his dumb comment. "Very funny. Will anything else work?"

"What about paper clips?" Rusty asked. "You got some of those?"

"I have some in my room."

I left my dad's room and ran up the stairs to my bedroom. I walked over to my desk and rummaged through my drawers. I wasn't the most organized person in the world, so it took a while. But I ended up leaving the room with a handful of paper clips. Once I returned to my dad's room, I ran over to Rusty and handed him the paper clips.

Rusty looked at my hand and gave me a strange look. "Only needed two." He carefully picked two of them out of my hand.

"Well, how was I supposed to know? It's not like I ever picked a lock before." I put the rest of the paper clips in my pocket.

Rusty started to pull one of the tiny pieces of metal into a different shape.

"Rusty would know how to break into things," he mumbled in a mocking voice. "He's *that* kind of guy."

I would've laughed if that hadn't been so annoying. "Okay, I think you're reading a little too much into this. Sensitive much?"

"Yeah ... yeah." He started poking at the lock with an altered paper clip. I could hear the metal scraping the inside of the lock. "I guess I am. I mean, the school wouldn't even listen to me when I said I didn't steal Mad Millie's stupid wallet."

"I'm not surprised." I leaned in closer to see what he was doing.

"I still can't figure out why she stood up for me," Rusty mumbled again.

"Who?"

"Maria." He stopped poking at the lock and looked up at me.

"Maybe she saw Emmett do something."

"You think it was him too?" His voice got louder. "I don't know why that guy has it out for me!"

"I do." I couldn't believe he was so oblivious. "Two words: Kristy Phillips."

"No way." Rusty grinned. "There's no way she would ever like me."

"You're kidding, right?" I asked him. I couldn't tell if he was being humble or fishing for a compliment.

He paused and stared into space for a second. "You really think she has a thing for me?"

"Do you not see her staring at you all the time?"

"Well, maybe," he answered. "But it's not like she would ever admit that she liked me to anyone."

I didn't respond to that because I knew he was right. It didn't matter how much she liked him; she would never really go out with him. Her parents would freak out, and she wasn't the type of girl who went against her parents. I decided to steer the conversation in another direction.

"Can we get back to the locks and discuss your love life another time? Who knows when those creeps will be back."

"All right. Relax." He put his head down and got back to business.

I paced the room impatiently. I didn't know what I would do if he couldn't get the chest open. My house kept those creeps out earlier, but they said they were bringing someone who could get in. How long would that take?

"You almost got it?" I asked Rusty, my anxiety level rising.

"Not yet, but I will. Keep your shirt on." Rusty leaned in closer to the lock as if he was trying to hear something, so I stopped pacing and stood still.

A click sounded, and Rusty leaned back on his heels as he looked up at me.

"The sound of sweet success." He pulled down on the lock, and it opened with ease.

"Wow! I admit, I'm impressed." I kneeled down next to him.

"My brother Dennis is the real master." Rusty removed the lock from the chest. "Taught me everything I know."

"Well, I'll have to thank him sometime." I reached over and began to lift the heavy lid.

"Can't. Unless you want to visit the juvenile detention center in Philly."

Rusty helped me with the lid. I probably would've asked what his brother had done to land in juvie if I wasn't so anxious to see what was inside the chest.

It creaked loudly as we yanked it open. Unlike the room, everything inside was jumbled together, papers, pictures, and clothing at the surface. I hesitated, not expecting the open chest to be so unsettling, but it was. This was my mother's stuff, and the pain of having to watch her lifeless in a bed for the last couple of years really hit me.

"Are we going to go through this stuff or what?" Rusty interrupted my thoughts, and I was grateful.

I nodded and then bent down and started to remove the items. Rusty kneeled next to me and plunged his hands inside the chest, grabbing a handful of books and placing them on the floor.

"Just be careful with everything," I said to him. I felt uncomfortable about him going through my mother's stuff. I barely knew the guy.

Rusty lifted his hands in the air dramatically, insinuating that I was overreacting.

I sighed. "It's just ... my mom ... she's been in a coma for a while, so this stuff is pretty important to me."

Rusty glanced at me, and to my surprise, his face softened slightly with compassion.

"All right," he said and reached back in the chest with a bit more care.

As I started to take things out of my side of the chest, I noticed a bunch of pencil and pastel drawings. I never knew my mother was an artist. Most of them were of plants. There were detailed descriptions of them with diagrams and notes about their characteristics. I wanted to examine them more closely, but I knew we didn't have time for that. I pulled out some pieces of clothing—long, flowy skirts, shawls, and blouses. Lots of them had flowers sewn into them. I was beginning to get the impression that my mother had a thing for plants, which was cool. And if there were clothes in the chest, maybe there were shoes. I continued to pull things out. Small boxes of jewelry and glass containers filled with seeds.

Rusty was examining something that looked like a telescope, and then he placed it on the floor. "Not finding any shoes in here," he said as he pulled out another pile of books.

"Me neither." I was beginning to think we weren't going to find the shoes. We were almost to the bottom. I scooped up the last pile of papers and laid them on the floor. The chest was empty, but there was a large, metal handle on the bottom.

"What the heck? Maybe it's like a secret compartment!" Rusty reached down, grabbed the handle, and pulled it upward.

I was expecting to see a shallow compartment inside, but instead all I saw was darkness. I remembered there was a flashlight in my dad's nightstand, so I jumped up and ran over to it and pulled open the drawer. I grabbed the flashlight and headed back to the open chest. I turned the flashlight on and leaned into the chest so the light could illuminate the darkness. There was no compartment. Rather, there was an opening at the bottom of the chest, and it appeared to descend downward into the musty earth. The floor of the chest was actually a door, and a ladder hung on one side, leading down into a dark space.

It seemed I didn't know everything about the shoe house after all.

CHAPTER 10
SECRET TUNNEL

Rusty looked at me. "Could this day get any crazier?"

"I don't think so, but you never know."

The crazy scale had been rising exponentially these last few days. I couldn't imagine what else was going to be thrown my way before the day was over.

"And you never looked in here before?" Rusty asked me.

"No, it was locked, remember?" I started to climb into the chest. Rusty grabbed my shoulder. "What are you doing?"

"I'm going in." I took the flashlight and shoved it under my chin so I could use both my hands. I climbed into the chest and put my foot on the first rung and wiggled it a little to make sure it was secure. I looked up at Rusty, who was peering inside from above.

"You coming?"

"Absolutely," he answered without hesitation.

I was glad. I would've gone down there alone, but I was happy he was coming with me. It was dark down there, and I preferred to have some company. It somehow made things less spooky.

As I started to go farther down, I could smell the earth. It was wet and musty, and the walls of the passageway seemed to be a combination of roots, rocks, and dirt. I tried to angle the flashlight with my chin to see how far I had to go, but it looked like the passageway went on for quite a while. I just kept moving one foot down a rung and then another. I looked up at Rusty.

"Don't fall on me!" I yelled up to him.

"I'm not making any promises. You're the one with the light," he said.

I finally hit something hard and flat. I planted both feet on the dirt ground and scanned the area with my flashlight. Before me was a long corridor carved out of the earth. The space was tight, but the ceiling was rather high. Both sides of the tunnel were constructed out of stone, and every so often, there would be a thick, round pillar. But the objects on top of the pillars freaked me out. Big, stone creatures perched up there. Gargoyles. If I had to describe one, I would say it looked like a combination between a lizard and a bird. Its body resembled a lizard, and a line of spikes extended all the way to the tip of its tail. The head and wings reminded me of a bird, but there were no feathers on this thing. Instead, it appeared to be covered in scales. And even though its mouth was shaped like a beak, I could see sharp teeth inside its opened snarl. All of these statues were in different poses, some curled up and others more alert.

"You gotta be kidding me." Rusty was now standing next to me, peering down the spooky corridor. "What kind of creep show is this?"

"No idea," I answered him.

He gave me a suspicious look. "How could you not know all of this was below your house? Are you being straight with me, Larkin?"

"I honestly had no idea any of this was down here," I replied, but he still looked skeptical. "I'm telling you the truth. My dad would prefer to lock everything up that reminds him of my mom and forget about it forever."

"Are you saying this place has something to do with your mom?"

"I'm saying it has something to do with her family."

I hoped he would stop right there and not ask me any more questions. I was suddenly feeling protective of my family and didn't want Rusty to judge us based on whatever we found down here.

I started to walk down the corridor. It was too dark to see how far it went, so I just kept walking, one foot in front of the other.

The flashlight allowed us to see what was to come, which was just more pillars and statues of strange creatures grinning with razor-sharp teeth.

"What if your family didn't want anyone down here?" Rusty asked quietly. He pointed at one of the gargoyles leering down at us. "These aren't the most inviting things I have ever seen."

"Why are you whispering?" I asked him.

He shrugged. "Just seems like I should. This place is creepy."

I couldn't disagree. It *was* creepy. I tried to keep my focus on the task at hand and ignore the statues. But then, I heard a sound. Like stone rubbing against itself. The sound drew my gaze upward, and I swore I saw one of those creatures move. When Rusty grabbed my shoulder, I nearly jumped out of my skin.

He leaned in toward my ear and whispered, "Did you see that?"

I had seen it, but I wasn't going to admit it to him. I needed to figure out what secrets were hidden in that tunnel, and I didn't want Rusty to hightail it out of there. Sure, I could continue forward on my own, but I'd be lying if I said I didn't prefer having some backup.

Instead, I tried to blow it off, saying, "I don't think that was anything."

"What?" Rusty was still clutching my shoulder, and his grip tightened. "You don't think that a moving statue is a big deal?"

"Rusty," I said as calmly as I could, "I thought you were the tough guy in school. Don't tell me you're actually scared of a few rocks. You wanna go back?"

Rusty paused, his grip loosening.

"No," he grumbled as he pushed me forward.

I started walking again, but a bit faster this time. I didn't want to stay in this corridor any longer than I had to. I refused to look up at the gargoyles. And if I could've, I would have covered my ears as I walked. But I wasn't about to do that in front of Rusty.

Finally, after a few minutes, I saw something up ahead. It was a door.

"There's something up there."

"It's about time." Rusty had stayed right behind me the whole way.

As we got closer, I could see more of the door's details. It was rather large and appeared to be covered with brown leather, which was embossed with an elaborate geometric design. Perched above the curved crown of the door was one of those creepy statues. It was curled up like a sleeping cat; even its eyes were closed. Once we reached the door, I looked for a handle, but there was nothing there.

Rusty nudged me. "What are you waiting for? Open the freaking door."

"There's no handle." I moved aside and positioned the flashlight to show him there was no way to open the door.

"Are you serious right now? I didn't walk through this tunnel for nothing." Rusty moved past me and started to feel around the edges of the door. "Maybe there is some secret latch."

I illuminated the door with my flashlight as Rusty examined the two pillars on either side of the door, the floor, and the surface of the door. I moved the flashlight upward, toward the top of the door. The stone creature was still perched up there, but something had changed. Its eyes were no longer closed. It was staring down at us; its beak was open, exposing its razor-sharp fangs. I inhaled sharply, unable to turn my gaze away from the creature for fear that it would jump off the ledge and attack us.

Rusty grabbed the flashlight from my grasp and aimed the light toward the bottom of the ledge where the creature was perched.

"It says something there. What does it say?"

He moved closer, and I could see a plaque directly below the creature. The words etched into the stone read, "Only the blood of Needlecoff can open this door and harness the power of the Vess. Beware, intruders. All others will endure the fury of the Vess."

As soon as I read the words aloud, the creature began to move its stone body. The sound echoed through the tunnel, a scratching vibration filling the deathly quiet space. The creature leaned over the edge, and then its long tail spun violently toward me. The sharp point at the end of its appendage was now directly in front of my face. Neither Rusty nor I moved. We were frozen, nervous that creature would move again.

Rusty's nerves must've gotten the better of him because he suddenly exclaimed, "I knew one of those things moved back there! I *knew* it! And you acted like I was crazy."

"Are we really going to argue about that now?" I shakily asked him as I stared at the terrifying point in front of me. "Seems like we have bigger issues to deal with."

"What did it say again? 'Blood of Needlecoff'?" Rusty pondered the meaning of the words I had spoken. "What's a Needlecoff?"

I had to swallow the lump in my throat before I could answer. "It's a last name. It's my mom's side of the family."

The name was written on various items all over my house: the backs of old photos, the interior page of ancient-looking, leatherbound books, and even some of the paintings in the house had my grandmother's name scribbled in the corner. I assumed she was the artist.

Rusty looked at the tail again.

"Well, if he was your grandfather, then you have the blood of Needlecoff." He pointed at the door. "I bet this thing is just like the front door. Only you or someone in your family can open it."

I glanced at him. "But there's no handle. How do you propose I do that?"

"Well, maybe this time it needs something more." He nodded at the point of the creature's tail.

I wasn't following. "What do you mean?"

"The blood of Needlecoff," he recited slowly. "Maybe it needs your blood."

"My blood?" I looked down at the point. "Well, that's disturbing."

"Have you looked around?" Rusty gestured to our surroundings. "This whole place is disturbing."

I looked at the pointed tail of the stone animal again and then up at the creature who was glaring down at me. "So you think this is a Vess?"

I could see Rusty nod out of the corner of my eye. "That would be my guess."

"What do you think the 'fury of the Vess' means?" I didn't like this plan. Technically, I was half Needlecoff and half Larkin. Would half be enough?

"I'm thinking fury isn't good. But hey, since you're a Needlecoff, we're good."

I nervously glanced back at him. "But how can we be sure?"

Rusty's eyes narrowed. "Who's the tough guy now? Do you want to see what's behind that door or not?"

I looked back at the pointed tail in front of my face. He was right. What else was I going to do? Go back upstairs, knowing this door existed, and try to not care about all this or figure out what was behind this door? That wasn't going to happen.

"I better not get tetanus or something," I grumbled.

"Don't think you can get that from stone, Einstein," Rusty chided. "That's just from rusty metal. Believe me, I've had to hear people joke my whole life about how you'd get tetanus if you got too close to me."

I held up my pointer finger and started to move it toward the tail of the stone beast, which looked as sharp as a needle. I pushed my finger down on the point and winced when it pierced my skin. A drop of blood trickled down the spiked tail. The tail suddenly swung back up, and the gargoyle let out a blood-curdling scream and briskly leaped off the platform. We ducked down to avoid getting hit and watched the stone creature descend the passageway, screeching down the tunnel. I tried to watch it for as long as I could, but its form was quickly overtaken by the darkness. We stood for a second in silence, waiting to see if something else would happen.

"Now what?" Rusty asked.

Just then, the door began to move and slide into the wall. Rusty directed the flashlight toward the widening gap. We both peered inside. There was a large table and a ton of shelves, and on those shelves were shoes, more shoes than I had ever seen in my life. Rows and rows of them.

"I think we found what those freaks were looking for," Rusty said, and I had to agree.

CHAPTER 11
BERTRAM'S WORKSHOP

Rusty gave me a nervous glance. His forehead was all scrunched up, and his eyes were really wide.

"If I get blasted by something for not being a ... Needle whatever—"

"Needlecoff," I corrected him.

"Yeah, that. Please drag my injured body back up top."

I rolled my eyes at him. "Quit being so dramatic."

Then again, he could be onto something. Those people up top were blown across my lawn just for trying to get into my house. What if he really did get hurt for trying to come into this room? I turned back quickly to stop him from following me into the room, but he had already jumped over the threshold. He turned his head in every direction to see if his action had caused some dire consequence. Luckily, nothing happened.

I looked around for some kind of light switch; a thick, metal lever stuck out of the wall next to the door. It didn't look like a normal light switch, but I didn't expect to find anything normal down there. I grasped it and pushed the lever upward. A loud buzz sounded, and then ancient-looking light bulbs hanging from the ceiling flickered on and off a couple of times until they remained lit. That was when I saw a carved wood sign hanging on the opposite side of the room. Carved into the wood were the words *Bertram Needlecoff's Workshop*.

"So this is my grandfather's workshop," I said mostly to myself.

"You say something?" Rusty asked me.

"This was my grandfather's place."

I was in awe. It was like something from another time. Nothing about this place felt current. In the middle of the room was a huge, wooden table. On the table sat instruments like scales and measuring devices as well as stacks of folded leather, a few shoelaces, hammers, metal and wood molds, and a variety of other tools. Every wall had shelves. Most had shoes on them, but others had fabric, leather, jars, bottles, paint, and books. Lots of books.

The whole place reminded me of the shoe house. It wasn't organized; things were strewn everywhere. Rugs of different patterns were haphazardly placed on the floor; there was an old couch in a corner that was ripped and torn. Next to the couch were hooks, and some overalls, aprons, and work jackets were hanging from them.

I looked at all the shoes that lined the walls—every kind of shoe you could imagine. Some looked old, and others looked new. There were boots, dress shoes, moccasins, ballet slippers, high heels, rain boots, and sandals. Some were big, others were small. Some were shiny, and others were worn.

"My grandfather was a shoemaker," I said out loud.

"Ha!" Rusty laughed. "Guess this explains why your grandfather built your house to look like a shoe."

I looked at him in amazement. "You're right! There actually *is* a reason why my house looks like a shoe."

"Was he cool?" Rusty asked.

"I don't know. I never met him," I said as I walked over to the shelves. "I wish I had."

"Yeah, me too." Rusty walked over to one of the shelves full of books instead of shoes. "When did he ... pass away?"

"Honestly? I'm not even sure if he's dead," I answered him.

"Oh, sorry. I just assumed ... ." Rusty shrugged his shoulders.

"He and my grandmother just disappeared one night," I told him. Then it occurred to me that I wasn't sure if even *that* was true. Maybe my dad had lied about that too.

"That sucks." I was surprised by how sincere Rusty sounded. "I find it hard to believe he just left this place. I wouldn't leave."

I could see his point. It made me think that maybe he didn't leave by choice. I started to look at the shoes closer. Below each pair of shoes was a plaque, and written on the plaque was a three-digit number along with some words. One of the plaques said, 761, Vision of Night. I took one of the shoes off the shelf to get a better look. I wasn't too well versed in shoe fashion, but I believed that the shoe I'd just grabbed was called a "loafer." I put the shoe back on the shelf and looked at the shoes to the right of them. They were women's shoes with rubber bottoms and a gray, canvas body. Below them read, 762, Exhaustion Repellant.

"So weird," I said out loud. "He gave them such crazy names."

"Yeah, I can see that," Rusty said from somewhere behind me. "Looks like he kept a log of all of his creations."

I turned around. Rusty was hunched over a giant book on the large table. I walked over to where he stood to see what he had found. He was right. Each page had a drawing of the shoes on them, their title, their number, and what looked like a list of ingredients. Why a shoe would need ingredients was beyond me.

I shook my head. "I don't understand. Why name them all?"

"Well, it must be for a reason." Rusty turned a couple more pages. "Look, this one says, Ability to Keep Secrets." He turned the page again and read, "Invisibility."

We both looked at each other.

"Do you think … ." Rusty paused.

I knew what he was going to say. Maybe these shoes actually made the wearer invisible. It sounded crazy, but a lot of crazy things happened today. It could very well be possible. I looked back down at the book. Number 224. Our eyes met again, and then we hightailed to the shelves, both of us eager to find the shoes first. Who doesn't want to be invisible? How cool would that be? I went to the opposite wall from where I had previously been since I was looking for a low number.

478 ... 398 ... 266 ... 241 ... 230—

There! Number 224, Invisibility. They were a pair of men's shoes, shiny leather with thin laces. Fancy! I grabbed them off the shelf and sat on the floor to put them on.

Rusty came running toward me just as I was pulling off my shoes. "You found them?"

He hunched down so he could see what they looked like.

"They look pretty small," I commented as I loosened the shoelaces.

I crammed my foot into the stiff shoe, and somehow, it fit. In fact, it fit perfectly. I grabbed the other shoe and realized the one I was wearing now appeared to be larger than the one in my hand. I slid on the second shoe, watching closely to see if it would expand before my eyes. But my attention was taken elsewhere because all of a sudden, I couldn't see my hands. They just weren't there. And let me tell you, it was almost impossible to tie the other shoe now that I couldn't see my hands or foot.

"Holy crap!" Rusty gasped. "It really works!"

He reached out and accidentally hit me in the eye.

"Ouch!" I yelled and batted away his hand. "I'm still here."

Rusty backed away slightly.

"That's insane. Can you imagine the things you could do with those shoes?" Rusty laughed. "You could go to the movies for free. Heck, you could go *anywhere* for free."

"You could spy on people," I added.

"You could play pranks on Mad Millie," Rusty sneered. "I need to borrow those."

"No way," I answered. "I can only imagine what kind of trouble you would get into."

He just shrugged as he stood up.

"Hey, she deserves it." He started looking through the shoes that were on a nearby shelf. "I need to find a pair to put on."

I grabbed one of the shoes with my invisible hands and pulled it off my foot. Once they were both off, I regained my normal appearance again. I carefully put them back on the shelf, but I took note of where they were—the number and the fact that they were between a pair of cowboy boots and some crummy-looking leather flip-flops. They would come in handy if I ever needed to be invisible someday, maybe when those people returned.

I looked back at Rusty as he took a pair of shoes off one of the other shelves. They looked like a pair of work boots.

"I think these can turn you into a giant."

I walked over to him. "You sure you want to be a giant?"

"Heck yeah!" He sat down on a rug that was spread out on the stone floor, ripped his shoes off, and began to pull on the boots. I watched, but I held my breath, feeling nervous about how this would turn out. I backed up and waited to see what would happen.

It started with his posture. He bent over a bit, and then everything started growing in every direction. His legs, arms, torso, and head. Even his hair was growing at a rapid pace. Not only were his limbs getting longer, but they were also growing thicker. His clothing started to rip into pieces, which was unfortunate and a little awkward. Why had we not thought about that before he put the shoes on?

He was so tall now that he was almost touching the ceiling even though he was still sitting on the ground. I looked up at the low-lying beams and started to panic. He wasn't going to fit in this room. Either the ceiling would break or he would. Shoot! His feet were now pushing against a row of shelves. The shelves broke, and a wall of shoes fell into a massive pile on the floor.

"Rusty!" I started to wade through all the shoes on the floor to reach him.

He slowly turned to me, and I saw that he had also grown a full beard.

"Take them off! You won't fit in this room!" I yelled and pointed toward the ceiling.

Rusty looked up and must've realized he was inches from reaching the ceiling beams because he then frantically yanked off the shoes. His huge elbow hit the table and sent it sliding across the room. Luckily, most of the things on top of it didn't fall off, but some of the tools came crashing to the ground. The last thing I wanted to do was trash the workshop; this was my grandfather's special place, after all.

Once the shoes were off, just like that, Rusty began to revert to his original size. The hair on his head and face receded back into his face and scalp. His body thinned, and his limbs shortened. When he was finally normal again, he was left lying on the floor, surrounded by his clothes that were now tattered pieces.

I ran over to the hooks on the wall and grabbed a pair of overalls and threw them at Rusty. "Please, for my sake, put something on."

"That wasn't nearly as much fun as I thought it would be," he grumbled as he slowly sat up and grabbed the overalls. "I'll tell you one thing though: these shoes are the real deal."

"Guess that's why those people want them."

I surveyed the mess we made and started freaking out. How were we ever going to find these Vinland shoes? It could take forever, and we didn't have forever.

"I hope the shoes we're looking for weren't on the wall you just completely destroyed."

"Yeah ... sorry about that." Rusty was now standing beside me in his newly adopted overalls.

I couldn't help it. I started laughing. "Wow! You look ridiculous, dude."

"Shut up, Larkin," he snarled at me.

"Well, it's your own fault. You should've thought about what would happen when turning into a giant." I walked over to the shelves that were still on the wall and began to go through them. "Let's not try on anymore shoes for now, all right?"

Believe me, I knew it was tempting. Heck, I wanted to try more on too. A world of endless possibilities existed in this workshop, but now wasn't the time. We needed to find the Vinland shoes and fast.

"I'm going to see if there's anything in the book."

I walked back over to the big, wooden table, careful to not step on many of the random items that were now laying on the floor due to the table being swept across the room during Rusty's giant transformation. I flipped over the heavy pages of the massive book so I could start at the beginning. This book was fascinating. The pages were thick and had a rough texture to them, and the pictures were beautiful. The titles were so outlandish, though.

Seer of Truth ... Comprehension of Foreign Tongues ... Memory Retention ...

I wanted to ponder all their meanings and carefully read each page, but I couldn't let myself. I made a mental note to thoroughly read the book when I had time. For now, I focused on the word "Vinland" and turned the pages quickly. One after another. I glanced up and saw Rusty going through each pair of shoes one at a time. It might take a while, but we would find them. I continued flipping the pages. Some of the drawings were in ink, others in pencil, and a few even looked like they were done in watercolor. My grandfather didn't seem to follow any rules. I hoped that didn't mean we would have any difficulty finding the shoes, but it didn't seem like my grandfather was very organized. I continued to leaf through the book, and Rusty was now across the room. It was so quiet, I could hear water dripping from the ceiling somewhere. *Drip, drip, drip.*

"Uh, Wren?" Rusty said. "I think you should come over here."

I paused my reading to look up at him. He was standing still with his back to me. "Did you find them?" I asked.

"Maybe." He turned toward me. "I am officially creeped out."

"What is it?" I let go of the page I was holding and walked to the other side of the room.

He just pointed to the wall, so I followed his finger. There on the wall was a small shelf more elaborate than the rest, thick with carvings. On the shelf was a box. The structure holding it together was wood, but the sides were made up of panes of glass so we could see what was inside. There were three pairs of shoes. One looked like a short woman's boot with a bit of a western flair. The middle one looked like a pair of very worn, high-top sneakers. There was even a hole on the side of one of them. The last pair looked like a pair of black, military boots, the kind soldiers wore.

I turned to Rusty. "Why are you showing me this?"

"Did you read what's under them?"

Rusty pointed to the interior of the box. Even though the lighting wasn't great, I could see three names and three titles etched into the wood in front of each pair. The first said, Maria Tovar: Clarity of Sight; the second said, Wren Larkin: Compass to Vinland; and the third said, Rusty Whitaker: Cunning Warrior.

I tried to speak, but I couldn't muster up anything more than a whisper. "I don't understand. Why is my name on there? Why is your name on there? And Maria's?"

"Crazy, right?" Rusty was shaking his head back and forth. "How would your grandfather even know about me?"

"Or Maria? It doesn't make sense."

I peered through the glass again, staring at the shoes that were made for me. I read the words under my name again. Compass to Vinland.

"Do you think those are the shoes they're looking for?"

"Obviously, but what's the deal about Vinland? I mean, Maria's and mine kind of make sense, but yours is weird."

I slowly shook my head as I recalled everything my aunt told me.

"My Aunt Bryn used to tell me about it. It's a mythological place. Kind of like Atlantis," I tried to explain.

"But earlier you said it was on a map—like it was a real place."

"Well, technically, my aunt told me it was on really old maps, and then it just disappeared from later maps and people weren't sure where it went."

"What's that supposed to mean?" Rusty asked.

"I don't know. That's just what she told me."

I told him what I could remember. "Supposedly, the Vikings landed there. Leif Erikson was the leader, I think. They used to call it Vinland, but I think historians now think they just landed on Greenland or Newfoundland."

"So it isn't real?"

"Well, I didn't think it was." I paused before saying, "But now I'm not so sure."

"Maybe it's just hidden. Kind of like this place." Rusty gestured to the room, implying that Vinland and the workshop may have something in common.

I nodded. "Maybe."

"Compass," Rusty said slowly, contemplating its meaning. "Maybe these shoes can lead you there."

I gave him an incredulous look. "Why would I *want* to go there?"

The serious tone in his voice took me by surprise. "Maybe it's not a question of wanting to. Maybe you're supposed to go there. And maybe I'm supposed to be a cunning warrior."

I scoffed. "Well, he definitely got that part wrong."

"No, I think he was spot on with that one," Rusty said with certainty. "Now how do we get in there to get our destined shoes?"

We both examined the box again. No latch or handle.

"Your grandfather is kind of irritating," Rusty stated. He knocked on the glass. "Do you think we should just break the glass?"

"Seems a bit extreme."

I slid my hand across the front of the box, hoping my touch would do something. It didn't. There were no sharp things to prick my finger on, either.

"How are we supposed to get this thing open?"

As the last word left my lips, the front panel of glass split in the center and began to slide in opposite directions. I could hear glass being dragged against the frame. It stopped moving when the panes of glass were protruding out of the sides of the box, leaving the front wide open.

Rusty gestured toward the shoes. "Well, grab them."

I hesitated. Magical shoes that were somehow intended for me seemed a bit overwhelming. I slowly reached in and grabbed them. They felt a bit flimsy. These were the shoes everyone was looking for? These shoes didn't look good enough to even be put on the shelves at Goodwill.

Rusty pointed at the other shoes. "Get mine too. And Maria's."

I gave him a questioning look. "You sure we should take hers?"

He nodded. "Yeah, I'm sure. They were together for a reason."

I reached in and grabbed the other two pairs of shoes. Rusty's were pretty heavy, but Maria's were so soft and slippery, they almost slid out of my hands. I turned toward Rusty with an armful of shoes.

"Okay. Now, there's gotta be something down here we can put them in."

Rusty went back to the table and shuffled through all the random objects. After rummaging for a few minutes, he came back with an old, leather saddlebag. He held it open so I could pile the shoes inside. As I was putting them into the bag, I noticed words etched into the soles of the shoes. I held up Maria's boots and saw her name along with the phrase "Clarity of Sight" below it. It was faint and could've easily been missed, but nonetheless it was there. I looked at my worn sneakers. My name was faintly scrawled across the rubbery surface.

"Dude, how long is it going to take you to put those shoes in there?" Rusty asked.

"There's writing on them," I explained as I pushed the shoes into the bag. "Our names."

"Cool." Rusty smirked, seemingly liking the idea of these magical shoes having his name on them. "Where's the flashlight?"

I remembered seeing it on the huge table. I looked around, and yep, there it was. I picked it up off the table and then headed for the door. I glanced back at Rusty as I put my hand on the huge light switch.

"Ready?"

"Yeah," Rusty answered as he made his way to the door. "Back to the tunnel of doom."

I pulled the lever down, and the workshop was once again hidden in the dark. It made me sad to think this place had been abandoned for so long, buried deep in the earth. I walked through the doorway, and as I did, I heard shrieking and the sound of stone grinding against itself. I shined the flashlight in the direction of the noise. The Vess was coming back. Rusty and I ducked down and waited for the intimidating beast to pass. It landed on the platform above the door, laid its head down on its clawed feet, and locked its eyes on us. The door emerged from the wall and slid back into place.

Rusty got back up and adjusted the saddlebag's strap on his shoulder. "Geez. Are all these safety precautions really necessary?"

I slowly stood back up and dusted myself off.

"I'm starting to think *everything* my grandfather did was necessary."

CHAPTER 12
REVELATIONS

We sprinted back to the ladder, the light from the flashlight bouncing erratically around the enclosed space because I was moving so fast. It cast strange shadows on the hovering creatures, giving the impression that they were moving—then again, they probably were. A couple of grinding sounds made me think they were repositioning themselves, but I ignored them and just focused on getting back to the ladder. Eventually, I could see a light shining down from the opening above. When I finally reached the ladder that led back to my father's room, I jammed the flashlight into my back pocket and began to climb. I paused and glanced back at Rusty.

"You got that bag secure? We don't need to lose any of those shoes."

Rusty nodded and positioned the strap of the bag across his body. I glanced back at the tunnel one last time and was shocked by how dark it was. How did the stone creatures survive in such darkness? I had to remind myself that they weren't real. They were animated due to some kind of magic, but it was still kind of sad.

I began to ascend the ladder again and eventually reached the top. Placing my foot on the small space of the floor inside the chest, I stepped out of the chest and was again standing in my father's room. All my mother's things were sprawled on the floor, surrounding the chest. Rusty climbed out of the chest and then leaned over and closed the hinged door so there was no longer a hole in the floor. He put down the bag full of shoes, and we both began to quickly pile all the drawings, books, and clothes back into the chest. Once we finished, Rusty closed the heavy lid and reached for the lock that was still on the floor.

"Wait!" I grabbed the lock from him. "Don't put it back on. I may need to get in there again. We'll just put the sheet on. I'm sure my dad won't even look."

"Fine by me." He bent down, lifted the gray sheet, and covered the ornate chest.

I pointed to his leather coat on my father's bed. "You'd better get that."

Rusty grabbed his coat and then looked down at the overalls he was wearing. "Hey, can I borrow some clothes? I look like a hobo."

I wasn't about to disagree. He did look ridiculous.

"My room is one floor up. First door on the left. And can you throw this on my desk?" I handed him the big metal lock from the chest.

"Sure." He sprinted out of the room, leaving the bag full of shoes behind. His footsteps echoed as he climbed the rickety stairs to the next floor.

"Top two drawers in my dresser! And can you grab my backpack?" I called after him.

I put the flashlight back in the nightstand and scanned the room to make sure we didn't miss anything. I grabbed the bag full of shoes and stepped into the hallway. That was when it occurred to me. I had no idea what to do next. Yeah, I had the shoes the strangers probably wanted, but now what? I was conflicted. Should I tell my father? Should I give those freaky people the shoes? My gut said "no" to that one. My grandfather had a reason for making them for me, and I needed to find out why.

A minute later, Rusty came down in my clothes. I was struck by two things. The first thing was that, even though my clothes were too small for me, they looked pretty big on him. The jeans he put on had to be cuffed at the bottom so they didn't drag, and the sweater hung down past his waist. The second thing, and this was what really bugged me, was that he looked cool in them. It seemed like he could wear anything and look cool—well, anything except overalls—and that was beyond irritating.

I took the shoes out of the old saddlebag and put them in my backpack. We decided we would find Maria and tell her about the shoes. In retrospect, we just didn't have a clue what to do and hoped that maybe three brains were better than two.

Since I only had one bike, and Rusty wasn't big on the idea of riding as my passenger, we began walking to Maria's house. As we did, Rusty quizzed me about my family. He didn't believe me when I told him I didn't know why those people came to my house or why my grandfather had built that creepy tunnel to hide his workshop. With the inexplicable events of the day, and Rusty's constant badgering, I finally ran out of patience. I stopped at the top of Ghost Hill to set him straight.

"Okay, listen. I honestly don't know who those people were. I told you that my aunt told me stories about Vinland and that we were Vins, but I, regretfully, thought she was nuts, so I didn't really believe that any of it was true."

Rusty's face was all scrunched up in confusion. "Vins?"

"Yes, Vins," I repeated myself. "From Vinland."

"So where is your aunt now? Maybe she's the one we need to talk to."

I just shook my head. "We can't. She's dead—I think."

"You *think*?"

"You wanna hear something really crazy?" I asked him.

"After the day we've had, might as well keep it coming," Rusty snickered.

"The other day ..." I paused, wondering how stupid I was going to sound. "The other day, I was riding my bike to school, and when I got to Ghost Hill," I pointed in the direction of the spot, "I swear, I saw my aunt."

"What do you mean?" Rusty gazed down the hill. "Like alive?"

"Maybe," I said slowly. "Or maybe not."

He started to laugh. "Are you saying you saw a ghost on Ghost Hill?"

I sighed and shrugged my shoulders. "I'm not sure." I was starting to regret sharing this with him. It didn't sound like he believed me. "After everything we saw today, is it so hard to imagine that a ghost might exist?"

He stared at me for a minute in silence. Then he nodded his head in agreement.

"I guess you have a point."

We continued walking in silence, occasionally peering into the dense woods for any sign of ghostly figures. Once we started walking down the hill, I saw three people standing at the bottom: Maria, Mrs. Tovar, and a man I had never seen before. He was wearing a navy coat and had dirty blond hair. He was probably in his thirties or forties. It was hard to tell from a distance. I squinted my eyes to see him better, but then the craziest thing happened. He just disappeared. There one second and gone the next.

Rusty grabbed my arm. "Did you see that? Where'd he go?"

"I have no idea," I replied. "Maybe it's another ghost."

Mrs. Tovar must have heard us because she turned her head in our direction. "What are you two doing here?"

"Where did that guy go just now?" Rusty was walking rapidly down the hill, pointing to where the man had been standing. "He just disappeared!"

She looked at him like he was crazy, but I could tell her expression was forced. Her face was too stiff.

"Disappeared? I don't know what you mean. Just me and Maria here."

"You're kidding right?" Rusty approached them. "There was a guy here a second ago, and then he was gone."

"I think you are mistaken," Mrs. Tovar opened her jacket, exposing the interior of the garment. Inside were tons of small glass containers nestled into rows of pockets that lined the inside of her jacket. She poked around for a second and then took one out and held it to the light.

Maria reached out and snatched the small container out of her grandmother's hand.

"What are you doing?"

"A little forgetting spell isn't going to hurt him," Mrs. Tovar said discreetly to Maria.

"Are you kidding me? After you just had to break one on me?" Maria shook her head.

Mrs. Tovar pointed at Rusty. "He's a Nullvin!"

"Like that makes a difference." Maria put the container inside her jacket pocket.

Rusty was clearly confused. "What's going on? What are you talking about?"

I quietly voiced my interpretation of the situation. "I think she wants to make you forget that you saw that man disappear."

"Seriously?" Rusty took a step back.

Mrs. Tovar rolled her eyes. "Oh please. It's no big deal. You wouldn't even notice."

"Why would you do that to me?" Rusty asked.

"The less you know the better," Mrs. Tovar answered and then turned her attention to Maria. "I mean, seriously, Maria. Now he's going to start asking all these questions. Is this really necessary?"

"Yes," Maria said strongly. "You can't just go around erasing people's memories because they aren't Vins. That makes you just like *them*."

"How do you know I'm not a Vin?" Rusty asked somewhat defensively.

They both looked at him and them back at each other and laughed.

"What?" he asked loudly, clearly exasperated. "What's so funny about that?"

Maria stopped laughing and approached him. "Nothing." She reached out like she was going to put her hand on his shoulder, but then quickly changed her mind and pulled it back. "You're right. That was rude. It's just that we can sense each other, and you are definitely a Nullvin."

"A what?" Rusty asked.

"A Nullvin. That's what we call you guys," she explained.

"All right, that's enough. If you won't let me erase Rusty's memory, then we at least need to move this conversation into the woods." Mrs. Tovar gestured toward the forest. "Anyone could come through the port."

Maria nodded in agreement. Mrs. Tovar then stepped into the woods and disappeared.

"Come on," Maria said as she gestured for us to follow her into the woods.

"You good with this?" I asked Rusty.

"Yeah," he said and took off after Maria.

I followed him into the wild. It didn't take long for Rusty to start grilling Maria again. Luckily, Mrs. Tovar was far enough away that if we spoke softly, she wouldn't be able to hear what we were saying.

"So let's go back to that guy disappearing into thin air. How did he do that?"

Maria glanced back at Rusty. She bit her lip, probably contemplating if she should answer him. Finally, she just said, "This is very confidential stuff, Rusty."

Rusty pinched his thumb and forefinger together and moved them across his tightly closed mouth as if he were zipping it shut.

Maria grinned. "My abuela would never forgive me for telling you this stuff."

"Who?" Rusty asked.

"My grandmother, Rusty," Maria leered at him. "It's Spanish."

"Oh." He nodded and then leaned in toward her and whispered, "I won't say a thing. You can trust me."

She glanced over at me. "Wren, can he be trusted?"

I wasn't exactly sure how to answer that. Sure, I had been in school with him forever, but I barely talked to the guy.

"I can't say for sure, but he's already seen some pretty messed-up stuff today at my house, so … ."

Maria stared at Rusty as if she could somehow tell if he was trustworthy just by looking at him. She held her hand out. "Let's shake on it."

"Shake on it?" Rusty smirked. "Okay, sure." Rusty planted his hand in hers and shook it vigorously.

Maria eventually let go. "Okay, fine." She glanced ahead of us to make sure her grandmother was out of range. "There are many places all over the world—gravity hills, mystery spots. They're like portals. We call them ports. The guy you saw was using one to go somewhere else."

"So you're saying that if I step on that exact spot, I'm going to disappear and end up somewhere else, too?" Rusty asked, clearly getting excited.

"I'm not so sure it would work for you since you're not a Vin," Maria said. "Wren, however … it would work for Wren."

"I don't know about that." It wasn't like I'd ever done anything magical in my life. As far as I was concerned, I was just like Rusty.

Maria looked confused by my statement. "You really don't think you're a Vin, do you?"

I shook my head.

"So when I came to school, you didn't feel, like," she glanced at the ground, "a connection to me?"

Well, that was an awkward question. How the heck was I supposed to answer that? Was I really supposed to admit that I couldn't get her off my mind for the entire day? Or that it drove me crazy any time she and Rusty acted a little too friendly with each other? There's no way I could say any of that without dying from embarrassment. Instead, I tried to play it cool.

I just shrugged and said, "I guess."

"Anyways, you're saying that your special breed of people, the Vins," Rusty exaggerated the last word, "can just stand there and then—whoosh!—they're gone?"

"It's not that simple. You need a coin. The coins are kind of like tokens. There's a different coin for every port," she explained.

I remembered the coins piled on Mr. Fitzgerald's bed. It was all coming together.

I ducked under a low-hanging branch as I asked, "So where did that other guy go?"

"Tristan?" Maria asked. "He's looking for my parents. Things have been a little ... intense lately." She turned away and started walking faster.

I tried to catch up with her. "What do you mean by that?"

Mrs. Tovar glanced backward. "What are you kids talking about?"

"Nothing," Maria lied. "I was just telling them that things have been a little crazy lately."

Mrs. Tovar stopped walking and turned back toward us.

"Maria," she scolded her.

"After what happened to me, we know they're around here," Maria argued and then gestured to me and Rusty. "They should be warned."

"Who's around here?" I asked.

Mrs. Tovar sighed and then said, "The Wrathful."

"The what?"

Poor Rusty.

"The Wrathful," Mrs. Tovar said slowly. "They aren't like us. They use magic for dark purposes. There are rumors that they're plotting something and are gathering up Vins for some sinister purpose. People are disappearing."

"Disappearing?" I couldn't help but think about my neighbor. "Like Mr. Fitzgerald?"

"What about him?" Mrs. Tovar asked me.

"He wasn't home, but his suitcase was there like he was in the middle of packing," I explained. "But there was no sign of him."

Mrs. Tovar's face paled, and she brought her hand to her forehead. She appeared to be briefly overwhelmed by the idea.

"The thing is, Wren," Maria continued for Mrs. Tovar, "that day, when you found me, a man stopped me on the road. He was asking about where you lived and if I knew your aunt."

"But I thought you didn't know what had happened to you."

"I didn't because he put a forgetting curse on me. My abuela broke it."

"Did you tell him where I live?" I asked her.

"No way!" Maria responded. "That guy seemed shady. I knew something was up. He got all angry at me and did something to make me black out and forget ever talking to him."

This was all getting way too freaky. "He asked about my aunt?"

Maria nodded.

"But why would he ask about her? She's been dead for a while now," I said.

"Dead?" Mrs. Tovar's voice echoed loudly through the forest. "What on earth are you talking about?"

"My aunt died in a car accident a few years ago," I answered her. "At least, that's what my father told me."

She shook her head with disapproval. "Honestly, your father makes no sense to me. None at all. What a horrid thing to say!"

"Well, if she's alive, where has she been?" I asked.

"She has been living on the West Coast," Mrs. Tovar explained. "When it was clear that the Wrathful were becoming a real threat, she came here to get you."

"To get me?" I couldn't believe it.

Mrs. Tovar nodded. "That is what I've been told."

"Then that *was* her! Back on Gravity Hill. I saw her just the other day." I pointed behind us. "I thought she was a ghost."

"A ghost!" Mrs. Tovar shrieked. "You really are a strange boy."

I ignored her comment. I was too excited about the idea that my aunt was still alive. "What else was I supposed to think? But then she disappeared in the woods, and there was a circle burned into the earth of the forest. There was another circle at Mr. Fitzgerald's house, and those people who came to my house ... they burned up the grass there too."

"What?" Mrs. Tovar and Maria asked at the same time.

"The grass just, like, died around one of them," I told them. "All ash-like and gray."

Both Mrs. Tovar and Maria exchanged looks. "Sounds like you saw a Drainer," Maria said.

"What the heck is a Drainer?" I wondered if Rusty was actually following along with everything that was happening.

Mrs. Tovar's tone suddenly turned very serious. "Drainers are considered one of the evilest creatures of our kind. They drain the life out of all living things. They are so feared that all of them were banished from Vinland back in the nineteenth century, leaving them to roam the rest of the world and torment the unsuspecting Nullvins. Rumor has it they have recently formed an alliance with the Wrathful."

"I think the Wrathful were there too," I added. "Back at my house."

"I knew we were entering dark times, but I never expected they would come to your house." Mrs. Tovar was now pacing back and forth in the small clearing where we had stopped. "The darkness has even come to Lewisberry. I fear that the Wrathful have Mr. Fitzgerald and possibly your aunt."

I held my breath. "What do you mean?"

"Like I said," she responded, "people are disappearing."

My stomach dropped. What a terrifying thought. The relief I had felt after finding out that my aunt was alive was quickly overtaken by the fact that there was a very real possibility her life was in danger. I could lose her all over again. It was like a sick joke.

"Do you know why they were at your house, Wren?" Maria asked.

"From the sound of it, they were looking for a pair of shoes."

Maria's eyes widened. "Did you talk to them?"

"No. We were hiding. Up in a tree," I answered her, feeling numb.

"And they couldn't get into the house," Rusty added. "His grandfather protected it somehow. It was wild."

"That sounds like Bertram," Mrs. Tovar commented.

"You knew about the things my grandfather could do?" I asked her.

"Of course, Wren. Vins stick together."

It blew my mind. All this time, I had no idea she was so connected to my grandparents. "And Mr. Fitzgerald?"

She winced when I mentioned his name. "Yes, Mr. Fitzgerald ... is a Vin. We were the fearsome four at one time."

"Four?" I asked.

"Me, Bertram, Fritz ... that's what we called Fitzgerald, and your grandmother, Genevieve."

"Wait," I put my hands up. "My grandmother was a Vin too?"

Mrs. Tovar stared at me intently for a moment. "You really were in the dark about all of this, weren't you?"

"Apparently," I said, more aggressively than I intended.

I was angry.

I was angry with her and Mr. Fitzgerald for not being more forthcoming. I was angry with my father. I was angry with myself for not seeing what was right in front of me.

Maria sensed my frustration and changed the subject. "What kind of shoes could they be looking for?"

"I think the shoes they want can lead you to Vinland," I answered her.

Both Mrs. Tovar and Maria turned to me, their mouths slightly ajar. Mrs. Tovar shook her head. "But that doesn't make any sense. Once you leave Vinland, you can never return. It's not possible."

"Well, I don't know if they work, but the shoes say, 'Compass to Vinland' on them." I felt the weight of the shoes in my backpack.

"Where did you find them?" Mrs. Tovar asked.

"In my grandfather's workshop. Did you know about that too?" I asked her.

"Of course I did."

"Why didn't you ever tell me about it?"

"It wasn't my place to tell you. If you were still clueless when your powers kicked in, Fritz and I decided we would explain things to you."

"Why would you wait?"

"We figured you would eventually catch on. Besides, Bryn said she already told you everything."

"But I didn't believe her. I thought she was insane or making it all up."

Her mouth opened slightly and she narrowed her eyes at me. "Well, whose fault is that, Wren?"

That shut me up. I immediately felt guilty for thinking my aunt was crazy.

Rusty broke the awkward silence. "So now what?"

"After Maria was attacked outside of your house, well ... I decided it was time to leave Lewisberry." Mrs. Tovar folded her hands together and bought them to her mouth. "But now that I know there were Drainers at Wren's house, I think he should come with us too."

"Wait a minute," Rusty interjected. "You knew bad dudes were lurking around Lewisberry, and you were going to just leave us here?"

"I didn't know there were Drainers in town," Mrs. Tovar defended herself. "I was planning on getting Wren eventually. And you certainly weren't in any trouble, Rusty. You're a Nullvin."

"You just said those Drainer things prey on unsuspecting humans," Rusty argued his case.

I had to agree with Rusty. "You *did* say that."

Mrs. Tovar sighed and put her hands up in surrender. "Listen, I'm sorry you got mixed up in this, Rusty, but this is Vin business. Wren is a Vin, and you aren't."

"What about my dad?" I asked.

"I suppose that he could come with us if he wants," she said, but I got the feeling she didn't actually mean that. Her words didn't seem genuine or sincere.

"But not me, right?" Rusty took a few steps closer to Mrs. Tovar.

The sun was now setting, and he was surrounded by a backdrop of dark trees with bursts of orange and red hues from the sunset filtering through the countless branches.

"Honestly, Rusty, you should just go back home and pretend like none of this ever happened. This doesn't concern you," Mrs. Tovar said.

"Doesn't concern me?" Rusty shouted incredulously.

He then walked briskly toward me and pulled my backpack off my shoulder. He flipped the flap open and sorted through the contents until he found his shoes. When he pulled out the combat boots and thrust them toward Mrs. Tovar, he reminded me of a lawyer presenting the courtroom with the smoking gun.

"What about these?"

Mrs. Tovar stood there for a second with a confused look on her face. "Boots?" she asked. "I'm not following. Are those the Vinland shoes?"

"No," Rusty said firmly, "these were made for me." He leaned toward her, pointing to the place where his name was etched into the sole. "By Wren's grandfather."

Mrs. Tovar reached into her interior pocket again. But instead of pulling out some potion, she pulled out her reading glasses. She put them on, took the boot from Rusty, and angled it so the remaining sunlight would hit the sole.

"Rusty Whitaker. Cunning Warrior," Mrs. Tovar read out loud. "Where did these come from?" She glared at him over her reading glasses.

"My grandfather's workshop," I answered her. "We found them in there along with the Vinland shoes."

"But that doesn't make any sense." Her gaze darted toward me like I had the answer to her unspoken question, which I didn't. "They wouldn't work on him. He's not a Vin."

"I think they'll work just fine," Rusty argued. "I put on a pair of shoes that turned me into a giant a couple of hours ago. Right, Wren?"

"That is true." There was no denying it.

"And he didn't just make a pair for me," Rusty continued. "He made one for Maria, and the Vinland shoes … those are for Wren."

He opened the bag to show Mrs. Tovar the shoes inside. "So it looks like we're all in this together. And there's no freaking way you guys are leaving me behind."

CHAPTER 13
DUSK

"He made shoes for me?" Maria approached Rusty and peered into my backpack. She reached in and pulled out the short, leather boots.

"It has your name on it." He pointed to the sole. "See, right there."

Maria read it quietly at first, then lifted her head.

"It says my name, and then it says, 'Clarity of Sight.' Which makes sense, considering the difficult time I've been having. These could change everything."

"But he never told me about any of this." Mrs. Tovar was clearly unsettled. She started pacing again in the middle of the forest. I could hear the sound of old, dried leaves crunching under her feet. "And yours, Wren. What is the title of your shoes again?"

"It says, 'Compass to Vinland,' " I answered her.

" 'Compass'?" she repeated and paused, letting the word sink in.

"I don't understand why he would make them for me," I commented. "Why would he want me to go there?"

"I don't know," Mrs. Tovar responded. "But there are a lot of exiled Vins who would do anything to get back to Vinland."

"What's the deal with this place exiling everyone?" Rusty asked. "Like, what do you have to do to get kicked out?"

"There are many reasons," Mrs. Tovar explained. "There are ridiculous politics in Vinland, just like here. People have been wrongly accused of crimes or have simply pledged allegiance to the wrong leader. The biggest expulsion involved the Drainers. When they were banished, they swore they would return to Vinland and seek vengeance on those who had cast them from their homeland. If those shoes truly lead you back there, then it makes sense why the Drainers are after them. The question is, how did they find out about their existence?"

Mrs. Tovar was still pacing, thinking. We waited in silence until she finally said, "I think I need to make a few calls. You three: don't move an inch." She walked a little farther into the trees and disappeared.

We were all still for a moment. We had a lot to think about.

Finally, I broke the silence. "This is a lot to take in. I don't know if I'm ready to leave Lewisberry."

Maria sighed. "I get it, Wren. I really do, but this is serious. I have no idea where my parents are and no idea how to find them. I don't think you should stay here alone, especially since they have already been to your house."

The weight of her tone was hard for me to acknowledge. It was one thing for an adult to lecture me about how dangerous something was, but hearing it from Maria, a peer, was more confirmation that things just got real.

"And that's exactly why you're not leaving me here," Rusty said. "If they know about Wren's shoes, they must know about mine too."

"Relax, Rusty." Maria put her hands in front of her, urging him to calm down. "I'm sure we'll be able to convince my abuela that you should come with us. We just need to be strategic about it. You need to plead your case *calmly*."

"Not exactly sure I know how to do that right now," Rusty said gruffly.

"I can tell."

Maria found a nearby stump and sat down with a huff. She still had the shoes my grandfather made for her in her hands. She was examining them, looking closely at the interior, the stitching, and the sole.

Rusty walked over and sat on the ground next to her. "You gonna put them on?"

"I don't know," she answered without looking at him. "Not sure what will happen if I do."

"I don't get it. What does 'Clarity of Sight' mean anyway?" he asked. "What's your superpower?"

She gave him an exasperated look. "Vins don't have superpowers."

"Kind of seems like it," he answered her. "At least from what I've seen."

"Well," she paused. "I'm not really that impressive. I can't do anything as cool as my grandmother. No casting or potions for me. I'm just a Cerebral."

"Am I supposed to know what that means?" Rusty asked.

"I guess not," she paused. "How do I explain this? There are many Vin categories. Some examples are Casters, Crafters, Potion-Smiths. My grandmother is a Potion-Smith."

"Okay. So what do Cerebrals do?" I asked her.

"The Cerebrals have psychic powers. Some have visions of the future, and others can move things with their minds, like telekinesis. And finally, there are others who can read people's minds."

"So which one are you?" Rusty was leaning forward, waiting for her to respond.

"I can read people's minds," she said with a sullen expression.

"That's amazing! How do you do it?" I asked, fascinated.

"I have to touch whoever it is I'm trying to read."

As soon as she said that, my mind raced back to the first day of school when I was completely infatuated with her. I could feel my face heat up by the idea that she may have been able to see how I was thinking about her. Had she touched me that day? By the bike rack? I couldn't remember. I knew she had touched me when we were in Rusty's room when I felt like crap. What was I thinking then? What had she seen?

Maria interrupted my thoughts. "Don't worry. I suck at it. I barely know what I'm doing. Cerebrals are pretty rare, and I haven't had anyone around to show me the ropes."

"Why do you think you suck?" I asked her.

"Imagine being inside of someone's brain. It's a mess in there. A lot to sort out," she responded. "And sometimes, it's better if you don't know what people are thinking about you. Believe me. Not great for your self-esteem."

"That makes sense. I can only imagine what people think about me," Rusty commented. "But then again, most of the time, I feel like I already know."

"Can you give us an example?" I was intrigued. "Preferably nothing to do with me."

Maria leaned back and gazed off for a second. "Well ... I read that jerk at school. I didn't mean to, though. The guy basically knocked me over."

"Which jerk?" Rusty asked. "There are a lot of them."

"That guy in Mad Millie's class. Emmett or something."

"The biggest jerk of all," Rusty said.

"Well, when he plowed into me, I knew he and his friends were planning on hiding Mad Millie's wallet in your desk. That's how I knew you didn't steal it."

"I knew it was him!" Rusty shouted as he hopped up. He thrust a clenched fist up in the air. "That jerk! I feel vindicated!"

I pushed myself off the tree I was leaning on and grabbed his arm. "Rusty, not so loud. There could be some Drainers around."

Rusty brushed my hand away.

"All right, all right." He put his hands on his hips and shrugged. "And all this time, I just thought Maria had a thing for me."

"What?" Maria exclaimed. "You're kidding, right?"

Rusty didn't answer her right away. He just glanced her way slyly. "You didn't have to stick up for me."

Maria huffed and crossed her arms in front of her chest. "It was the right thing to do."

Rusty let out a laugh. "Who does that anymore?"

"I do," she said firmly. She then shifted her body so her back was to Rusty.

"Anyway, Wren, as you can see, my powers are pretty useless. I can't cast spells or make magical shoes. I can just see people's inner thoughts. Kind of lame."

I shook my head. "I don't think that's lame at all. I think being able to see people's thoughts is killer. You can tell who's telling the truth and who's lying. That's amazing!"

I couldn't believe she thought that was lame. As far as I was concerned, having any kind of power sounded pretty cool. I doubted I even had any powers. All I had were these lousy shoes. I mean, what was I supposed to do with them anyway? Walk endlessly to some mythical land? Besides, the way my aunt had described it, this place sounded like it was an island. How was I supposed to get there? Walk on water?

Suddenly, I heard the crunching sounds of leaves being stepped on. Someone was coming.

Even though I all knew it was probably Mrs. Tovar, I waited anxiously for her to come into view. I released my breath when she emerged from the woods, holding a small, glass vial that contained something that was glowing green. Now that the space was illuminated by the neon light, it made the forest beyond appear dark and ominous. Mrs. Tovar's face was eerily lit from below.

"I got a hold of Tristan."

"Who's Tristan?" Rusty asked.

"A friend," was all Mrs. Tovar said.

"What about Mom?" Maria asked her.

"Still no word," Mrs. Tovar said, avoiding eye contact with her granddaughter. "Here's the plan. I'll go with Wren. Together we'll tell his father that we are leaving."

"What a minute," I interjected. "I never said for sure that I was leaving."

"I think it's for the best, Wren," Mrs. Tovar said without any regard for my rejection of the idea.

Rusty stepped forward. "I'm coming too, right?"

Mrs. Tovar glanced at him. "I'm conflicted. It's not like I can just take you with us. That's called kidnapping."

Rusty angled his head downward but kept his gaze on Mrs. Tovar.

"You can't leave me here. There is nothing for me here. There never has been, and there never will be. No one believes in me in this town." Rusty then raised his head a little and pointed at me. "But for some reason, his grandfather thought enough of me to make me these shoes. You have to let me see what that means. Believe me, my parents aren't going to miss me. Heck, my dad left home a week ago to god knows where, and now my mom just stays at the bar every night. They won't even notice I'm gone, and if they do, they honestly won't care."

Even though Mrs. Tovar didn't say anything at first, there was a look of concern on her face.

Finally, she said, "Okay. But you need to tell your mother something. No mother deserves to think her child just disappeared."

Rusty nodded. "I'll leave her a note. Is that good enough?"

"All right. Maria, you go with him. You'll be safer at his house than at Wren's." Mrs. Tovar pointed at my backpack, which Rusty was held. "And the shoes. You two should take the shoes. Keep them safe."

"Of course," Maria said, and she put her shoes back inside the backpack. Rusty zipped it closed and slung it over his shoulder.

"Stay out of sight," Mrs. Tovar said firmly. "Woods only. We'll meet back at Ghost Hill in a half hour. Tristan will be there waiting for us. Got it?"

Maria and Rusty nodded and then went in the opposite direction. Mrs. Tovar led the way through the dark forest with her glowing vial. We stepped over fallen trees and ducked under thick, horizontal branches. I had walked in the woods at night before, but that was before I knew what was out there.

The woods seemed different now.

Everything did.

CHAPTER 14
SINKING IN

"You do realize that if my dad thought my aunt was crazy, he's going to think that you're completely insane," I said as I followed Mrs. Tovar through the woods.

She glanced over at me. "Your father might surprise you."

That was an odd thing to say. My dad never surprised me. He was the most predictable person in the world—same clothes, same food, same conversations, same bedtime, same weekly routines. I wasn't buying into the idea that he would surprise me.

As we approached my house, we were careful to stay out of sight. Even though it was dark, the moon provided enough light that I was able to see the large burn circle on my front lawn. It reminded me of who had been here and who could be coming back. It blew my mind that this was even happening.

"How do we know that none of them are around?" I whispered.

"We don't." Mrs. Tovar had a stern look on her face as she looked around. "But I can usually sense other Vins nearby, and I'm not sensing anything."

"That's the thing I really don't get. If I'm a Vin, shouldn't I have sensed something about you and Mr. Fitzgerald?" I asked.

"Did you not feel an attachment to Mr. Fitzgerald?" she countered. "And, to some extent, me?"

I had to think about it, but if I was being honest, I kind of had. They had always felt familiar, comfortable.

"I guess."

We walked along my driveway, hiding behind various trees and bushes. Her hand was inside her jacket, and I wondered if she was contemplating which magical potion she would pull out if we were confronted or attacked. I hoped she was. Once we got closer, I could see that the large shed my dad used for a garage was open, and my dad's car was inside. We quickly ran to the side door and opened it. As usual, it wasn't locked, at least not for me. Mrs. Tovar followed me inside, and I made my way to the kitchen. I knew my dad would be there on his computer. As I walked into the room, my father looked up at me. He must have realized I wasn't alone because he leaned his head to one side so he could see who was behind me.

"Camilla?" He had a surprised tone to his voice. "What are you doing here?"

Mrs. Tovar walked around me and approached the table. "We need to talk, Ben."

"Did something happen?" My father looked slightly concerned as he leaned back in his chair and waited for her to respond.

"Ben," she began slowly, her tone remarkably gentle, "you and I haven't really talked at length. I mean, not since Abigail fell into that awful coma."

My father's gaze moved to the table. Anytime my mother's name came up, a look of discomfort washed over his face.

"I think we both know that Abigail and her family were ... special." She waited for my father to look up, but he didn't, so she continued. "The thing is, some people were here earlier, some people who I believe have bad intentions. Your son is in danger."

My father finally looked up. "What do you mean?"

"I think you and your son should leave Lewisberry," she responded.

I tried to read his face. I was expecting him to be more confused or claim that what she was saying was outlandish, but he didn't look confused at all.

"Did those people burn up the grass on the front lawn?"

Mrs. Tovar just nodded and remained quiet.

My father pushed his chair back, trying to create some distance. It made a loud scratching sound as it skidded across the floor.

"It just so happens that I got a job offer. Wren and I are leaving town anyway."

"What?" My worst fear had come true, although it didn't matter anymore. I would be leaving Lewisberry regardless, but for some reason, I was angry. Maybe it was because he never asked me how I felt about any of it. Or maybe it was because Mrs. Tovar was telling him I was in danger, and all he still seemed to care about was his job, his future.

"The job came through," he said. "I was planning on us leaving in a week or two, but if we have to leave now—then so be it."

I was so frustrated with him that I could barely contain myself. "Didn't you hear what she just said? There were people here, and they were looking for me and some shoes. They could do crazy things, or even hurt someone. Why are you acting like this is no big deal?"

He didn't respond. He didn't even look at me.

"Did you know about Vins?" I asked him. "Or the workshop under the house?"

His head shot up once I mentioned the workshop.

"You know about the workshop? You went into my room?"

"Are you kidding me?" I couldn't believe him. After everything he had kept from me, he thought I should feel bad about going into his room? "You knew all about this stuff, didn't you? The workshop. What my grandparents were. What my mother is. You told me Aunt Bryn was *dead*!"

My dad abruptly stood up. "It was better for you to stay out of it. Look what happened to them!"

"I don't *know* what happened to them. You've never been honest with me!" I walked over to the table and slammed my hands on the hard surface, leaning toward him. "How could you keep this from me?"

He sighed. "Listen, I stayed out of all of it. I knew there were things about your mother's family that were strange, but I never asked about any of it. I never got involved. And you should do the same."

I couldn't believe him. "How is that possible? How could you not want to know?"

"Because I didn't," my father said bluntly.

"So what? You just ignored who your wife is?" I couldn't understand it. How could you love someone yet not want to know everything about them? "You lied to me."

"It was for the best," he said wearily. He was rubbing his forehead, like the conversation was giving him a headache.

I wasn't going to let him off that easily. "How could not knowing the truth be for the best?"

"Look around, Wren," he said as he glared at me. "Everyone is missing, and honestly, I really thought your aunt was dead. Everything these people touch turns bad. It's like they're all cursed. It was best to keep you out of it."

"Shouldn't that have been *my* decision?"

"Last I checked, you're the child, and I'm the adult!" he roared.

I jumped, startled by his sudden anger. I had never heard my dad speak with such intensity. He always seemed numb to everything. Detached.

Mrs. Tovar cleared her throat. I had forgotten she was in the room.

"Ben," she said softly, "am I to understand that you intend to leave town for your new job?"

"Yes," he answered her. "It's in Pittsburgh."

"I have some concerns." She glanced my way as she spoke. "I am not sure you can keep Wren safe. I feel like, for the time being …" she hesitated before continuing, "it may be better if he came with me. We can protect him."

My dad crossed his arms in front of his chest. I thought he was going to argue, but then his face softened and he said, "I can't say that I disagree with you."

"Wait," I interrupted. Again, I was shocked by his response. "You're not coming with us? You're still going to Pittsburgh?"

He didn't look at me. He was staring down at the table again.

"She's right. She can protect you, and I don't belong with those people. I never have. No matter how hard your mother wanted me to, it never worked."

"So that's it? You're just handing me off?"

"I'm not handing you off. She said you're in danger." He looked at Mrs. Tovar. "She can protect you—I can't."

I threw my hands up. "Fine! Go to Pittsburgh. Go on with your life. That's what you always wanted anyways, to pretend like you never met my mom or had me."

I could see hurt in his eyes, and I almost felt bad.

"That's not fair. I loved your mother ... and I love you."

He had never said that before. It was what I had always wanted to hear for as long as I could remember, but for some reason, it didn't seem to matter anymore. I looked at him and wanted to feel something from his words. But I didn't.

I turned to Mrs. Tovar. "What should I bring?"

"Just some clothes, I guess," she said tentatively, watching my father out of the corner of her eye. "You should hurry."

She pulled out her phone and looked at the time.

I left the room without glancing at my father and climbed the stairs. Once I reached my room, I stopped and looked at it. *Really* looked at it. I saw all the strange things I had collected around the house—a scroll with some foreign text, a statue of a dragon with fur instead of scales, and a table lamp that looked like a giant glowing feather. I walked over to my desk and thumbed through the huge packet from US History. It seemed totally weird that I didn't have to worry about finishing it anymore. Next to the packet was the pile of random gifts I had gotten from the crows. I sifted through the items and grabbed a four-leaf clover pendant and shoved it in my pocket for luck. That was when it finally hit me. I was leaving, and who knew how long it would be before I could come back.

I grabbed an overnight bag that had been sitting on the bottom of my closet for years and opened it. I walked over to my dresser and pulled out some clothes. How much would I need? Would it be hot or cold? I grabbed random pieces of clothes and shoved them into my bag. I went over to my nightstand, opened a drawer, and took out the picture of my mother with her parents and my Aunt Bryn. I would definitely bring that. I took a couple of my favorite books and a wad of cash I had kept hidden in my top drawer.

I went to the door and glanced back at my room one last time. I would miss it.

I left my room and looked down the narrow hallway toward the stairs that lead to the roof. The crows would be pissed when I stopped showing up in the mornings. That made me feel crappy. They would be waiting for me to open the door every day, but it would never open. At least, not for a while. I kept telling myself this was just temporary. I didn't know how, but I had to believe I would be back soon. I couldn't accept the idea that I was never coming back. That this was final.

I turned my gaze away from the stairway that led to the roof and walked in the opposite direction. I paused by my father's bedroom on my way back downstairs. I saw him inside, his back to me as he filled a suitcase. I wondered how much he would take with him. I doubted he would pack much; he hated the shoe house and everything in it. He would probably prefer to leave everything behind and start over. I kept walking.

In the family room, Mrs. Tovar waited for me. "Are you all right, Wren?"

I could tell she felt bad for me. She had a look of pity on her face. I knew she was just trying to be nice, but it was embarrassing and uncomfortable.

"I'm fine. Shouldn't we get going?"

"Yes," she answered. "Here comes your father now."

I saw him come into the room with a suitcase. He glanced at me and then set his suitcase down.

"Listen, Wren," he said as he awkwardly shuffled closer. "Let me get settled in Pittsburgh, and when everything calms down, you can come live with me there."

I didn't answer him. He was more like his family than I ever realized. They abandoned him, and now he was abandoning me. He hugged me, but I remained stiff as a board. Once he let go of me, he handed Mrs. Tovar a piece of paper.

"Here is my number. Keep in contact," he said. "And keep him safe."

"Of course," she said.

Then my father walked out the front door, leaving the shoe house behind for good.

CHAPTER 15
CAUGHT

I was such an idiot. I asked Mrs. Tovar if I could say goodbye to my plants, which, in retrospect, seems like a really dumb thing to do. I just felt so bad about the fact that I took care of them for so long, and now they were just going to shrivel up and die. Plus, I wanted to grab some seeds so that, wherever I ended up, I could regrow what I had created in the greenhouse. I shoved some seeds into my pockets and headed for the front door. I reached for the handle and pulled the door toward me right when I heard Mrs. Tovar's voice behind me. "Wait!"

But like I said, I was being such an idiot. I wasn't thinking about the fact that no one could get into my house unless I let them in. It didn't occur to me that I should look outside before I opened the door. I just opened it like I had done a thousand times before, and when I did, I immediately regretted it. There, standing in front of me, was the tall Drainer who had burned my grass. He looked as surprised to see me as I was to see him. His fist was raised as if he were preparing to knock on the door.

The stunned look on his face slowly morphed into a smirk.

"Wren Larkin," he said smoothly.

He was taller than me and, frankly, looked perfect. His clothes were perfect, as were his hair and face. He didn't look real.

I mentally slapped myself for just standing there, staring like the idiot I was, and tried to slam the door shut, but the Drainer was quick. His hand caught the side of the door, and he prevented it from closing.

"Well, that was rather rude. Do you always treat your guests so disrespectfully?"

"Not all of them," I grumbled under my breath.

I looked at his hand grasping the door and thought about what Mrs. Tovar had told me. All it took was the touch of a Drainer, and you would pretty much be dead. The Drainer pushed the door inward and bent down slightly as he walked into my family room. Behind him were more people. I recognized the balding guy who had tried to get into my house earlier that afternoon. As for the others, they could have been there earlier, or maybe they were new. It was hard to tell. But the person who stood out the most was a woman. If I had to describe her, I would say she looked like a real-life anime character—petite with large eyes and thick, dark hair that was pulled into a high ponytail. She was wearing all white, which didn't seem right. These were the bad guys; shouldn't they be wearing all black? But the weird thing was, she didn't look all there. Her eyes were glossed over. It was almost like she was on drugs or something.

They all entered my house, and suddenly the room felt too small. The door remained open, and for a second, I considered just hightailing it out of there. But even if I had managed to slip away, I knew I couldn't leave Mrs. Tovar behind. So I turned away from the door and faced what was to come.

Mrs. Tovar grabbed my arm and pushed herself in front of me, which was kind of pointless since she was shorter than me.

"What do you want?" she asked them.

The tall Drainer sneered down at her. "Nothing of great importance. All we seek is a pair of shoes. Give us what we want, and we will be gone. Simple, right?"

Mrs. Tovar's neutral expression gave nothing away. She wasn't going to let on that she knew about the shoes. "What shoes?"

"Well ..." he said as he started to stroll around the room. He moved so fluidly, he almost appeared to be floating. "The thing is, it has come to our attention that the resident shoemaker made a pair of shoes that has the ability to lead the wearer to Vinland. Can you believe it?" He glanced at Mrs. Tovar. "Who would think that such a thing was possible?

"I wouldn't." Mrs. Tovar's voice was steady. "Doesn't seem possible."

"I thought so as well." The man was now standing by the entryway to the kitchen. "But I have been assured that they are indeed real."

Mrs. Tovar cleared her throat. "Could you be kind enough to tell me your name?"

"But of course!" He walked toward her. "My name is Ashford. Thomas Ashford."

He put his hand out as if he wanted to shake hands with her. Mrs. Tovar looked down at his hand but didn't move.

"There is nothing to fear, dear lady," Ashford assured her. "Just two Vins greeting each other. We are not at odds, are we?"

I wondered how he knew she was a Vin, but then I remembered that Vins could sense each other.

"No," she answered him, but she kept her hands to her side.

He slowly put his hand down.

"Do you live here?" he asked her. "Are you the shoemaker's wife?"

"No, I am a friend. Mr. Needlecoff and his wife no longer reside here," Mrs. Tovar answered.

"But his shoes are still here, right? His creations?" Ashford looked around the house. "Where did he keep them?"

"I was rather close to the shoemaker, and he never once mentioned anything about shoes that could lead the wearer to Vinland. I question whether you have been led astray." Surprisingly, Mrs. Tovar was rather convincing. She could've been an actress. "Perhaps your sources were untrustworthy."

Ashford grinned at her. "I don't think so. Our source would know; she is his daughter after all."

"What?" Her voice was strained. "Who is your source?"

"Bryn Needlecoff." Ashford tilted his head to the side. "Are you familiar with her?"

Mrs. Tovar froze. "That can't be—"

"I mean, it took a while." He gazed up at the ceiling for a minute. "It's not like she volunteered the information. But the shoes *are* here, and we *will* find them."

I couldn't help but think about seeing my aunt on Ghost Hill and how it looked like she was pulled into the fog. What if that was when they got her? Just a moment before we were reunited ... .

Ashford once again turned his attention toward me. "What about you, young man? Do you live here?"

Mrs. Tovar nervously glanced back at me. I stepped to the side so she was no longer blocking me. "Yes, I live here."

"Do you know where the shoes are?"

"Up until earlier today, I didn't even know my grandfather was a shoemaker. I don't think I can help you."

My heart thumped loudly in my chest. I hoped he would believe me.

He titled his head and squinted his eyes at me. "You didn't know your grandfather was a Crafter? I find that hard to believe."

"It's the truth," I answered him. "I have pretty much been left here on my own, raised by a regular ... Nullvin."

He nodded his head slightly. "Interesting. So you have a limited understanding of the Vins?"

"Yes, very limited."

"Then do you know what I am?"

I lied and shook my head.

He smiled at me and then walked over to a nearby plant that was cascading over a side table. He glanced over at me to make sure I was watching him, and then he reached out and touched a leaf on the plant. Before my eyes, the leaf began to shrivel, and it turned from an emerald green to an ash gray. The dead color began to travel toward the center of the plant. One by one, the leaves turned gray and then to dust. The stems were the last to survive; the plant now looked like a charred skeleton reaching out in all directions for help.

But then the fragile structure collapsed, and gray dust particles filled the air and slowly descended to the floor. Thomas inhaled deeply with his eyes closed as though he just had a refreshing drink. He then turned back to me.

"Amazing, isn't it?"

I didn't answer him. I found it annoying that he thought I should be in awe of him. What a freak.

He came closer to me, looking a bit irritated that I wasn't more impressed.

"You do realize that what happened to that plant could happen to you," he said gruffly. "Or even to your elderly friend here."

I remained quiet.

Mrs. Tovar quickly spoke up. "Mr. Ashford, we don't have the shoes. What would you like us to do?"

"I would like you to find them!" he shouted, finally having lost his patience.

At that moment, I realized more than just his loud voice filled the room. Through the open door, a cloud of black had suddenly burst into the enclosed space. My crows! The others were trying to fend them off, waving their arms frantically.

I glanced at the open door. This was our chance. We could escape while the crows attacked the intruders. I grabbed Mrs. Tovar by the wrist and started to run for the door. As I got closer, I heard Ashford's voice shouting, "Caterina, do something!"

Out of the corner of my eye, I saw the young woman with the huge eyes step forward. She pulled out a rather large Asian fan and snapped her wrist. The fan unfolded; it was white just like her clothes, except for the back design and black spines that extended past the fabric. She moved her hand swiftly to the side and then downward and said, "Obtundo."

A cool mist filled the room. My body went limp, my legs going out from under me. I collapsed onto the floor, and Mrs. Tovar collapsed behind me. I was so close. I could see the outside, but I couldn't get there. I couldn't move. All around me, I could see the others had collapsed as well. Only Ashford and the girl who had cast the spell remained standing. Even the crows were lying motionless on the floor, silent and in contorted positions. One was lying close to me, its black eyes focused on me, pleading for help. It was terrifying to not be able to move. I was completely at their mercy, and I hated the feeling.

"Thank you, Caterina," I heard Ashford say. "What did you do to them?"

"I stunned them." Her voice sounded cold and emotionless.

"How long until they regain their strength?"

"Ten, fifteen minutes," she answered him. "The birds, however, will take longer. They may not recover at all."

Oh no ... my crows ... .

"What was that anyway? Why did they fly in here like that?" Ashford asked her. "Was that a spell? Did someone command those crows to attack?"

Caterina's answer was monotone. "I don't know. Birds are not easy to control. If someone did, I would be impressed."

"Well, I am an impatient man, and this has already taken too long." I could hear someone, probably Ashford, walk farther away from me. "Let's look for his workshop. The shoes are supposed to be there."

The woman didn't answer, but I heard more than one pair of footsteps leave the room. I glanced out the door again. If I could just regain my strength, I could somehow get out the door. I would drag Mrs. Tovar to safety if I had to. My gaze fell upon the bird closest to me again. Its feet were like sticks poking out of its body. Past the bird stood the balding man. Thankfully, his face was turned away from me.

I angled my head to get a better view of how far away Mrs. Tovar was, and that was when it dawned on me that I was moving my head. I was already getting my movement back! I looked back at the crow lying next to me. Would he regain his strength, or would he never move again like she said? I wanted to reach out to the crow and comfort him. I put all my focus on moving my hand toward him and—yes! My hand moved, and I was now caressing his wing.

It'll be okay, I thought. I couldn't tell the crows apart that well, but I recognized this one. It had a dent on its beak that I had always wondered about. I called him Tough Guy because I imagined he'd gotten it in a fight. I wondered if he was scared, if all the crows were scared. I wished there were something I could do.

That was when it happened again. The tingling started in my chest and traveled down my arm. I blinked because my vision had suddenly become blurry. My head felt heavy as the tingling intensified. I closed my eyes for a second, hoping the strange sensation would fade. I honestly didn't want to experience that again. Then I felt movement under my hand. I opened my eyes; the bird was on its feet, stretching out its wings. It then came closer to my face and nudged my cheek with its dented beak.

Had I done that? Had I somehow made the crow better? Was this what I had done to make Maria better that day? The crow backed away from me, turned toward the door, and then flew out into the darkening sky.

I breathed in deeply, tightening all my muscles as I tried to move again. I wasn't as drained this time, so I was able to roll on to my side. No one else was moving. I looked down toward my feet. Mrs. Tovar was lying on her stomach, her hand outstretched in my direction, but I couldn't see her face. I slowly pushed my upper body off the floor and scanned the room. It was an eerie sight. Bodies and black crows lying motionless in silence.

I somehow got into a seated position and then eventually to my feet. I felt weak and off-balance, swaying a bit as I stood, but I knew this was our best chance to get away from these people. Those who were facing me followed my movements, but they couldn't do anything to stop me. Not yet.

I moved toward Mrs. Tovar and bent down. I looked into her eyes and smiled at her, trying to reassure her that we were going to get out of here. I grabbed her under the arms and pulled her upward. It was awkward, but somehow, I was able to get her off the ground and was now carrying her toward the door. I was almost there when I heard something behind me. I glanced backward, and my heart sunk. The dark-eyed woman with the fan was right behind me. A strong swoosh of wind hit my face as the front door slammed shut.

"Where do you think you're going?" she asked.

So close... .

CHAPTER 16

THERE AND BACK AGAIN

The others were coming around; I could see them starting to move. I had put Mrs. Tovar on the couch and was sitting on a chair next to her.

"But why did he come around before the others?" Ashford was asking Caterina. They were both standing in front of me, trying to analyze my abilities. "Isn't he just a Crafter?"

"Maybe he's just stronger," she answered him, but she was staring down at me. She nudged my foot. "What's your story, boy?"

I looked up at her. "I don't have a story." I didn't like that she had called me boy. She didn't look *that* much older than me. Maybe twenty?

Ashford approached me. I could tell he was starting to lose his patience with us again. This guy seemed like he had two different gears: ultrasmooth or superpissed.

"Listen, this could end very badly for you and your friend. I could kill you both in an instant. Also, I have her." He pointed at Caterina. "Do you know who she is?"

I just shook my head.

"She's known as The Mother of the Unbreakable. Do you know what that means?"

I shook my head again.

"It means that her magic is permanent. If she makes you sleep, you don't wake up. If she makes you feel pain, it doesn't go away.

If she renders you motionless, you stay motionless. Forever. Lucky for you, what you just experienced was temporary." He gestured to the people now regaining their movement on the floor. "If it had been an unbreakable spell, you would all still be lying there until you rotted into the floorboards."

I looked at all the bodies on the floor and thought about how disturbing his words were.

He continued. "Before Caterina, all casts could be broken. Not anymore. She's training more of our followers in her revolutionary magic. So you see, there is no point in resisting us. We are invincible. Luckily for you, we wish you no harm. We simply want the shoes that will lead us to our homeland so we can finally leave this Nullvin-infested place. We are the rightful rulers of Vinland. So just tell me where your grandfather's workshop is, and then we will be on our way."

My mind was racing. At that point, if I'd had the shoes, I might've just given them to him. I would've grabbed a marker, scratched out my name on the sole, and written, "Happy trails." But I didn't have the shoes, and if I told him where they were, I would be leading them to Rusty and Maria.

"Or like I said," Ashford continued, "Caterina can leave your friend in an unfortunate eternal state. It's up to you."

I didn't look up at him. I kept my gaze straight, toward the door. I decided I would play along for now, but I was determined to find a way for me and Mrs. Tovar to get out of there.

"I'll take you to the workshop." I stood up and began to leave the room.

"Hold on, young man," Ashford said as he grabbed me by the shoulder. It was unnerving to think he could drain the life out of me in that very moment if he wanted. "Hessel, we're headed to the workshop."

The balding man was slowly getting to his feet. He looked slightly dazed, but then he began shouting orders to some of the others.

"On your feet! You heard the man. We're going to the workshop!"

Ashford's eyes darted to Mrs. Tovar. "Caterina, stay here with our new friend."

His hand was still on my shoulder, his grip firm.

"All right." His voice was too close to my ear. "Lead the way, young man."

I walked quickly so I could get away from his grasp. I headed for my father's room. I walked through the doorway; many of the drawers were still open, and some things were left on the bed. It was strange to see his room like this. Even though I was mad at him, I was glad he had gotten away before these creeps showed up. I walked over to the chest and pulled the sheet to the side. It fell to the floor in a heap. I opened the lid. It felt like a violation, showing these people my mother's belongings. And I definitely didn't want to show them the secret passageway, but I didn't feel like I had a choice. I leaned over and began to take out all the contents again. It was strange. These things probably hadn't been touched in years, and now they were being sifted through twice in a single day.

"What is the meaning of this?" I could hear Ashford's voice behind me. "Where is the workshop?"

"The passageway is through the bottom of this chest," I said as I continued to remove the contents.

Ashford shoved a man toward the chest. "Help him clear it out."

The man leaned over, grabbed my mother's stuff, and threw it on the floor. That made me crazy mad. I wanted to tell him to back off. But I didn't. When the chest was cleared out, I reached in and opened the secret door. The dark opening was revealed.

Ashford eyed the opening. "Quite clever, actually. How do we get down?"

"There's a ladder." I stood back up and glanced over to the nightstand where the flashlight had been before. "We need a flashlight."

Hessel scurried over to the chest. "I have a firebird feather, Mr. Ashford."

He opened his jacket and reached inside an interior pocket. He pulled out a thin metal container and unlatched it. Once the lid was opened, a golden light emerged from the case. With his other hand, he pulled out a rather large, glowing feather. I leaned toward it to get a better look. It not only glowed but also gave off heat. Surprisingly, it looked just like the lamp that had been on my nightstand since I was a child.

"Lead the way, Hessel." Ashford gestured for the balding man to climb down into the earth.

Mr. Hessel awkwardly climbed into the chest and almost fell into the hole. Another man grabbed his arm to prevent him from tumbling into the darkness. Mr. Hessel looked nervously back at Ashford and then began to descend into the chest.

Ashford nudged me. "Why don't you go next?"

I begrudgingly walked over to the chest and climbed inside. The farther down I went, the more trapped I felt. I could lead them to the workshop. I could even open the door for them. They would spend hours searching the workshop, but in the end, they wouldn't find the shoes. I reached the bottom, where Hessel glaring at me. The amber light gave his face a strange appearance. It looked orange and angry. I waited for the others to enter the cramped space. Ashford was last to come down. He dusted off his long overcoat with a scowl on his face, as if he wasn't happy about being in such rustic conditions.

"Where is it?" Hessel said gruffly.

I pointed down the long passageway. "It's at the end of this tunnel."

Hessel turned and began walking, and the rest of us followed. There were five of us all together. Ashford, Hessel, me, another man, and a woman. Hessel glanced back at me.

"There better not be any funny business down here, boy. Does your grandfather have this place booby-trapped?"

"Not that I know of." I wasn't about to make it easy for him. Let him wonder and be nervous.

"What's up with these creatures?" Hessel held up the feather so it illuminated one of the stone statues on top of the pillars.

"They resemble the ancient Vess, creatures of Vinland," Ashford said. "They no longer exist, but they were known to be vicious creatures. It was said that if one was able to train them, they would be extremely loyal and protect their master with a vengeance."

He laughed lightly. "Rather interesting choice for this passageway. I have to say, I like your grandfather's style, young man."

I looked back at the tall Drainer. What did he want me to say? Thanks? Did he think we were buddies now? Whatever. I shook my head and kept moving ahead, trying to figure out what I was going to do once we reached the workshop. I needed a plan. If I let them into the workshop, they would see the glass box where my shoes had been kept, which meant they would see the title and my name as well. If they knew the shoes were made for me, they probably wouldn't be so willing to let me go on my merry way.

I anxiously looked around me. Could I escape? Hessel was leading the way with the glowing feather; another man was following him, and I was following that man. Behind me was the woman, and towering in the back was Ashford. How was I going to get out of this?

As I walked, drops of water dripped from the ceiling. One landed on my cheek, which directed my gaze upward. My eyes fell upon one of the Vess creatures. Maybe they could help me. I peered around the people in front of me to see how much farther we needed to go. The door was not too far ahead of us, and above the door was the stone Vess that had taken my blood. It had flown away once the door opened when Rusty and I were down here before. Just like that, I had an idea. It was crazy, and I knew it might not work, but it was worth a try.

I kept my head down and walked in silence until we reached the door at the end of the passageway. I watched as Hessel frantically searched for a way in.

He eventually turned to me and spat out, "How do we get in, boy?"

I looked up at the Vess staring down at me. It was in a different position than it had been when Rusty and I first encountered it. Its head lazily hung over the perch it was sitting on, staring down at us.

"Open it," Ashford commanded.

"Can you hold that feather up?" I pointed upward. "I need to read the plaque that's up there."

"A plaque?" Hessel's eyes searched the area until he saw the plaque. He then held his feather as high as he could, but he couldn't quite reach it. Ashford took it from him and extended his arm toward the creature. The plaque was now illuminated.

"Well, go ahead," Ashford instructed me. "Read it."

I walked closer to the door so I was directly under the beast. I looked up at it. Would it do what I asked it to?

I read the words aloud: "Only the blood of Needlecoff can open this door and harness the power of the Vess. Beware, intruders. All others will endure the fury of the Vess."

Just like before, the stone Vess moved briskly. The sound of stone rubbing against itself echoed down the corridor. The creature pulled itself up on its legs and whisked his tail toward me like it had done before.

"They move!" Ashford exclaimed. "How brilliant!"

This was it. This would be my opportunity to escape. The creature was staring at me, waiting for me to prick my finger on its sharp appendage. Could I really harness its power? Did that mean it would listen to my command? If my plan failed, Ashford would be in a rage. I was pretty sure it wasn't a good idea to make a Drainer angry, but it was a risk I was willing to take.

I looked into the dead, gray eyes of the Vess. I took a breath to calm my nerves and then said as firmly as I could, "Take me on your back and get me out of here!"

The Vess showed its teeth slightly and then moved swiftly like a lizard. It jumped down from its perch, and as it did, its tail whipped sideways and knocked the woman down. I jumped on the stone back of the statue, careful to not impale myself on one of the spikes that protruded out of its back. The creature was cold, and the stone was rougher than I thought it would be. I grabbed two of the spikes that protruded out of its neck and leaned in close to its ear.

"Fly!" I commanded it. "*Go!*"

The creature jumped up, and before I knew it, its wings extended outward and filled the narrow space. Ashford immediately reached his long, bony hand toward me, but I pulled my leg up just in time. His hand grazed the creature as it flew past him, but it presumably did not affect it since it was made from stone. There was no life to drain.

I heard Ashford shout to the others behind me, "Stop him!"

Beams of light were quickly being directed at me. I ducked down and hoped nothing would hit me. Something hit the wall, and pieces of brick shattered, some of the debris flying toward me. I covered my face with my arm and felt a few pieces of stone pierce my skin.

I squeezed the gargoyle's spikes, though it probably didn't even feel it. "Faster!"

The passageway echoed with shouts, crumbling walls, and the flapping of the Vess's wings. We were gaining speed, but I could hear the others shouting behind us, and when a sudden, bright light filled the space, the creature fell to the ground as if it were wounded. We skidded to a stop on the cobblestone walkway. The sound of the beast hitting the floor was intense. I fell to the side, but I kept my grip on one of the spikes.

I could feel something wet over my eye. I wiped it with my sleeve and, in the faint light, realized it was blood. I must have gotten cut somehow. I looked behind me; the others were trying to catch up, running down the corridor toward me. Hessel was holding the glowing feather up high, and in the shadowy light, I could see the other Vess creatures staring down at the intruders.

"Stop them!" I yelled, hoping the statues that lined the passageway would hear me. "I command you to stop them!"

One by one, the stone creatures left their pillars and flew toward Ashford and his followers. Their stone forms blocked the intruders from my view as they darted down the passageway. I turned to the Vess that I had been riding. Was he hit? In the dim light, I tried to see if anything was wrong with him. It looked like one of its wings was damaged. A large piece of it was now on the ground in clumps of concrete and dust.

"Can you still fly?"

The Vess grunted and pulled itself back on its feet. It shook its head back and forth violently and then pushed off from its hind legs. Once again, we were flying down the corridor, though not as gracefully as before. The damaged wing resulted in him occasionally hitting the walls and ceiling. I held on as tightly as I could and hoped I would make it out of there in one piece.

I glanced backward at the beams of light shooting in every direction, and there was a lot of shouting. I didn't want to think about what was going on back there. What if I unleased something terrible on Ashford and his followers? Sure, they weren't the best people in the world, and they had threatened to kill me and Mrs. Tovar, but I wasn't used to inflicting pain, or maybe even something worse, on another human being. That wasn't something I ever contemplated before, and I wasn't so sure I wanted to contemplate it now.

I turned away from the chaos behind me and focused on the pillar of light beaming down from the opening that led to my father's room. We were almost there. I figured the Vess I was riding would stop when we reached the end of the corridor, and I would climb up the ladder. But I was wrong. Instead of slowing, the creature accelerated.

"Are you not going to stop?" I shouted at the stone creature.

His wing hit the wall again. A few sparks flew from the stones colliding. The Vess jolted to the left violently. I held on, anticipating the worst. We reached the opening and suddenly, the Vess changed course. It was going upward.

"You're not going to fit!"

But the Vess didn't listen to my warning. The stone creature was stronger than I expected. It was somehow forcing its way up through the narrow passageway, carving through the earth as it traveled upward. I hunched down and covered my face as bits of stone and dirt flew in every direction.

We burst into my father's room. I looked back quickly and saw the chest was now shattered, and there was a huge hole in the floor of my dad's bedroom. But the Vess still didn't stop. It crashed through the ceiling of my father's room, through the room directly above, and then we burst through the roof. Bits of shingles, wood, and stone cascaded down the slanted roof and took out most of the birdhouses.

Suddenly, I was flying through the night sky, surrounded by stars. "Where are you going?"

We were really high, and his flying was so erratic with his busted wing that I was beginning to think I was going to end up splattered on the ground. Why was he going up farther? We needed to go down, toward the ground. Then it occurred to me that I shouldn't be asking it what it was doing. I should be commanding it.

"Put me down over there in the woods!" I pointed toward the willow and moved my hand as far forward as I could so the creature could see where I wanted it to land.

But then something else caught my attention. There was a man on my front lawn who was urgently walking toward my house. The guy must've been a Caster because I could see bright shades of browns and greens shooting from his hand toward another figure standing directly in front of my house. It was dark, but the light pouring out of the windows of my house provided enough illumination for me to see that the figure was Caterina, the crazy chick who was able to cast unbreakable spells.

Both Caterina and the man turned their gazes upward. They were looking at me.

Crap! I thought. *They're going to blast me right out of the sky.*

Thankfully, the Vess chose that moment to begin its decent toward the earth. We glided past the willow and landed in the brush on the edge of the woods. The weight of the stone beast cracked branches and leveled the surrounding bushes. I slid off the Vess, grateful I hadn't fallen to my death or been impaled by one of its stone spikes. I walked to the front of the Vess to look into its stone eyes.

"Thank you. I mean it."

It nodded as if it understood and then lay down with a loud *thud*. The creature rested its head on its front paws and looked like it was going to sleep.

Bang!

A deafening sound echoed through the woods. I caught my breath and covered my ears. I had no idea what had caused that thunderous boom, but it was so powerful that it left my ears ringing. As much as my instincts told me to run in the opposite direction, I knew I needed to find Mrs. Tovar. I lowered my hands, and once I started running in the direction of my front lawn, I realized I hadn't escaped Ashford without injury. I had both a cut on my forehead and a pretty deep gash in my leg. I tried to ignore the shooting pain as I moved through the brush and peered out from behind the willow tree. What I saw was something I'd never seen before.

A magical battle was taking place on my front lawn.

CHAPTER 17

BATTLE

Now that I could see him better, I realized it was the man who had disappeared on Ghost Hill. Mrs. Tovar had said his name was Tristan. He didn't look exceptionally powerful—average size and height. But one thing was for sure: he looked determined to defeat his opponent. He briskly walked forward with his hand outstretched, a line of broken earth before him. The line started to move rapidly away from him toward the woman, as if there were a giant mole under the ground. The ground violently broke apart under Caterina's feet, sending her and pieces of earth flying backward toward the house. She landed hard on her back, but she wasn't defeated yet.

She rolled over, got on her knees, and then held her fan up high in the air. Glimmers of light darted out of the spines of the fan, and a piercing whistle filled the air. The sky was now full of huge pieces of ice that resembled large icicles. They were thick, smooth, and very sharp. More and more of them shot out of her fan and were flew toward Tristan at an alarming speed. He crouched down before they had a chance to reach him. An amber-glowing shield appeared, and he hid behind it. The ice shards ricocheted off the shield with a hissing sound, leaving fragments of ice all around him. It must've been made of fire. Now my yard was covered with huge ice stakes sticking out of the ground where the sharp point had pierced the soil.

I jumped when someone pulled at my arm and whispered, "Wren."

It was Maria. She was panting and out of breath. "Oh my gosh! Are you okay? You're bleeding." She pointed toward my forehead.

My hand automatically went to the wound, and I winced from the tenderness of it. "Just a cut."

Rusty came up behind her with Mrs. Tovar.

"Dude, that was the coolest thing I have ever seen. Busting out of the roof like that? So sick! How did you get that thing to fly you out of there?"

"I took a chance that the Vess would listen to my command," I answered him. "And it freaking worked."

Mrs. Tovar's hand was on her chest. "The stars must be aligned in your favor tonight, Wren."

"What about you?" I was so relieved to see her unharmed. "How did you get away from the crazy lady?"

Mrs. Tovar smiled at me. "Well, between her fight with Tristan and you flying through the house, I was able to take advantage of the situation and get out of there. But now that we're all accounted for," she glanced toward the lawn, "we need to get Tristan's attention and get as far away from these people as possible."

We all moved closer to the edge of the woods to get a better look at what was going on. Tristan was standing still with both hands outstretched on either side of him. Then he snapped his arms inward so they were directly in front of his chest. With that movement, leaves began to pull away from the trees and lift from the ground. They were flying through the air, rapidly moving toward my house. It became difficult to see because of all the leaves and debris in the air. It reminded me of a tornado, but instead of a circular motion, everything was moving in one direction. And the target was Caterina. The leaves began to cover her body, clinging to her skin, clothes, and hair. Layer upon layer of rotting and fresh leaves were now concealing the woman, rendering her incapable of inflicting any more dark magic on Tristan.

Rusty watched in awe, his mouth slightly ajar. "What on earth?"

"Tristan!" Mrs. Tovar called out to him. He turned and saw us in the woods. Mrs. Tovar gestured for him to come to us. *"Vamanos!"*

He looked back toward my house. I followed his gaze, and my stomach dropped. The others had come out of the front door and were now standing on the front porch. Ashford was in front of the group, glaring at Tristan. Then a bloodcurdling scream pierced the night air. It sounded as though it was coming from Caterina. The leaf-covered form looked like a monster now—thick limbs trying to move, wiggling, straining to break free from its organic restraints. Abruptly, the leaves exploded away from her body. The dark leaves were replaced by rays of bright, white light emerging from her form. The bursts of light began to morph into animals resembling glowing dogs or wolves. It was hard to tell. The creatures were not solid. They were ethereal, ghostly really. But they were fast, darting between the huge ice spears that were scattered around my entire front lawn. They were terrifying. They began to bark ferociously as if they were part of a hunting party. And it looked like Tristan was their prey.

"Trauma hounds," Mrs. Tovar said, more to herself than to us. "Tristan! Hurry!"

Tristan began to run toward us.

Mrs. Tovar took out a leather pouch and frantically poured the contents into her hand. It looked like a pile of coins. "We need the ones for Lake Wales. Help me find them, Maria!"

Maria started to anxiously sift through the pile of coins. She was moving so frantically, some of the coins fell to the ground.

"What in god's name are you two doing?" Rusty asked. "Those ghost dogs are coming our way. Shouldn't we be running?"

Mrs. Tovar answered without looking at him. "Yes, we should. Do you have enough?" she asked Maria.

She gave a firm nod. "Yes, I have four."

Mrs. Tovar shoved the rest of the coins back into the pouch and pulled the leather straps to close it. She opened her jacket and put the pouch inside somewhere.

"Now, listen to me. We need to get back to Ghost Hill. Those hounds will hunt us down, so we need to escape. These coins will take us to Spook Hill."

Maria put an octagon-shaped coin into each of our hands. "Whatever you do, don't drop them."

I glanced back toward my front lawn. Tristan was almost to the woods, but then he stopped.

"What is he doing?" I shrieked.

The hounds were almost to us. He needed to run. We all did. But he was standing perfectly still, eyes closed.

"Tristan!" Mrs. Tovar yelled. "We have to go!"

Keeping his eyes closed, he slowly lifted his hands in the air. He then brought them back down swiftly, and it looked like some translucent force was moving away from him. A force that, as it moved, leveled everything in its path. The pillars of ice protruding from the earth all crashed to the ground like dominos, falling toward the house. The trauma hounds that were racing toward him were blown to the ground with a whimper. When the force hit Caterina and the others, they were thrown to the ground as well, where they remained motionless. The force continued until it reached my house. As it hit, all the windows shattered, and the structure fell backward, landing on the earth with a loud, rumbling crash. All that remained standing was Ashford. His tall, shadowy figure stood motionless, surrounded by debris. Bits of my house were slowly falling around him.

My house was gone. Leveled to the ground. I stood in disbelief for a minute, absorbing what had just taken place. I was devastated; my place of comfort and safety, whatever comfort and safety I'd had, was no more.

Then through the haze of the crash, I saw movement. Ashford was walking in the direction of where Tristan stood. His intense stare and determined steps made me break into a nervous sweat. As he passed a couple of the hounds, they began to pull themselves from the ground, shaking their heads back and forth as if they were trying to shake off the blow they had just endured.

That was when Tristan finally reached the woods and yelled, "Run! If that didn't take him down, nothing will."

He had a British accent. I hadn't expected that.

Way off in the distance, I caught a glimpse of the others running through the woods. Tristan ran past me, and I followed him, ducking under branches and jumping over fallen trees. I struggled to keep up due to the gash in my leg. Pain shot through my leg every time my foot hit the ground. I heard strange noises behind me, a combination of hissing sounds and muted thuds. I didn't dare look back, though. I just focused on moving forward.

Suddenly, a loud crash made me jump. Tristan turned his head so he could see what was lurking behind us.

His eyes widened, and he yelled, "Bloody hell! Hurry up, mate!"

I turned to see what was happening and froze. The forest was turning to ash before my eyes. The trees, grass, vines, bushes, everything was withering away, dying. The towering trees disintegrated, their tree limbs crashing to the ground. All that remained was gray ash and soot, as if a fire had scorched the earth. The decay was spreading like a sickness, getting closer and closer, and it was accompanied by an eerie, sizzling sound.

Far behind us, I could see a dark figure emerging out of the cloud of dust that had filled the air. It was Ashford; he was getting closer. Surrounding him were the trauma hounds, their white glow piercing the darkness of the forest. Their snarling growls were getting closer.

I could barely hear Tristan's voice over the pounding sound of trees falling to the ground. "What are you doing? Move!"

He was right. What was I doing? I needed to run.

I turned around and ran faster than I had ever run in my life, jumping over rocks and dodging branches. I was truly running for my life. As I passed hundreds of trees, I thought about how they were going to disintegrate right after I passed. Their time was coming to an end.

My lungs were burning. My legs felt like jelly. My wound was throbbing, making me want to scream. There was a sharp pain in my chest. I regretted never participating in any sports in school, never building up any stamina.

The barking and the sizzling sounds were getting closer.

Thanks to my long legs, I was able to catch up to the others.

"Are we almost there?" I yelled out to Tristan. My voice sounded weak and winded. "Can you see the road?"

"I think it's up ahead!" Tristan yelled back at me, his eyes never straying from the destination ahead of him.

I clenched the coin in my hand, the one that was going to transport me to someplace called Spook Hill. I felt its hard edges push into my palm, keeping me grounded and focused.

Finally, I could see the road up ahead. I quickly glanced back to see how far away the Drainer was. He was close, but there was still a distance between me and the death that surrounded him. As for the hounds, they were gaining on me. One trip or fall and I would be in serious trouble.

My eyes shot forward as my feet hit hard concrete. I could now see everyone else. Rusty was yelling for us to hurry, and Mrs. Tovar was pulling Maria down the hill by her arm. I followed Tristan down the hill. I was ready to disappear.

But once Tristan and I joined the others, the hounds emerged from the woods. Their backs were down, and they began to circle us, determining the best angle to attack from. Mrs. Tovar grabbed a vial from the interior of her jacket and threw it at one of the hounds. A green fog surrounded the hound; I could see the white, glowing form of the hound struggling inside the fog. It was howling as if it were in pain.

Mrs. Tovar grabbed Maria by the wrist and pushed her toward the bottom of the hill.

"What are you waiting for? Get through the port!" she yelled.

Maria ran down the hill. One minute she was there, and the next, she was gone.

Tristan's left hand was outstretched, keeping the hounds at bay. I could now see that he had an elaborate tattoo covering most of his left hand. I couldn't see it very clearly, but it appeared to be mostly text intertwined with a swirling design, and a portion of the text was glowing. He was focused on one of the hounds directly in front of him. It was pacing back and forth with its teeth bared.

Tristan quickly glanced back at Mrs. Tovar. "What are we waiting for?"

Mrs. Tovar grabbed Rusty by the sleeve. "You got the coin?" she asked him.

"Yeah." Rusty's eyes were wide. "Is it going to hurt?"

"Oh for heaven's sake!"

She pushed him toward the spot where Maria had disappeared. Rusty stumbled down the incline, and then he wasn't there anymore. I was grateful it actually worked since he wasn't a Vin. Who knows what we would have done if he couldn't get through?

One of the trauma hounds must have decided it was the right time to attack because it suddenly leaped toward Tristan. A bright light shot out of Tristan's hand and collided with the glowing creature just in time. The hound fell to the ground, unresponsive.

"What did you do?" I asked him.

"I shocked him." His eyes were locked on something behind me. "Watch out!"

I turned quickly to see that another trauma hound had emerged from the forest. It had pounced on Mrs. Tovar and pushed her to the ground. It snarled at her, its fangs inches from her face. Mrs. Tovar was trying to push it away. She was trying to reach inside the interior of her coat while also attempting to keep the creature from biting her. But the hound managed to dig its fangs into her arm, and she screamed out.

I ran toward her and kicked the hound as hard as I could. It didn't budge. It was too solid. Even though it looked translucent, it definitely didn't feel like it. I kicked the hound harder just as Tristan appeared next to me. He grabbed a clump of fur between its shoulder blades with his tattooed hand and pulled the creature away from Mrs. Tovar. The hound howled in pain. Where Tristan's hand was touching the animal was no longer white. Traces of red were spreading outward, overtaking the whiteness of the animal.

He threw the animal to the side of the road, where it attempted to lick at its wound.

We both looked down at Mrs. Tovar. She was lying motionless on the pavement. Blood was pouring out of the wound on her wrist. Tristan bent down and picked her up.

"Let's get out of here," he said, but I could hear the defeat in his voice. "They went to Spook Hill, right?"

"Yes," I answered.

The trees by the side of the road were collapsing into dust. The Drainer was almost here.

"We have to go," Tristan said. "Follow me through."

And then he took a few steps and was gone.

I sprinted toward the spot where he had disappeared, and that was when I realized my hands were empty. My coin was gone. I must've dropped it when the trauma hound was attacking Mrs. Tovar. I ran frantically back to the spot where Mrs. Tovar had been attacked. The hound that had attacked her was still trying to lick its wound, but it noticed me approaching and began to stand up. Out of the corner of my eye, I could see the other hound that had been surrounded by the green mist was also staring at me. The last of the green mist was dissipating, and soon the hound would be free. To make matters worse, the Drainer was getting closer. I could see him heading my way with a few more faithful trauma hounds on either side of him. The glow from the creatures allowed me to see a cloud of ash hovering around his dark form. There was nothing left behind him. He had incinerated everything in his path.

I was in serious trouble. I was just a kid with no powers and no weapons. How could I ever hope to fight off both the trauma hounds and the Drainer? I didn't stand a chance. The only way I was going to survive this was by going through the portal. I needed to find that coin. I fell to the ground and began to run my hand across the pavement. It had to be here. I felt something small and round and picked it up, holding it toward the moonlight. It was only a flat stone covered in Mrs. Tovar's blood. One of the trauma hounds was growling at me, slowly approaching. I stood back up and looked for a way to escape.

Should I just run? Where can I go that they won't find me?

Just then, something dark flew past my face and landed on my shoulder. It was a crow, the one with the dented beak that got away back at my house. Tough Guy. And in his mouth was a single coin. I took it from him and felt the octagon shape of it. It was the coin! Tough Guy had brought it to me in the nick of time. I didn't know where he'd found it, and I didn't care. I just ran toward the port, hoping the hounds wouldn't be able to catch up with me before I disappeared.

I closed my eyes, and before I knew it, I was breathing warm air.

I opened my eyes and saw the moon again. Except this time, it was partially covered with palm trees. Tough Guy pushed off from my shoulder and flew into the night sky.

CHAPTER 18
SPOOK HILL

I was at Spook Hill in Florida. The portal had worked! I had traveled to another place using magic. Thankfully, it hadn't hurt. In fact, I didn't feel anything at all.

I was standing on a road; trees were sporadically placed on either side of the street. The landscape was relatively flat, which was something I wasn't used to. The trees looked strange, like they were from another planet. Long, branchless trunks stretched up toward the stars. I had seen palm trees in pictures but never in real life. Other trees looked a bit more familiar, but they were covered with some kind of moss that swayed slightly in the gentle breeze.

Tough Guy was sitting in one of those trees. I couldn't believe it. The crow had saved me. The crows had brought me gifts before, but bringing me the coin was truly incredible. And now he was here in Florida, miles from home.

The air felt sticky and heavy. It was hard to pull it into my lungs. And the bugs were crazy loud. I couldn't see them in the darkness, but judging from the sound, there were a lot of them around us. There was a sign by the side of the road. The words Spook Hill were written in black across the top of the white sign and more words followed, but I couldn't make it out. I started to move toward the sign to read what else it said when someone grabbed me by the sleeve. I turned briskly and was relieved to see it was Rusty.

I yanked my arm away from him. "Geez, man! You scared the crap outta me."

Rusty held his hands up.

"Relax. Tristan told me to grab you," he said.

"I doubt he meant that you should literally grab me," I replied, my heart still pounding in my chest.

"He said they could follow us here. I mean, the odds aren't good since there are a ton of these gravity hills, but still ... ." Rusty began to quickly walk in the other direction. "What took you so long anyway?"

"I had a bit of an issue." I put the coin in my pocket. "I barely got out of there in time."

I glanced back at the spot where I had entered through the portal. There was nothing there. It was creepy to think that the Drainer could follow us here and just appear out of the darkness. Rusty led me behind a group of wild bushes; Tristan was kneeling next to Mrs. Tovar, who was lying on the ground. A soft, blue light was oozing out of Tristan's tattooed hand and spreading like a cloud around her body. Maria was at her grandmother's side, her gaze directed at Tristan, who appeared to be concentrating. His eyes were closed, and it looked like he was quietly speaking to himself. His eyes opened suddenly, and he quickly looked down at Mrs. Tovar. Disappointment washed over his face.

"It's not working."

His words were soft, as though he didn't want Maria to hear them.

"What do you mean it's not working?" Maria's voice was shaky. "Do it again!"

Tristan hesitated for a second and then closed his eyes again. A pale, blue light once again covered Mrs. Tovar's motionless body. We waited. No one spoke. I could hear my heart thumping in my ears. The light eventually faded away, but Mrs. Tovar remained still.

"I don't understand." Maria looked up at Tristan. "You can break everything."

"I can't break the unbreakable," Tristan said solemnly.

The words hung in the air. None of us wanted to accept that they were spoken.

The blood drained from Maria's face. She looked as though she'd seen a ghost; her eyes were wide with fear.

"No, it can't be." Maria looked down at her grandmother and pulled the woman's hand to her heart. "There's no such thing. It's only a rumor."

"This shouldn't have happened," Tristan said as he stood up.

I now had the chance to see him better. He had a slender face and dirty blond hair, and I would guess he was about forty years old. There was an air of elegance about him. There was nothing fancy about his clothes, and his hair was unkempt, but he looked regal for some reason. Though I probably came to that conclusion because he had a British accent.

"But I thought you said it was just a bite from the trauma hound?" Maria asked.

"The trauma hounds came from the Mother of the Unbreakable." Tristan looked down at Mrs. Tovar. "I'm afraid her body is in trauma. Indefinitely."

Rusty was standing still next to me. "Is Mrs. Tovar going to be all right?" he whispered to me.

"I'm not sure," I whispered back. "That Drainer was talking about unbreakable curses back at my house, and it didn't sound good."

Maria turned her head our way. She must have heard us because she explained, "All magic is breakable. Nothing is absolute. But there have been rumors that the Wrathful are now capable of casting unbreakable spells."

She shook her head. "Who would do something so horrible?"

"The people who came to my house," I said.

Tristan was standing with his arms crossed in front of his chest. "Yes. Why *did* they come to your house?" Tristan asked me.

"They were looking for shoes," I answered, knowing full well how ridiculous that sounded.

He raised an eyebrow. "What kind of shoes?"

"Shoes that can get you to Vinland."

"Vinland?" Tristan scoffed. "You've got to be kidding me. That's not possible."

"Well apparently, they think it is."

I gestured over my shoulder as if Lewisberry might be just behind me, but it wasn't. They were way up north. I put my hand down, hoping no one noticed my mistake.

"Where are these so-called Vinland shoes?" Tristan asked.

Rusty took my backpack off his back. "Right here."

He walked over to where Tristan stood and opened the bag so he could look in.

"Looks like a lot more than just one pair of shoes to me," Tristan said as he began to shuffle through the contents.

"My grandfather made a pair for each of us. Wren, Maria, and me," Rusty explained.

"All three of you?" Tristan asked, this time raising a skeptical eyebrow.

"Yep," Rusty replied.

"So who are the Vinland ones for?" Tristan looked at the three of us, probably already knowing the answer to his question.

I just lifted my hand slightly like I was raising it in school but didn't really want the teacher to pick me.

"And we don't know why he made these shoes?" he asked.

I shook my head.

Tristan pulled out one of the sneakers and examined it. He was running his finger along my name, which was written on the sole. "He had to have known that making those shoes for you would've put you in danger. Of course the Drainers would want them. That's all the Drainers have ever wanted. To get back to Vinland."

"Why would the shoes put me in danger?" I asked.

He put the shoe back in the bag. "Because if he made them for you, they'll probably only work while they're on your feet."

I hadn't thought about that.

"But those people who came looking for them didn't seem to care about me," I said. "They only wanted the shoes."

Tristan didn't answer right away. "They must not know they were made for you. Most of Bertram's shoes will work on anyone—that is, unless they were made specifically for someone."

"Oh." This was getting more insane by the minute. I didn't think my head would ever stop spinning.

"How did they know about them anyway?"

I paused before I spoke. "It sounds like my Aunt Bryn told them."

"What?" He grabbed my shoulder and was looking at me rather intensely. "They told you that?"

"Yes." I was surprised by his reaction. "But I got the feeling that she didn't volunteer the information."

Tristan let go of me and started pacing back and forth. He looked more intense than he had before, if that was even possible.

"But that would mean they have her."

"That doesn't mean anything has happened to her," Maria said from where she sat next to her grandmother. "She could still be all right."

"But she would never tell them about the shoes ... unless she didn't have a choice." Tristan turned away from all of us.

After a few moments of silence, Rusty asked him, "You okay?"

Tristan turned back around and looked at Rusty, *really* looked at him. "What's your story?"

"Me?" Rusty's hand went to his chest. "What do you mean?"

"Why are you here?"

"Well," Rusty paused before saying, "I go to school with Wren, and I guess you could say that I just got mixed up in everything."

"But you're not a Vin," Tristan said flatly.

Rusty threw his hands up in the air. "You know what? I take offense at that. I'm getting really sick of everyone acting like I have no part in any of this. If that were the case, then Wren's grandfather would have never made me a pair of shoes."

Tristan was glaring at Rusty. "Right, these shoes he made for you ... what do they do?"

"They say, Cunning Warrior," Rusty said proudly. "I'm thinking it will make me into some kind of amazing ninja."

"Okay." Tristan was rubbing his chin with his hand. He turned his attention toward Maria. "What about you?"

"Mine say Clarity of Sight," she answered him. "Honestly, I was excited. I thought it may help me. But now ... I couldn't care less." She looked down at her grandmother. "When I touch her, I see nothing. Only darkness."

No one said anything after that. What could we say? Maria had used a piece of cloth to bind her grandmother's wound, but I could see the blood seeping through the material.

"What are we going to do?" Maria wiped a tear from her cheek. "If you can't break it, then who can?"

"There is only one person I know who has the potential to break the unbreakable," Tristan answered her.

"You're talking about the Eradicator, aren't you?"

A dark shadow had come over Maria's face as she looked at her grandmother, but the whites of her eyes widened as she asked the question.

"Yes," Tristan answered her. "I know no other."

"But what about my parents?" Maria asked.

Tristan kneeled next to her. "I think we should focus on your grandmother right now. And the Eradicator is our best hope. I think we should go to Underfoot."

"Will they even let us in?" Maria asked.

"Leave that to me." Tristan took out a leather pouch from his pocket and began to pour coins into his hand.

Maria grabbed his arm to get his attention. He stopped what he was doing and looked at her.

She had an ominous tone as she spoke. "After the Eradicator wakes up my abuela, they will they let us back out, right?"

I was struck by her words. What did she mean by that?

Tristan closed his hand that held the coins and put the pouch back in his pocket.

"I'll handle it, Maria," he answered her softly.

She gave him an exasperated look. "You know I can read you right now, right?"

Tristan pulled his hand away. "Then you know I can't say for sure."

Rusty sighed. "Where are we going this time?" he asked.

"Prosser Hill," Tristan answered him.

"Where's that?" I asked.

"Washington State." Tristan stood up and placed a new coin in each of our hands. This one was oval, and the letters *P* and *H* intersected to create a strange design.

"Lead the way, Maria," Tristan said as he lifted Mrs. Tovar.

Maria peered out from behind the cover of a bush and then started to make her way toward the street. Tristan followed her with Mrs. Tovar in his arms. I looked up at the palm trees one last time. I didn't know if I would ever see one again, so I wanted to remember what they looked like.

I saw the white sign again. I figured it explained the mystery of the sight, but it was still too dark to read it from a distance. I knew all the information written was wrong anyway. I'm pretty sure that it didn't say anything about Vins or spells or traveling from one gravity hill to another. I'm sure it talked about ghosts or something paranormal. If I had read something like that a couple of days ago, I would have pondered its validity. Now I knew the truth. People didn't appear and disappear because they were ghosts, they were simply Vins traveling from one port to another.

I looked back at the others and saw they had gone through. I scanned the trees, looking for Tough Guy. I didn't really want to leave him alone in this place. Finally, I saw movement in the night sky. The crow swooped down and landed on my shoulder again. "Time to go," I said to him, and we disappeared.

CHAPTER 19
PROSSER HILL

And just like that, we were across the country. Somewhere in Washington State. It was dark, and a road stretched out before us. Maria was acting like a schoolteacher on a field trip, counting us to make sure we were all accounted for.

"Dude?" Rusty pointed at me. "You have a flipping bird on your shoulder."

"I know." I could see its sharp beak out of the corner of my eye. "He kind of followed me here."

"What? From Lewisberry?" he said in disbelief.

"He actually helped me get out of Lewisberry." The crow pushed off from my shoulder again and disappeared into the night sky once more.

"Seems to be rather attached to you," Tristan commented. "I seem to remember your mother having a thing with crows as well."

"Really?" I wanted to know more, but Tristan didn't say anything else.

It was much colder than where we had been a second earlier, although the air was lighter and easier on the lungs, so that was nice. The land was flat like it had been in Florida, but instead of palm trees, electric poles lined the street. Dark, thin poles that loomed upward toward the sky. Unlike Florida, no stars could be seen here. I assumed they were hidden by clouds. Fields of long, golden grass extended outward from either side of the street. All I could see was a dark, strange building up ahead. It looked like a barn, but a tower-like structure jutted out of the roof.

"What is that building?" I asked Tristan.

"It's a grain elevator." He was walking briskly up the center of the road.

I thought we should get to the side of the road in case a car came, but I remained silent since I didn't see any lights. In fact, other than the barn and grain elevator, I didn't see anything. It was like the place was deserted. The stillness made me wonder what time it was. I had absolutely no idea. The night seemed like it was going on forever, and now that we were on the West Coast, we were probably in a different time zone.

Rusty was walking next to me. "This place is kinda creepy, don't ya think?" he asked softly.

"It seems deserted," I answered him.

"What do you think it's going to be like when we get there?"

"Where? Underfoot?" I asked.

He nodded.

"How should I know?"

He shrugged. "Well, you *are* one of them."

Here we go again. This was getting seriously annoying. "How many times do I have to tell you that I didn't know anything until today?"

"Okay, okay," he said. "Sheesh."

We were quiet as we followed Tristan down the street. Once we were by the strange-looking building, he turned and started to walk out into one of the fields. As we turned off the road, the long, golden strands parted like the Red Sea, creating a path for us to follow.

"Wow. I don't think I'm ever going to get used to how cool this magic stuff is," Rusty said with a big grin on his face.

I felt the same way even though I wasn't "normal" like him. I was having a hard time accepting the fact that I wasn't. I was somehow a part of this foreign world. A world that seemed to have endless possibilities. How could I ever prepare myself for what we were going to face?

"Where are we going?" Rusty blurted out.

"Just ahead," Tristan said with his back to us. "My truck is parked in the field."

I squinted my eyes to see into the darkness. Tristan laid Mrs. Tovar down gently in a tuft of grass, and then I realized there was a truck parked there. It wasn't an ordinary truck; it looked ancient. Well, I guess not ancient, but if I had to guess, I would say it was from the 1940s or 1950s. Tristan went to the front of the vehicle and came back with a large, glowing feather. It looked just like the feather that Hessel guy had back at my house.

Now that I could get a better look at the truck, I concluded that at one time, it had been painted blue, but there were so much rust and so many dents in it, it was pretty hard to tell. The curves on the truck were rounded and exaggerated, and the windows were much narrower than modern cars. The bed of the truck had long planks of wood that made up the sides. A thick tarp, secured with some hooks that protruded out of the wood, covered the top of the bed. Tristan unhooked the tarp and pulled it back, flipping it backward. Then he unlatched something, and the wall that made up the rear of the truck bed swung outward. We all peered in to see what it looked like inside. All I could see was that the floor was covered with hay.

Rusty and I bent down and gently lifted Mrs. Tovar. I didn't like picking her up; she was so limp, it reminded me of my mother. Tristan climbed into the bed of the truck, and once we were closer to him, he grabbed Mrs. Tovar by the shoulders and gently laid her down. Once he jumped out of the back, Maria jumped in and sat down next to her grandmother.

Tristan leaned into the bed of the truck and handed the feather to Maria. "This should keep you warm."

Maria took the feather, and the interior space was now glowing. The soft light made the hay look like a nest of glistening strands of gold.

"I'm sitting in there," Rusty said before he hopped up into the bed of the truck.

I couldn't blame him. It looked cozy and warm. I wanted to lay my head down and maybe get some sleep. I was exhausted.

"All right." Tristan started to close the back door of the truck bed when Tough Guy flew in and settled into the straw.

"No way!" Rusty scurried to the other side of the truck bed. "That thing can't stay here."

"Guess that means you and the bird are sitting in front with me." Tristan hit my back as he walked past me toward the front of the truck.

I was nervous, though I didn't know why. I leaned in and put my arm out for the bird to climb onto.

"I think you need to put those shoes on now," I said to Rusty. "Maybe it would increase your bravery."

"Shut up, Larkin." He leaned back in the hay. "Maybe you should work on making friends who aren't freakin' birds."

"Maybe you both should shut up," Maria interjected. "Close the door, Wren. The sooner we get to Underfoot, the better."

I closed the door, fastened the tarp back down, and walked to the front of the truck with the crow on my shoulder. I looked at the handle on the door. It was so weird. There were no buttons or anything. I grabbed the handle and pulled it out, but nothing happened. Then I tried to pull it up and then down. I must've done something right because, eventually, it opened. As I pulled the door toward me, I cringed when it made a loud, guttural sound.

I was shocked by how small the interior was. It was the narrowest front seat I had ever seen. The steering wheel was much larger than modern steering wheels, and there was a long pole sticking out of the floor, which I assumed was used to switch gears. I climbed up into the truck and slid into the front seat. Tristan was staring at me, clearly annoyed by how long it was taking me to get into the truck. I quickly pulled the door shut, sensing that he was ready to get going. Tough Guy climbed onto the seat back and nestled into a small space between the seat and the back window. Tristan started the engine, and it sounded much smoother than I expected. With the headlights on, beams of light extended out toward the field. The field went on much farther than I imagined, like an endless sea of swaying, golden grass.

Tristan did something with the gear shift, and the car started to move through the field. The ground was rough, and we bumped along until we reached the pavement of the road. I glanced back at the field we had come from and saw the grass spring back to life so there was no evidence of the tires having crushed it.

I thought about asking Tristan about how he had done that, but when I glanced over at him, he looked super intense and focused, so I decided to just keep quiet. His eyes darted around in the darkness as we neared the port. Once we had passed it, his focus was on the rearview mirror until we turned off the road onto another relatively deserted street.

That was when Tristan let out a deep breath and unclenched a little. "Okay, I think we're clear." His face looked more relaxed now.

"Clear?" I echoed.

"There's always a chance one of them followed us here." Tristan glanced at me. "If any of them had recognized me during our battle, they would have most likely figured I would come here."

That kind of creeped me out. I never wanted to see any of those people again, especially that Drainer.

"How're you holding up?" Tristan asked, concern washing over his features.

Was I that easy to read? I'd have to work on perfecting my poker face.

"What do you mean?"

I tried to sound unfazed even though I was *totally* fazed. But I didn't want him to know that. Tristan came across as the kind of guy you wanted to impress.

"Well ... a lot has happened," Tristan said. "I know your aunt told you about this stuff, but to see it in real life, that's a whole other thing."

"Yeah, but it wasn't like I believed her. I just thought she was crazy," I answered him, but then I regretted my words.

"Crazy?" he said slowly. "You thought your aunt was crazy?"

I really didn't want to talk about this again, so I tried to change the subject. "How do you know my aunt anyways?"

Tristan held up his left hand, and I could see a ring on his finger. "I'm married to her."

"What?" I couldn't believe it. "But that would mean that you're my—"

"Your uncle," he finished my sentence for me. "Yep, we're family, mate. That is, if I decide to forgive your aunt when I see her."

He paused for a second before continuing, his voice soft. "I hope I get to see her again."

His words faded into the night. He didn't say anything for a while. I assumed he was trying to process the fact that the Wrathful had his wife. I just stared ahead and tried to consider what that meant. I wanted to ask him, but I decided against it.

"You know what?" Tristan broke the silence, startling me. "When I think about it, you're right. She is crazy. Leaving Underfoot how she did."

"What do you mean?" I asked him.

"She snuck out in the middle of the night. Turned herself into a Scale, of all things. Still don't know how she pulled that off." He smirked as he spoke.

"Scale?"

"Aquatic creatures that originated from Vinland." He was staring straight ahead at the road. "I always seem to underestimate her. You'd think I would've learned by now that nothing will stop her when she's set her mind to something."

"Why did she leave?"

He took his eyes off the road for a second and glanced at me. "To get you."

"Right ..." Guilt washed over me. "That's what Mrs. Tovar said."

"Here's the thing," Tristan began. "We started to hear that things were getting pretty bad up top with the Wrathful. Then, when we heard they had allied with the Drainers ... well, everyone went into a panic. The council decided to close all entrances in Underfoot. No one coming in and no one going out. The intention was to keep everyone safe, which I understood. But your Aunt was determined to get you and bring you to the settlement."

"So it's my fault she's missing?"

Tristan didn't respond right away. "You can't think like that, mate. She did the right thing even though I wished she had chosen a different course of action. You can't blame yourself."

I tried to take his advice, but in the end, I couldn't help myself. "But if she hadn't left, you and she would've been safe in this Underfoot place."

"I doubt it," Tristan responded. "Your aunt doesn't like to be told what to do. Once they forbade her from going up top, she became hell-bent on finding a way to get out."

"Why do you keep saying up top?"

"Underfoot is underground. Mostly caves. Your aunt came down there to live with me after we were married. But we always came back to visit you while your mum was still … ." Tristan paused as if he didn't know how to finish his sentence.

"Awake?" I finished for him.

He glanced over at me. "You don't remember me, do you?"

I just shook my head.

"Well, I didn't make many trips back once your mum was unresponsive." Tristan looked back at the road. "Your dad drove me bloody crazy. I couldn't stand him."

Tristan paused, then added, "No offense."

"None taken." I lied. I wasn't a fan of my dad either, but it still stung a little to hear people talk so badly about him.

"Your dad was cool at first, but then he decided he didn't want Bryn to have anything to do with you," Tristan continued. "He started telling her she couldn't see you. He even called the cops and told them she was trying to abduct you. He went as far as getting a restraining order against her. It was absolute rubbish."

"What?" I couldn't believe it. "My dad did that?"

"Sure did," Tristan nodded his head. "I've never seen so much animosity. You'd think he hated Vins. I could never understand how or why he married your mum."

"I'm not sure he really got all this magic stuff."

Tristan gave me a weird look.

"I mean, maybe he didn't know as much as you think." It felt strange to defend my dad.

"I find that hard to ... ." He paused and looked over at me, perhaps changing his mind about what he was going to say. "Yeah, maybe."

I knew he just agreed with me because he didn't want to upset me. He thought I was a kid who needed to believe that my dad was not as bad as he was, but he really didn't need to bother. Deep down, I knew what he said about my dad was true.

We continued down the road in silence for a while. My mind was all over the place. There was too much to take in. I couldn't stop thinking about what we were up against and what had happened to Mrs. Tovar.

"Can you tell me more about the Wrathful?" I asked.

"They're Vins, just like us. They just chose a darker path. They are full of vengeance and have a hunger for power. If the rumors are true and they really have found a way to cast the unbreakable curse, well ... we're all in serious trouble."

"What about the Drainers?" I asked him. "What's their story?"

Tristan's body tensed up. His hands clutched the steering wheel so hard, his knuckles turned white.

"They are the epitome of evil. Ruthless, without empathy. Vinland had the right idea when they banished them all from their land."

"Have you had to deal with them very often?" I was hoping that running into Ashford was a fluke. A rare occurrence.

"The first time I ran into a swarm of them," Tristan spat out, as if just talking about them was poison, "I was in the military."

I waited for him to continue, completely surprised by his revelation.

He was quiet for a moment, staring straight ahead. His Adam's apple bobbed up and down as he swallowed hard, recalling bad memories.

I wasn't sure if he would continue, but then he said, "We were hit with an IED. It was gruesome."

An IED?

My mind went to the images I had seen on television, tanks mangled by bombs that had been planted on the road. I looked over at Tristan, trying to imagine what he had been through, what he had seen.

"My squad," Tristan swallowed hard again, "I couldn't help them. I was pinned under a piece of metal. Then some people approached. At first, I thought they were coming to help. I thought they were checking how bad we were injured. But ... that wasn't what they were doing."

"They were Drainers?" I asked.

He nodded. "One by one, they were draining them. I would have done anything for them, but I was helpless, trapped."

He was still clutching the steering wheel.

"I realized something was wrong, and I screamed at them to stop. One of them looked at me, and then he left my friend and started to approach me. I'll never forget it. This tall, dark form gliding toward me with the most wicked grin on his face."

"How did you get away?" I asked him.

He glanced my way. "I was saved by a Caster. He was able to cast a temporary repulsion spell. It was enough time for him to get me out from under the piece of metal and check on my squad, but ... ."

I waited for him to finish, knowing it must be hard to recount this dark moment in his life.

"But they were all gone, every last one of them. Those creatures," he seethed, "those *devils* sucked the very last bit of life from them. They could have made it through, they could've recovered, but those vile things took away any chances for survival."

"I'm sorry," I said, but it didn't feel like it was enough. It felt insufficient and pointless.

"You know what really gets me riled up?" he asked. I didn't answer because it seemed as though he was just talking out loud rather than to me. "It's the fact that they're all such cowards. They wait until their victims are injured and unable to defend themselves. As if it isn't pathetic enough that they prey on defenseless humans, they also wait until they're gravely injured. It makes me sick."

I didn't know what to say. The Drainers had taken away his friends, and nothing in the world could make him feel better about that.

"After that day, I made a promise to myself that I would avenge my squad," he added.

The air was quiet and heavy in the car. The beams of the headlights pierced the blackness and exposed a limited view of where we were headed. Tristan reached over and turned the radio on. The music was staticky, but it filled the space and lightened the mood just a bit. Tristan grunted and began to turn the dial, clearly still agitated. Finally, he stopped on a song that sounded as if it were from another time.

Tristan put both hands back on the large steering wheel. "You like Johnny Cash?"

"I'm not sure."

I didn't mind it though. The man's voice was deep and gruff and sounded a bit tortured. He was saying something about falling into a ring of fire. Suddenly, I felt tired. I leaned back in the stiff chair and let my eyes close. The song filled my mind until sleep eventually consumed me. My dreams were filled with rings of fire, glowing trauma hounds, and forests withering into piles of dust. Needless to say, it wasn't a restful slumber.

CHAPTER 20
DESCENDING

I felt someone shake me. Their grip was firm. Someone hovered over me, reaching in from outside the truck. Once the fog of sleep cleared, I realized it was Maria. I couldn't completely make her out because there wasn't a lot of light, but her corkscrew hair was a dead giveaway.

"Wake up, Wren."

Her voice had an anxious tone to it. She quickly turned and disappeared toward the back of the truck.

I rubbed my eyes and looked around, trying to get my bearings. It looked like we were parked inside a barn. There were clumps of hay and rusty tools lying around. It must have been an old, rundown barn because light poured in through the gaps in the wall.

I started to pull myself out of the cramped confines of the vintage truck. It was rough; the tight space had been challenging for my tall frame. Right away, I felt a kink in my neck, and my leg felt like it wasn't completely attached to my body. It felt all numb and tingly. I tried to wiggle it around to wake it up and hopped around a little bit when Rusty approached.

He was walking like a newborn deer, all wobbly and stiff. "What's your excuse, Larkin?" he asked me. "I mean, *I* have a reason to be walking like a freak, but—"

"What are you talking about?" That was when I looked down at his feet and realized he had put on the boots my grandfather had made for him. "Are those ...?"

"Yes!" Rusty was clearly disappointed. "So much for me being a cunning warrior. I can't even walk! It's like they have a mind of their own. When I take a step, my foot moves much farther than I want it to go."

I pressed my lips together to stop myself from smirking. "Why did you put them on?"

"Tristan told me I had to." Rusty jerked his head toward the front of the truck where Tristan was standing. "Guess the people in Underfoot don't like my kind. Seems like wherever I go, it's the same story."

That was a can of worms I didn't feel like opening right now. "What are the shoes going to do?"

"I guess the shoes will hide who I am," Rusty tried to explain.

"How can shoes hide who you are?"

"I don't know how it works!" Rusty started moving again, looking ridiculous. His steps were overexaggerated, and he almost fell at one point. "You guys can sense each other or something. He said the magic in the shoes will mask that I'm a Nullvin."

Maria walked up to us. "Can you hurry it up, Rusty?"

"Well, excuse me!" Rusty sounded frustrated. "It's not like I put on magic shoes every day. And these things are almost impossible to walk in."

Maria's eyes narrowed. "Oh please. It can't be *that* hard."

"It is, actually." Tristan said as he approached with a bag on his shoulder. "Bertram's magic can be a bit overpowering. It will take a while for Rusty and the shoes to understand each other."

Maria shook her head. "We don't have time for that. We need to get my abuela to the Eradicator as soon as possible."

"Just relax, Maria," Rusty said, trying to calm her nerves.

"But what if she's scared?" She scanned all our faces. "What if she's in pain? We don't know what's happening to her. I can't see anything!"

"I understand, Maria," Tristan responded. "He doesn't need to master the shoes, but he at least needs to not look like a complete idiot. Now let's see how you're getting on, Rusty." Tristan gestured for Rusty to show us his progress.

Rusty tried to walk across the dirt floor of the barn again. His steps were huge, as if he were lunging across the room. Rusty threw his hands up in frustration. "It's no use!"

"We could just leave him here," Maria suggested.

"Hey!" Rusty interjected.

"We're staying together," Tristan said firmly. "You have fifteen minutes to get those shoes under control, mate. As for you," he turned toward me and pulled a first aid kit out of his bag, "let's clean up that cut on your forehead."

"Oh yeah." I had forgotten about the cut. My hand went to my forehead, and I could feel the dried, crusty blood, but it didn't hurt nearly as bad as it had before.

"Did something happen to your leg?" He pointed to my pants, where blood had seeped through the fabric to give away the fact that I was injured there as well.

"Yeah." I tried to pull up my pant leg to get a better look, but the material seemed to be attached to the wound. That wasn't good. "I got cut on my leg too."

He gestured for me to follow him and then directed me to sit on a bale of hay. He kneeled in front of me and opened the first aid kit.

"That was pretty cool what you did, you know." He started to wipe away the dried blood on my forehead. "Getting out of there by riding one of those stone creatures."

"Um ... thanks." Weird. I wasn't used to being complimented. "I wish I didn't have to crash through the house to do it, though."

The reality of the shoe house being gone hit me again. Images of my former home flashed through my mind—the greenhouse, my bedroom, the birdhouses. I still couldn't believe it was gone. Something about the house had seemed timeless, like it would last forever. It didn't seem possible that it no longer existed.

Tristan pulled his hand away. "Sorry about trashing the shoe house. Truly. I got caught up in the moment and didn't think about it when I cast that leveling spell. I know how much it meant to your family. I assume it meant a lot to you as well."

"Yeah ... ." I paused for a moment. "It did mean a lot."

Now everything was in a heap of rubble on the ground. How would the people of Lewisberry ever make sense of it? Or the charred forest, for that matter?

Tristan didn't say anything more. He just went back to cleaning the wound again. Eventually, he pulled away the last bit of red gauze to examine the wound.

"That's odd." He was close enough that I could see a faint scar on his chin.

"What is?"

"Considering the amount of blood on your head, I would have thought your wound would have been more substantial. It's quite long, but it already looks as though it's sealed itself up." He pulled out some disinfectant, and I braced myself for the burn, but I actually didn't feel much of anything. "Do you always heal so fast?" he asked.

I shrugged my shoulders. I hadn't really paid much attention to how fast my wounds healed.

"I guess."

He bandaged my forehead, then leaned down to look at my leg. "This may hurt when I pull your pants away from the wound."

I again braced myself for some discomfort, but once again, it didn't hurt that bad. The skin tugged a bit when Tristan pulled my jeans up toward my knee, but the wound didn't sting like it had the night before when I was running through the woods.

Once the lesion on the leg was cleaned, it also proved to not be as bad as expected.

"I think you got lucky. Both cuts look like they're already healing nicely," he said. He finished cleaning out the wound and pulled out a bigger bandage. "Do you feel better after getting some sleep?"

"Sure," I answered. "I mean, it wasn't the most comfortable sleeping arrangements, but I think I needed it."

"I think you did too," Tristan said as he finished applying the bandage. "You were completely knackered. I tried to wake you a couple of times, but I couldn't get you to budge. Of course, Maria wasn't so gentle."

I smirked. "Sounds about right."

Even though I didn't know my travel companions that well yet, it was clear Maria wasn't easily deterred when something was important to her.

Tristan rearranged the first aid kit, closed it, and slid it back in his bag. I pulled my jeans back down and watched as Tristan walked over to a large barn door and slid it open. Sunlight flooded the dark interior of the barn. I followed him to the door and had to shield my eyes with my hand because the light was so bright. When my eyes adjusted to the brightness, I walked outside to take a look around. That was when I saw that I was standing on a cliff. Everywhere I looked, all I could see was water. It looked like it went on forever. I walked closer to the edge and looked down. Far below, violent waves crashed against the rocky shore. It was killer. I had never seen the ocean before. I had only seen lakes, which always seemed calm and peaceful, as though content with their own existence. But this ocean below ... well, it seemed restless to me, unsettled. I heard a crow squawking above me. I looked up and saw one circling overhead. I knew it was Tough Guy.

Out in the distance, some large rock formations poked out of the churning water. They were dark and oddly shaped. All around me on land were emerald green trees and bushes. There were more pine trees than I had ever seen in my life. They towered above me and gently swayed in the breeze. Off to the side of the barn stood a large, white farmhouse against a green backdrop. On one end of the house was a tower that resembled a lighthouse, but it wasn't nearly as tall.

Tristan joined me on the edge of the cliff. "Better soak up the sun while you can."

"What's that supposed to mean?" I asked him.

"Well, you'd be surprised how much you'll miss it once it's gone." He was looking out at the ocean as he spoke.

"They really don't let people out?" It sounded so crazy. "Even to see the sun?"

"They used to," Tristan nodded as he spoke, "but fear is a powerful thing."

"So where is this place, Underfoot?"

"We'll have to hike down to the water." Tristan walked closer to the edge and pointed down to an area where the ocean was pelting the rocky shore. "There's a cave down there that will lead us to it."

"How are we getting down there?" I asked.

"There's a path." He didn't sound too fazed by the idea of climbing down a cliff, but I definitely was.

Maria came out of the barn and walked briskly toward us. "I think Rusty's almost got it."

"Think he can make it down the path without falling off the side of the cliff?" Tristan asked.

Maria looked down the side of the cliff, then back to us and shrugged. "Sure."

Rusty was suddenly right behind her. Once he reached the edge of the cliff and saw how high up we were, his face went pale, and he completely lost it for, like, the hundredth time that day.

"Are you freaking kidding me?" Rusty looked at all of us as if we were crazy.

I felt bad for the guy, but Tristan promised him that if he fell, he would somehow use his magic to prevent Rusty from getting too injured. That didn't sound very reassuring to me, but it seemed to be enough to convince Rusty. Honestly, I didn't know how Tristan was going to save Rusty from falling off the side of a cliff while he was carrying Mrs. Tovar, but I decided to keep my mouth shut. We grabbed our stuff and started our descent down the cliff, and while Rusty did stumble a couple of times, he managed to not completely fall off.

As we continued down the path, the vibrant green trees and plants became less frequent. Eventually, we were surrounded by nothing but rock walls. The path became narrower, and, at times, it almost disappeared. I sometimes had to find a place to put my foot between the jagged rocks. I didn't realize how nerve-wracking the whole experience was until the path opened onto a small beach up ahead. I was relieved that all of us had somehow survived.

The beach was amazing, and I have to say that standing on an endless body of water was quite humbling. The waves on the beach approached the sand with more grace than the ones that were hitting the rocks so violently on either side of the secluded beach. There were a few trees and washed-up debris from the ocean, and all around us were towering rocky walls that reached toward the sky. Some shade on the beach had been created by a rock that jutted out of the side of the cliff. Tristan walked over to it and laid Mrs. Tovar. Maria and I followed him and collapsed on the sand next to Mrs. Tovar. We both took out the water Tristan had given us before we started the trek down the cliff wall and guzzled it. It was irritating how Rusty seemed completely fine, no sweat, no heavy breathing. I decided it had to be the shoes.

"So now what?" Rusty asked.

Tristan just pointed over to the right. I squinted my eyes and followed his gaze. He seemed to be pointing at a dark cave in the middle of the cliff wall. But the thing was, there was no land around this cave. Only water.

"How the heck are we getting over there?" I asked. Did he think we were all going to swim over there? God, I hoped not. As embarrassing as it might be, I had never learned how to swim.

"There's a boat hidden over here." Tristan walked across the sand toward a pile of dead trees and twigs. He moved some of them away and started to tug at something.

"Hey, muscle boy, why don't you give me a hand?" Tristan yelled back our way.

I assumed he meant Rusty, so I stayed put.

Rusty sprinted over toward him. At first, he almost lost his footing, but he quickly caught himself and walked more carefully across the sand. They pulled together until an old rowboat eventually broke free from under the dead trees. It was colorless and gray and definitely didn't look seaworthy. Heck, it didn't look like it would hold together sitting there on the beach.

"We're going to Underfoot in that?" I asked, feeling my stomach turn a bit as I stood up.

"She'll get us there," Tristan said as he patted the side of the boat like he was its proud parent. One thing was clear: this guy obviously had a soft spot for old, beaten-down things. The boat looked even worse than his truck.

"FYI," I added, "I'm not the best swimmer."

I wasn't a swimmer at all, so I figured it was just a half lie.

"I got ya." Tristan smiled at me. "Don't worry. As long as you're with me, you'll be fine."

I wasn't so sure I bought into this superhero image he was trying to project. I mean, if nothing bad ever happened around him, Mrs. Tovar wouldn't be in the state she was in.

Tristan went back toward the shade and retrieved Mrs. Tovar. I helped Rusty drag the boat to the edge of the water. The boat moved as the waves hit it, and it was a bit challenging getting in. I helped with Mrs. Tovar, and we set her down next to Maria in the back of the boat. I sat down in the front, hoping the aged wood would hold my weight. Tristan and Rusty pushed the boat farther out into the water and then hopped in before the water reached their feet. The boat swayed back and forth, and I nervously held my breath as it regained its balance. Tristan sat down on the middle bench and grabbed the oars that were inside the boat. Rusty sat down next to me. It was definitely a tight fit. Tough Guy landed on my knee for a second. He nudged my hand and gave me a small seashell. I put it in my pocket. He seemed satisfied and then flew up into the sky again.

The bright rays of the sun created pockets of glistening light on the rippling water. I looked back at the cliff we had hiked down. It towered over us, overwhelming and intense. Part of me couldn't believe we had climbed down it. But here I was, in the middle of the Pacific Ocean in a rickety, old boat, heading toward a dark cave. We would soon be entering a strange new world, and I had no idea what to expect.

CHAPTER 21
IN THE MURKY DEEP

Once we got off the shore a little way, the water became rough, and it was clear that Tristan was having a hard time fighting the waves that were trying to force us back to the shore.

"Is this how you always get in?" I asked. It seemed kind of crazy and unnecessary to me.

"No," Tristan answered. "All the other entrances have been shut down."

"And they didn't shut down this one?" I asked him.

"No." Tristan's breath was strained. "No way the Scaled would allow that to happen."

"The what?" Rusty asked.

"They are an aquatic species that live in Underfoot."

"Gotcha. You want me to paddle for a while?" Rusty asked.

Tristan shot him a scowl. "You think I'm too old to row a crappy rowboat?"

"No," Rusty answered. "I think these waves are intense, and we should take turns."

Tristan thought for a moment then said, "Fine."

He handed Rusty the oars, and they somehow managed to change seats. Rusty took the oars and began to paddle. Surprisingly, the boat started to cut through the waves swiftly.

"Am I doing it right?" Rusty asked.

"Yeah," Tristan grumbled. "You're doing fine."

Then he leaned toward me and whispered. "You know it's the shoes, right?"

I gave a firm nod. "Oh yeah."

Rusty glanced over his shoulder to see how close we were to the cave entrance, clearly unaware of our bitterness. Up ahead was a dark cave, and Rusty veered the small boat toward the direction of the opening. As we got closer to the cliff wall, shade overtook our boat, and the temperature dropped at least ten degrees.

"Say goodbye to the sun," Tristan commented, which was a depressing thought.

We were closer to the entrance now. The interior looked black. Seriously, you couldn't see a thing.

Tristan looked around the inside of the rowboat. "Now, where's my bag? Ah, there it is." He leaned down and picked up the leather bag from the curved floor of the boat. He took out a long tin box and pulled out the firebird feather. "Think we're going to need this again."

Rusty looked over his shoulder one more time as he carefully navigated the rowboat between the cave walls. The temperature dropped again, and the air felt heavy. The sound of the water hitting the walls echoed throughout the cave. I looked back and watched the opening to the outside world get smaller and smaller until, eventually, the only light that could be found was coming from the firebird feather. I wondered for a moment about Tough Guy, but then I figured he would be better off on the outside.

"How far in does this go?" Maria asked from the front of the rowboat.

"Just a little bit farther," Tristan answered her, his voice echoing throughout the chamber.

We rowed for a while in silence. I think we were all contemplating what we had gotten ourselves into. At least, I was. There was something unnerving about getting farther and farther away from the outside world. I knew the sun; I knew the sky. But this deep, dark cave felt foreign, and I had no idea what it would be like in

Underfoot. Each time the oar hit the water and pulled us closer to the unknown, my apprehension grew.

"Hey." Maria pointed ahead of her. "The cave ends up there."

She was right. As we got closer, I could see a wall of rock before us. "I don't get it."

"Well, we can't have pesky Nullvins stumbling upon this place, can we?" Tristan said.

He took off his jacket and laid it on the floor of the boat. Then he stood up and jumped into the water without warning. We all leaned over the side of the boat and tried to see into the murky depths. The boat tilted to the side from our combined weight, so we all scrambled to the other side in order to keep it from tipping over. Since Tristan was still holding the firebird feather, we could see the light grow smaller as he swam deeper and deeper into the watery depths. Eventually, it stopped moving.

"Do you know what he's doing?" Rusty asked Maria.

She shook her head. "No idea."

"How the heck is he holding his breath for so long?" Rusty asked.

Suddenly, a loud, guttural sound filled the small space, and the stone wall started to move upward into the ceiling of the cave. The water from both sides of the wall violently came together in a crash, and Maria shrieked as we were all sprayed with cold water. Once the wall had completed its ascension into the roof of the cave and the water settled down, we all peered inside, anxious to get a glimpse of Underfoot.

Beyond the entrance, the interior space was enormous. The roof extended way up, and hovering directly under it was a huge orb of light. It looked like a ball of energy; it was fuzzy, like it didn't have a crisp edge. It wasn't hard to look at it like it was to look at the sun. It was more like a soothing light that radiated a soft glow. Under the orb was a huge body of water. It was bizarre because it was as though there was a lake inside the cave. Sporadically placed throughout the lake were numerous statues covered in bright green moss. Beyond the statues was a waterfall pouring out of an opening in the upper portion of the cave. The sound of rushing water falling into the lagoon echoed throughout the space.

"Wow," Rusty said as Tristan emerged from the water and grabbed the side of the rowboat.

I reached over, grabbed his arm, and pulled him back in. Rusty quickly leaned the opposite direction, trying to prevent the boat from flipping.

"Easy there."

Tristan's clothes were dripping with water. He handed me the firebird feather and began to ring his shirt out. I expected the feather to be hot, but it wasn't. Even though it was wet, it was warm to the touch.

"Okay, Rusty." Tristan pointed beyond the statues. "Just head toward the shore."

"Shore?" he asked.

"Yeah," Tristan said. "Just past the statues is a beach. Can you see the pier?"

"Yeah, with all those ships?" Rusty asked. Up ahead, lines of ships were tied to a long pier that jutted out into the water.

"Yeah, head toward the pier," Tristan answered him. "Best not to linger."

Rusty just nodded and started to move our boat toward the shore. We were all on edge, knowing there were some kinds of aquatic creatures swimming below us. As our boat crossed the body of water, I could see areas of the lake where ropes were suspended over the surface. Hanging from the ropes were various objects—sharp pieces of metal, wads of seaweed, and a variety of fish. I was going to ask why those things were hanging like that when something moved in the water. A loud splash drew my attention, and I caught a glimpse of something large and shiny break the surface of the water before disappearing.

Rusty pulled the oars close to him. "What the heck was that?"

Tristan seemed unconcerned. "Nothing to worry about. Just the Scaled. They're inspecting us."

Tristan wasn't kidding because, suddenly, the boat was surrounded by a whole bunch of them. I could see thick, snake-like forms moving in and out of the water. They were circling the boat, making it impossible for Rusty to continue rowing.

"How big are these things?" I asked as one of the Scaled broke the surface. Its large, black eyes were glaring at me. They were the biggest eyes I had ever seen—almond-shaped and completely black, no white surrounding the pupil. Heck, there was no pupil at all. The face resembled a human, but it was covered in scales, the nose was pushed back into the face, and the nostrils were elongated. It had long, wild hair that reminded me of clumps of seaweed.

More of the Scaled pushed through the surface of the water, all of them glaring at us aggressively. Their faces were a variety of muted colors: lavender, celadon, and salmon. The color became darker as it traveled down toward their webbed hands. They were pointing spears, daggers, and other sharp weapons at us. Rusty somehow stood up without flipping the boat over and looked ready to start whacking them with one of the oars. Maria shielded her grandmother from the Scaled with her body, and I searched the floor of the boat for a weapon. I grabbed the long, tin, feather container and prepared for an attack. It wasn't much, but it was all I had.

"Now hold on, Tomo," Tristan said as he thrust his body between Rusty and one of the Scaled.

The Scale's mouth was slightly open, and I could see they had a lot of teeth crammed in there. They were razor-sharp, in multiple rows like those of a shark.

"Tristan," the Scale answered him, but his voice was strange. It sounded like he was speaking and hissing at the same time. "Why would you come in this way? Did you want to get killed?"

Tristan shrugged his shoulders. "Not really. But how else did you expect me to get in? All the other entrances have been closed."

"You shouldn't have come unannounced," the Scale replied. "Unannounced and with strangers. It could've been ugly."

"How was I supposed to announce us?" Tristan countered. "You guys have completely shut yourselves off from the outside world."

"And for good reason!" another Scale spoke. This one sounded angry. "How could you bring those strangers in here?"

"They're just some children in danger and a cursed woman," Tristan said, trying to downplay our presence.

"No one is allowed in, Tristan," the Scale named Tomo hissed. "You know the rules."

"I couldn't just leave them out there," Tristan pleaded his case. "They were in danger. And as for this woman," he glanced toward Mrs. Tovar, "I believe she may need the Eradicator. She has a curse on her I haven't been able to break."

They all began to speak with each other. Even though they were difficult to understand, it was clear they were no longer speaking in English.

Tomo then sneered at Tristan. "That is precisely why they closed the entrances. To prevent the dangers of the outside world from entering our settlement, like curses that can't be broken."

Tristan nodded as if he was agreeing with them. "Very true. But I still couldn't leave them there." Tristan pointed at me as he said, "This one's family."

"Family?" Tomo questioned him.

"Yes." He glanced toward Mrs. Tovar. "Family and a close friend."

"Ring the bell," Tomo said to the creature next to him. "Summon the guard."

The Scale he spoke to dove into the water. I could see his body briskly slide through the water, away from us. It reminded me of when I once saw a water snake in a lake back in Lewisberry. I'd thought that snake was pretty creepy-looking, but it was not nearly as creepy as this guy.

"So can we proceed to shore?" Tristan asked with a bit of sarcasm.

"We will escort you in," the Scale hissed.

"Fine." Tristan sounded like he thought the Scale was completely overreacting. "Go ahead, Rusty. Row us in."

Rusty looked a little freaked out, but he put the oars back in the water and began to move the boat again. The Scaled started to move with us, but they kept their black eyes just above the water, watching our every move.

CHAPTER 22
UNDERFOOT

"So, are we ... good?" I asked Tristan.

"Good?" he tilted his head.

"They don't seem too excited about us being here," I said as quietly as possible. Even though the Scaled were mostly submerged in the water, I had no idea how good their hearing was.

"They're never excited about anything. Very serious species," he said. "No worries. We're good."

I wondered if he really believed what he was telling me, or if he was just trying to convince us it wasn't a mistake to come down here. At that moment, I wished I had Maria's power so I could just grab his arm and see what he was really thinking.

"You sure this was such a good idea?" Rusty asked.

"You just keep quiet and try to walk as gracefully as possible," Tristan instructed.

Rusty must've realized Tristan was getting annoyed because he just nodded his head and said, "Got it."

"What's the deal with all of these statues?" I asked.

"They represent the various residents of Underfoot," Tristan said as we approached one of them. "There are tons of species down here. For example," Tristan pointed toward a moss-covered statue to our right, "this statue represents the original inhabitants of Underfoot. We call them Moles, but I think their formal title is Gray Dwarfs."

"Dwarfs? You're joking," Rusty said and leaned to the left side to get a better look.

It didn't really look like how I imagined a dwarf to look. No big beard or stocky build. This guy actually looked a little sickly; he didn't appear to have much hair and had these huge goggle-like glasses that covered most of his face.

"Why does it look like they have something covering their eyes?" I asked.

"Moles hate bright lights," Tristan gestured to the glowing orb hovering above us, "which is a big point of contention down here. They think it is too bright, but we would like it to be a little bit more intense. They wear these huge goggles to protect their eyes."

Rusty pointed to the orb. "You can control the intensity of that thing?"

"Yes, it's the product of magic. Nothing like the real thing, but it serves a purpose." Tristan gazed up at it. "The Moles hate it. I think, deep down, they regret ever letting the rest of us in."

"They let you guys in?" I asked.

"The Moles have been here forever," Tristan explained. "They're the ones who created this settlement. They've always lived underground. This is their domain. We're basically their guests."

"Even these guys?" Rusty asked, nodding toward the swirling, aquatic bodies that continued to surround our boat.

"Kind of. They live exclusively in the lagoon." Tristan waved his hand to the surrounding water. "This is their section of Underfoot. Rumor has it they found this place long ago, when the seas were full of warships. This became a safe haven for them. The Moles and the Scaled formed an alliance. The Scaled protected this entrance from intruders, and the Moles allowed them to stay."

"So what would these Scale creatures have done to us if we hadn't been here with you? If we had come alone?" Rusty said very quietly.

"Well, let's just say they are known to be rather aggressive," Tristan answered Rusty. "It could have been a bit dodgy."

"What else are we going to find down here?" I asked. "Any other aggressive creatures?"

Tristan hesitated before he said, "Not really. Mostly just entities who are seeking a secret place to live so they don't have to deal with the outside world. There are Vins who have been banished, many mythological creatures of the Northwest and Alaska. Heck, there are even a few banshees down here. The deal is, they just have to keep their mouths shut."

"Why is that statue so small?" Maria was pointing to a statue that looked more like a pillar coming out of the water with a small person on top. It only looked to be about eight to twelve inches tall.

"Have you ever heard of the Nim?" Tristan asked her. "Formal name is Nimerigar."

"No," she answered him. "Are they small?"

"Yeah," Tristan explained. "They are a miniature race. Supposedly, they came from the Rocky Mountains. Don't be fooled by their size, though. They're great archers, and their arrows are dipped in all sorts of potions. Some are rather deadly."

"Geez ..." Rusty looked up at the statue. "Maybe Mrs. Tovar was right. Maybe I should've stayed in Lewisberry."

"She *did* try to warn you," Maria commented.

"Yeah, but if I hadn't come," Rusty glanced back at her with a smirk, "just think how heartbroken you would've been."

She scoffed. "Oh yeah," she said sarcastically. "I would've been devastated."

What was going on? Were these two flirting? I didn't know how I felt about that.

We passed a few more statues. Some were hard to decipher since they had so much moss and algae growing on them. Some looked relatively normal, and others completely freaked me out, like the rather small person who wore a cap and had talons for hands. Or another one that looked like a woman, but there was something about her features that reminded me of an owl. I knew that once we reached the shore, I most likely would be shocked by what I was going to see.

I looked beyond the statues at the approaching shore. There was a long dock with many boats lined up on either side. Tall masts emerged from the center of the boats, but the sails were all rolled up. There were rows of long oars suspended above the water on either side of the ship. They kind of reminded me of Viking vessels, long and low with sweeping curves and elaborate carvings on both ends of the boat. There was also a group of long, slender canoes tied to the dock, which were painted with elaborate Native American designs.

Large tapestries hung down from the enormously high ceiling. The imagery on the tapestries represented many of the residents of Underfoot. I could see that one of them had something to do with the Scaled because the image looked like one of them with a three-pronged spear. But what surprised me the most was seeing green plants and trees on the far end of the cave. It was strange to see plants thriving in this underground environment. I concluded that it must be a result of the magical sun hovering above us. Large, gray rocks were randomly placed on the shore, and many more were poking out of the water near the shoreline. Next to one of the rocks in the water was a large bell suspended on a thick, wooden armature. The Scale who was sent to alert the others of our arrival had pulled its way onto one of the rocks by using its arms. It reached up to pull a lever that allowed the bell to ring. Its sound echoed loudly through the chamber.

"What's going to happen when we get to shore?" Maria asked. Her tone was all business, like she was preparing the best plan of action in her head for getting them to help us.

"We'll be greeted by the guard," Tristan responded. "Then I'll try to convince them to summon the Eradicator."

"How do you think that's going to go?" she asked him.

Tristan could sense her uneasiness. "Relax, Maria. I can be very convincing. It's not like they're going to kill us or anything."

Rusty's eyes widened. "Well, that's ... reassuring."

Tristan took the firebird case from me and opened it. He placed the feather inside the case and closed it. I then realized his clothes were almost dry. "Did the firebird feather dry your clothes?" I asked.

"Like I said, firebird feathers are quite handy," he responded.

Rusty nodded to another statue as we passed by it. "Why does that guy look like a Native American?"

"Oh yeah." Tristan grabbed his coat from the bottom of the boat and put it back on. "There's some of them down here. Shamans mostly."

"Why would they be down here?" Rusty asked.

"Can you blame them?" Tristan asked. "After they were pushed farther and farther west, coming into the settlement was an assurance that their ways would not be forgotten."

I was just glad there would be some people down here that were human and relatively familiar. A few of the non-Scale residents were now standing on the edge of the shore, trying to get a better look at us, the intruders. I spotted one of the Moles. I knew it was a Mole because he was wearing huge, steampunk-looking goggles. The thing I wasn't expecting was their skin to look so gray. It was like the color of concrete.

As if that wasn't crazy enough, the Scaled were dragging their bodies onto the beach. Their heads tended to be light, pastel shades, but the tones became much deeper down the length of their bodies. The gradation continued until it reached the tips of their tails and webbed fingers, which were as black as their eyes.

"Well ... we are definitely not in Lewisberry anymore," Rusty commented.

I couldn't agree with him more.

CHAPTER 23
UNWELCOMED

We had reached the dock where two guards were standing on the end and watching us approach. They both looked like normal human beings except they were dressed in black with several weapons hanging from their belts. The larger one had a sword so long, it almost touched the ground. Everything about him was intense—his oversize beard, his turban, the scowl on his face. If I were a betting man, I would say his scowl was a permanent feature. The other one was much leaner and looked more like a model than a guard—perfect features and hair. It made me wonder if there was some kind of magic involved. Behind them on the shore were five other members of the guard.

"What's up with these guys?" Rusty grumbled, glaring up at the guards. He had placed the oars inside the boat, and his hands were balled into fists.

"Just play it cool," Tristan said softly and then directed his attention to the guard with the turban. "Anik." Tristan climbed out of the boat and put his arms out like he was going to hug the guy.

"Not in the mood for your games, Tristan. You know the rules. Coming in here like this with outsiders." He shot a disapproving glance toward the rest of us. "It's not allowed."

"Come on, they're a bunch of kids," Tristan said casually.

"I don't care if you brought a boatful of newborns," Anik replied. "Rules are rules, and you and your wife seem to have a hard time following them."

"You can leave Bryn out of this." Tristan's expression turned dark, and his voice no longer sounded friendly.

Anik walked right up to Tristan, their faces inches apart. "No, I really can't. Her actions may have put us all in danger."

At that moment, Rusty jumped out of the boat and landed next to Tristan. The guard turned quickly, his hand reaching for his sword.

"Now hold on," Tristan said firmly. "You need to calm down, Anik."

"And you need to quit making stupid decisions," Anik spat.

"I didn't have a choice this time." He glanced back at Maria and Mrs. Tovar. "The Eradicator may be the only hope for that cursed woman in the boat."

Anik looked past Tristan to Mrs. Tovar. "What happened to her?"

"She was bit by a trauma hound," Tristan explained. "But the problem is ... I haven't been able to break it."

Anik's eyebrows went up. "You can't break it?"

Tristan just shook his head in defeat.

"So ... it's real." Anik's voice slowly rose. "The unbreakable is real."

"Maybe," Tristan answered him, but he was looking down when he said it, as if he knew he would be in trouble.

"You brought an unbreakable curse down here?"

Tristan glared at the guard. "It's not like it's contagious."

"It's dark magic!" Anik was shouting now. "It's unpredictable."

The other guard gave Anik a disapproving glance. "Tristan may have faults, but he would never bring enemies into this place."

"We don't know that for sure, do we?" Anik asked. "Fintane, what do you think?"

I followed Anik's gaze. He was talking to a Scale in the water next to our boat along with several other Scaled. We were surrounded again.

"He can't be trusted," he hissed. "The way his wife deceived us all. I wouldn't put anything past him."

"You're just angry because Bryn was able to get past all of you undetected," Tristan snarled at him. "Seems you guys are really great at guarding this entrance," Tristan said sarcastically.

"You think this is a joke?" The Scale moved closer to the pier. "We are protecting our kind from the dangers of the outside world."

"What do you think *I'm* doing?" Tristan motioned to us. "They're no threat. They are simply people in need of help. Isn't that how this settlement came into being? A safe haven for those seeking shelter from their enemies? Have we really strayed so far from our roots?"

"It was a different time," Anik said.

"Was it?" Tristan questioned him. "Our people were under attack, threatened, seeking protection in dangerous times. I don't see the difference. Maybe the only difference now is that we are ruled by fear. Our ancestors were not."

"It's not a matter of fear. It is a matter of survival," Fintane snarled. "We know nothing about these people. They could be spies. There could even be a Drainer among them."

"Right," Tristan laughed. "Like I would ever bring a Drainer down here. If I did, they wouldn't be breathing."

"Enough!" shouted a strong voice.

I turned my head to see who had spoken and was surprised to see it had come from a rather frail-looking, female Mole. She was walking toward us on the pier, and I realized it wasn't just her voice that was loud, so were her footsteps. The sound of her steps echoed loudly through the cave. She was wearing a simple, brown dress, and her salt and pepper hair was twisted into sections and piled on top of her head. "Tristan, what trouble have you gotten yourself into this time?"

Tristan's voice was a bit gentler when he addressed this woman. "I didn't really have a choice, Gwen."

"Of course you didn't," she said as she approached. The two guards moved out of the way to let her through. "Why have you come unannounced?"

"How was I supposed to bloody announce myself? You closed all the entrances," Tristan said, exasperated.

Gwen cleared her throat as if his answer wasn't acceptable.

"Sorry," he mumbled.

Her head turned our way. It seemed like she was looking at us, but since her huge goggles covered the top half of her face, it was a little hard to tell. "What about Bryn. Did you find her?"

Tristan shook his head in defeat. "No."

"They could have taken her. She could be leading them to us as we speak," Fintane said from the water.

These guys really didn't trust anybody.

Tristan glared at the Scale. "She would never do that."

"Maybe not voluntarily," another one of the Scaled commented.

"I've had enough of your double standards!" Tristan's voice rose again. "Your kind swim out in the ocean every day while the rest of us are cooped up in here like prisoners. It's ridiculous."

"We won't be seen in the water," Fintane responded. "Our kind can't be contained like that. We need the open water."

"I can't be contained, either!" Tristan roared. "What rubbish. There are sightings of you guys all the time. You know how easy it would be for one of your kind to lead the Wrathful here."

"Yet it has never happened, has it, Tristan?" the Scale hissed. "We have never brought outsiders into this settlement. *You* have done so time and time again. You brought Bryn here, and look what happened as a result."

"This discussion is pointless," Gwen intervened. "Tristan, tell me who these people are."

"The tall boy," Tristan pointed at me, "is my nephew. Wren Larkin."

I held up my hand slightly, not sure if I should wave or not. Gwen leaned in to get a better look at me.

Tristan gestured to Maria and Mrs. Tovar. "The girl is the daughter of some close friends, and her grandmother ... I haven't been able to revive her—"

"She has the unbreakable," Anik interrupted. "He brought dark magic down here."

"What was I supposed to do, Gwen?" Tristan asked quietly. He leaned down a bit toward the Mole and lowered his voice. I had to strain my ears a bit to hear what he was saying. "I couldn't leave the woman like this. That's her granddaughter for god's sake. What was I supposed to tell her? That there was no hope for her grandmother?"

The Mole didn't reply. She seemed to be pondering his argument.

"You have to help her," Maria spoke. "If there is a possibility that the Eradicator can wake her, you have to let her try. Please."

The Mole remained quiet for a moment more before saying, "Tristan, bring the woman with you. We'll take her to the council. Anik, take the young ones to Tristan's house and make sure they stay there."

Maria stood up in the boat. "I'm not leaving her. I'm coming with you."

Gwen crossed her arms in front of her chest. "Young lady, what is your name?"

"Maria," she responded. "Maria Tovar."

"Are you always so forthcoming with your demands?" she asked her.

"Yes," Rusty answered for her.

Tristan jabbed him the ribs.

"And we can't forget about you." Gwen was now focused on Rusty, which made me nervous. "How do you fit into all of this?"

"Me?" Rusty turned to me and then to Tristan for help. "I'm a friend. That's all."

"They're just a bunch of Vins," Tristan interjected. "Nothing fancy."

Gwen was again quiet, probably contemplating what was to be done with us.

"Very well," she said abruptly. "Come along, Maria Tovar. I'm sure the council will appreciate your outspoken nature."

She turned around and began to stomp down the pier. Tristan reached into the boat and, with Maria's help, was able to lift Mrs. Tovar into his arms.

Rusty helped Maria out of the boat. "Good luck," he said to her.

"You guys behave." She looked back at me. "Keep an eye on him," she said, pointing at Rusty. Then she ran after Tristan.

"Well? What are you waiting for, kid?" The intimidating guard was glaring me. "Are you getting out of the boat or what?"

"Y-yeah." I grabbed my backpack full of shoes and climbed out of the boat.

CHAPTER 24
WEAPON OF CHOICE

"What were your names again?" the guard who looked like a model asked.

"My name is Wren, and this is Rusty," I introduced.

"Nice to meet you. My name is Marcus." He smiled at us.

He was probably the first person to smile at me in Underfoot. I immediately liked the guy.

Rusty and I had followed Anik down the pier steps. Once we reached the sand, the crowd cleared a pathway for us and watched us closely as we passed. I had never felt so unwelcomed in my life. Seeing the residents of Underfoot up close was jarring. The Moles were crazy weird-looking, as were a lot of the other residents. Some had skin that looked more like leather; others were so pale, you could see all their veins through their skin. A couple of them wore masks over their faces, and I wasn't so sure I wanted to know what was under them. I realized quickly that if you were walking in Underfoot, it was best to look down because I had almost stepped on a couple of the Nims, the tiny people Tristan had told us about. If I hadn't heard them yelling at me or realized I was about to step on something, there would have been some seriously injured Nims along the way. And since Tristan said they liked to shoot poison arrows, who knew if I would have even made it to Tristan's place.

We then entered a tunnel where torches were hung sporadically on the walls, lighting our way. Strange formations were growing out of the cave walls. I remembered reading about them once. They were called "stalagmites" or "stalactites." One grew from the floor, and the other descended from the ceiling, but I could never remember which was which. They looked like hardened forms of lava or something from a sci-fi movie. I reached out and felt the surface of one of them as we passed. It felt so smooth and damp.

We had reached the end of the tunnel, and now we were standing in a rather large, open space. The ceiling extended even higher than the one in the lagoon, and there was another glowing ball of light hovering above us. Directly in front of us was a huge fountain. It was at least three tiers, and there was a burst of water flowing out of the top that cascaded down the various tiers until it settled in a large pool of water. It looked like people were filling containers from the fountain, and I wondered if this was the main water source for the creatures who lived down here. Surrounding the fountain were buildings. But they didn't look like ordinary buildings, more like large objects. One building looked like a teapot, and another looked like a dress with a rather full skirt. A few others resembled a bag full of tools, a huge loaf of bread, or a pile of books.

Rusty nudged me hard in my side. "Look familiar?" He was pointing at the other side of the road.

I turned and saw a building that looked like a shoe. It didn't look exactly like my shoe house—this shoe was more of a dress shoe, but I couldn't help but be reminded of my ruined home.

I turned to Marcus. "Hey, what are these places?"

"This is the Crafter row," he explained.

"But why do the buildings look like things?" I asked.

"Oh, well, the building looks like whatever they sell."

"Huh." I looked at the shoe building again.

"There used to be too many different languages between us in the early days of the settlement. To make things easier, the vendors built their stores to resemble the wares they sold. Supposedly, the tradition goes way back. Guess they used to do the same thing back in Vinland long ago," he explained.

"Marc, the less they know, the better," Anik growled.

COMPASS TO VINLAND   183

Marcus shrugged off Anik's aggressive tone. "Don't think I was giving any vital information, Anik."

I didn't really care whether Anik was angry or not. What I cared about was the fact that my grandfather had a reason for making our house look like a shoe. He was a Crafter, like the rest of the people down here. A maker of magical things. He wasn't odd or weird. He was a Vin, and that was what Vins did.

We walked past a few more storefronts. There was so much to take in. The buildings were rather detailed and appeared to be covered with a painted clay substance. Some of the buildings were colorful, and others were painted in muted tones. Between the stores, elevated walkways led to tiny entranceways. More of these walkways continued upward along the cave wall toward small structures that were positioned on rocky crevasses. I figured that must be where the Nims lived, which made a whole lot of sense to me since I almost trampled some of them back on the beach.

I turned to Rusty and realized he was quite far ahead of me. I sprinted a bit to catch up with him.

"Why are you walking so fast?" I asked him.

He gave me a puzzled look. "Am I?"

"It's probably because of those—" I was going to say "shoes," but, thankfully, I stopped myself before the word left my lips.

He gave me a guarded look. "Use your brain for once, Larkin," he grumbled.

I wanted to be offended, but I knew he was right. We had to have our wits about us if we were going to survive down here. We were passing a rather large building that looked like a bag full of weapons. In front of the building were tables covered with every kind of weapon you could imagine—knives, swords, hatchets.

"Anik!" someone yelled. It was a Mole. He was standing in the doorway and looking rather short surrounded by the darkness of the entryway. Anik went up to talk to the Mole. Marcus lazily leaned up against a wall. Word must have spread that we were outside the building because a group of Moles came out of the shop and were pushing each other out of the way to get a good view of us.

"They are freaky-looking, aren't they?" Rusty whispered to me.

"Sure are," I agreed. They reminded me of short zombies without all the blood and guts hanging out of them.

One of them came charging toward us with his finger pointed at Rusty. "Hey! What do you think you're doing?"

We gave each other a confused look.

"Do you know what he's talking about?" Rusty asked me.

"No idea." I was as confused as he was.

The Mole glared at Rusty. "Who do you think you are coming down here and stealing from us?"

Rusty exhaled sharply. "You have *got* to be kidding me. Even down here, I'm accused of being a thief."

"What's going on?" Anik had broken away from the Mole he had been talking to.

"That kid," the Mole said, still pointing at Rusty, "took a weapon! It's hanging out his coat."

"What?" Rusty looked down at the pockets of his leather coat. Sure enough, there was a silver object sticking out of the left pocket. Rusty grabbed it and pulled it out. It was a slender tube about twelve inches long.

"Now wait a minute!" Rusty defended himself. "I didn't put this thing in my coat."

Anik walked up to Rusty and grabbed the object from him, but the funniest thing happened. The object slid through his fingers and went flying back toward Rusty. It hit Rusty square in the chest and then fell to the ground.

"What kind of magic are you playing at, kid?" Anik asked, looking super angry.

"I'm not doing anything!" Rusty backed up a few paces, but the object followed him and started to climb his leg.

"What the heck?" he yelled. "Get this thing off me!"

He batted at it, but the object continued to climb and nestled itself back into his pocket.

Some of the Moles had gathered around us and were talking among themselves.

"Did you see that?"

"How'd he do that?"

"It's behaving like a well-trained pet."

One of the Moles walked up to Rusty and peered up at him. Now that he was so close, I realized he had a layer of soot covering his face and hands. His hair was thinning, and long, gray strands of hair barely covered his wrinkled head.

"What is your name, boy?" the Mole asked him.

"Rusty," he answered tentatively. "Rusty Whitaker."

"What are you? A Caster? A Potion-Smith?" the little Mole asked.

Rusty looked to me for help.

"Okay, listen." I drew everyone's attention away from Rusty. "He doesn't know what he is yet. Neither do I. We didn't even know we were Vins until a couple of days ago."

"I don't believe this innocent act!" Anik shouted at the crowd, not being helpful in the slightest. "I bet he's doing something to steal the weapon. We should check him for charms."

He began to reach into Rusty's pockets, but Rusty pushed the guard away. It was just a small shove, but the guard went flying backward. Seriously? The huge guard flew through the air and hit the wall of the next building, landing hard on the ground. He even knocked over a few Vins on his way.

"Whoa … ." Rusty looked nervous. "I didn't mean to do that. Honestly." He started to walk toward the guard with his arm outstretched as if he was going to help him up.

"Did you see that?" one of the Mole's whispered.

More and more of the Moles were getting antsy.

"I swear I didn't mean it, and I didn't steal anything." Rusty looked anxiously at the crowd surrounding him.

"He doesn't know his strength, is all," I defended my friend. Wow. I never thought I'd consider Rusty a friend, but here we were.

Everyone began talking at once.

"How is he so strong?"

"How did he enchant that weapon?"

"This is why we closed the entrances in the first place!"

"Hold it!" It was the soot-covered Mole. He held up his hands as though to appease the crowd. "I don't know anything about his strength, but perhaps the enchanted weapon is intended for this young man."

Anik was now standing, brushing away the dirt from his uniform. "What are you saying?"

"I have seen it before. When there is a warrior with substantial power, an enchanted object may attach itself to its preferred master. They may be destined to be together."

Anik wasn't buying it. "This snotty kid is no warrior."

"Well, he pretty much took you down, didn't he?" the Mole responded.

That shut Anik up real quick. Marcus was laughing discreetly as he watched from the sidelines.

"Perhaps we should test it out?" the Mole said.

"Test it out?" Rusty questioned him. "How?"

"See how you work together," the Mole answered him. "There is a training arena just behind my store. Maybe you can show us if you are the warrior this weapon thinks you are."

"Wait a minute." Rusty grabbed the object that had made its way back in his pocket. He held it out to the Mole. "That's all right. I don't want this thing anyway. I mean, no offense, but it doesn't look like the most impressive thing I have ever seen. I can't even figure out what it is."

The gray Mole didn't take it back. "Why don't you try pulling that little lever on the side?"

Rusty looked at me and then back at the Mole, not sure what to do. He held the silver object closer to his face and examined it to see if there was truly a lever on it. He must have found something because, suddenly, the object extended and grew into a long shaft with a dagger at the end. It was a spear. And not only that, it also glowed so brightly that we all had to shield our eyes. Rusty stared down at it in disbelief.

"Are you a bit more impressed now?" the Mole asked him. He obviously didn't like anyone questioning the quality of his goods.

"I still think this punk swiped it," Anik said.

"Well, since it's *my* store," the Mole said, "I think I should be the one who decides how we handle the situation."

Anik scoffed. "That's not exactly how things work." He went to grab the spear from Rusty, but the Mole got in his way.

"You keep with what you know." The Mole grabbed Rusty by the arm and started to lead him down an alleyway before the guard could strip him of his weapon. "And I will handle things when it comes to my enchanted weapon."

"Hey, uh, I never agreed to this!" I heard Rusty say as a group of Moles surrounded him, pushing him farther down the alleyway.

His head towered over the swarm of Moles. I shoved my way into the crowded alley and followed the swiftly moving sea of Moles into the arena.

CHAPTER 25
THE ARENA

Space was weird down here. The arena was larger than I thought it would be. It appeared to be divided up into a variety of obstacle courses. Within the courses were figures made of straw, which were totally bizarre-looking. They were like scarecrows without fields to protect. On the far end, there was a line of targets where a girl about my age practiced her archery skills. The commotion had caught her attention, and she turned around to see what was going on. She didn't look like she belonged down here. One side of her head was shaved, and the rest of her black hair was going every which way. And it wasn't just her hair that was edgy, so were her clothes—cut up and ragged. I would bet big bucks she made them herself, which probably wasn't that much of a stretch. It wasn't like there were malls down here. At first, I thought she was standing next to a guy, but once I looked closer, I realized she was alone. She joined the crowd to see what was going to happen next.

"All right, young warrior," the sooty Mole spoke, "enter the arena, and we shall see if the weapon really chose you, or if you are the thief Anik wants you to be."

Rusty's face was all scrunched up with uncertainty. "What's going to happen when I enter it?"

"The course is designed to demonstrate your abilities," the Mole answered him.

"So you just want me to go in there and stab those straw dudes?"

"If you think you are capable," the Mole answered him.

Rusty looked confused. He was probably wondering what that was going to prove, stabbing a bunch of stationary, straw men. He scanned the crowd until he found me. I gave him a thumbs-up and hoped for the best. It didn't seem like we had much of a choice unless he wanted to end up in Vin jail.

"Okay. Here goes nothing." Rusty positioned the spear firmly in one hand and turned toward the entrance of the course.

I pushed my way forward so I could get a better view. Once Rusty entered the course, everything happened at once. Logs were released from an elevated ramp and rolled swiftly toward him, hanging bags of sand around him began to swing violently, and the faceless straw figures magically came to life. The figures drew various weapons of their own from their stuffing. All these things descended upon Rusty at once, and there was nothing I could do but watch.

Shockingly, my anxiety was short-lived because Rusty handled everything that came at him with ease. His body moved so fast at times that he was nothing more than a blur. He would spin, duck, and jump with unbelievable agility and strength. He used the spear as a ninja would use a stick, spinning and flying and blocking objects before they reached him. The spear easily cut through wood, fabric, and even other weapons. It was like nothing I had ever seen before and most likely nothing the others had seen before either— everyone was standing perfectly still, the look of awe on their faces. In just a few short minutes, Rusty reached the end of the course. Pieces of wood, straw, and metal fragments lay in his wake.

"Bravo!" the sooty Mole cheered and began clapping loudly. "I think we have just witnessed what happens when a warrior and an enchanted weapon are united."

Rusty's eyes found mine in the crowd, and a huge smile spread across his face. I smiled back. I was proud of the guy. If only all the people back in Lewisberry who didn't believe in him could see him now. Finally, Rusty had proved he was capable of something. Something quite incredible.

Rusty was a star that day, at least as far as the Moles were concerned. At one point, they even lifted him in the air and paraded him around the course. Everyone seemed to think he was a big deal. Everyone except Anik, of course. He didn't seem too impressed. He stood at the entrance with his arms crossed and a scowl on his face. The cooler guard, Marcus, smiled broadly, clearly enjoying all the hoopla.

There was so much going on, I didn't even notice that the girl with the edgy hair was suddenly standing next to me.

"Hey, can I ask you something?" she asked me, her dark eyes outlined by thick, black eyeliner.

"Uh, sure?" She was seriously the coolest-looking girl I have ever met. Her choppy hair half-covered her face, and she had multiple earrings migrating up her ear.

"Are you guys the ones who came from up top?" Her eyes darted to the top of the cave as she asked the question.

"Yeah," I answered her.

Her eyes grew wide. "What's it like up there?"

"What's it like?" I echoed.

"Yeah. I've never been up top," she said. "I've only seen pictures in books."

"You've never left this cave?" I found that hard to believe. I tried to imagine spending my entire life underground. "Like, *ever*?"

"Most of us have been up top, but not me. I was never allowed," she said with a sour look on her face.

"She's special," a male voice said. Out of the corner of my eye, I could see a guy about my age standing next to me, but when I turned my head, all I could see was a sea of Moles.

Where did he go? Had I imagined him?

The girl cocked her head. "So ... can you tell me what it's like?"

I was still a little freaked out by the disappearing guy. "Wait a minute. Didn't you just hear someone?"

She looked at the crowd of people around Rusty. "I hear a lot of things right now."

"Right," I said, feeling my face grow hot with embarrassment. "Yeah, sorry. I just—"

"Have you seen horses? And snow? What is snow like? Can you really catch snowflakes on your tongue?" She word vomited these questions before I had a chance to answer any of them.

"Eyota, you need to calm down. You're going to freak him out."

There it was again! A male voice.

I turned all the way around in a full circle. I felt like someone was standing next to me, but as soon as I turned my head, he disappeared. I knew there was a presence there. Maybe it was a ghost!

"I'm sorry, but I *swear* someone is standing next to me and talking."

"Oh, that's just Pan," the girl said with a shrug. "He's a Tariaksuq."

"A what?" I was never going to get used to any of this.

Her eyebrows pulled together. "You don't know what a Tariaksuq is?"

I just shook my head. I was about to ask her to tell me more when an angry voice called her name.

"Eyota! What do you think you are doing?"

The girl turned swiftly toward the shrieking voice. It was coming from a woman who was standing by the entrance of the arena. She looked like an older version of the girl, minus the shaved hair and ripped clothes.

"Come with me now! You have been summoned."

"Of course I have," the girl grumbled. She rolled her eyes and slumped her shoulders as she started heading toward the woman. She turned back around so she was facing me as she walked backward. "Hey, can you tell me more about your world later?"

"Eyota!" The woman sounded angry. "Now!"

When Eyota was close enough, the woman reached out and grabbed her roughly by the arm. "Why would you talk to that stranger? We don't know anything about them!"

"Yes, Mother," she answered insincerely.

As I turned my attention back to the arena, I swear I saw a boy walking past me.

"Hey!"

I turned quickly and reached out to where he had been. But was nothing there. It was official. Either I was crazy or this place was.

Rusty was weaving his way through the Moles to reach me. "Dude! Did you see that?"

"Yeah, man. Pretty impressive," I answered him. "I guess those shoes are no joke."

"No, they are definitely not." Rusty was looking down at them like they were the crown jewels.

"Hey, you done showing off?" Anik burst his way into our conversation. "My orders were to get you back to Tristan's place."

Marcus was nearby, watching everything play out.

"Gordon!" he called out to the sooty Mole who owned the shop. "We good? You all right with this kid keeping that weapon?"

The Mole joined us and patted Rusty on the back. "By all means! The weapon is his. They are meant to be together."

"Really?" Rusty looked down at the Mole. "I get to keep it?"

"Absolutely," the Mole said. "Besides, now that it has found you, I don't think it's going to quit following you."

"Wow! Thanks."

The Mole grinned with a mouthful of yellow, jagged teeth.

"Thank *you*, young man. I've never seen such unity between a warrior and a weapon before. I can only imagine the adventures you two will have together."

"All right, all right." Anik had clearly had enough. He grabbed Rusty by the collar of his jacket and dragged him toward the exit.

I followed Rusty through the cramped alleyway and then through the winding streets of Underfoot until we reached a section that looked more like an apartment complex than a cave. From the ground to the ceiling were doorway and window openings. Many of the doors were rather small, and others looked normal. Some had ladders or steps that led to the dwellings perched up high, while others had stairs that descended into the ground.

Tristan's house was ground level and didn't require any stairs. Anik reached the stone porch, opened the door, and put his arm out, directing us inside. It was rather dark; there were no windows except for the ones in the front of the dwelling. The cave walls were curved in some places, and I found myself ducking so I wouldn't hit my head. On one side was a rather large fireplace with a pile of wood stacked next to it. There was a rustic-looking table in front of the fireplace and two overstuffed couches off to one side.

I jumped when Anik slammed the door. We could hear scraping noises on the other side of the door. I leaned out one of the windows so I could see what was going on. Anik was doing something to the door because it was glowing.

"Hey!" I called out to him. "Are you locking us in?"

"Yes," he growled at me. "Back up."

I did what he said, and the shutters on the window slammed shut in my face, leaving us in total darkness.

CHAPTER 26
SPRIGS

Eventually, Maria and Tristan came back with a fully awake and restored Mrs. Tovar. After Tristan unlocked the door and all the windows—and reamed out the guards for treating his house like a prison—he went out again and brought back a ton of food. We had a feast that night to celebrate having Mrs. Tovar back. Honestly, it was probably one of the happiest nights of my life. The only thing that got me down were the pictures of my aunt throughout the house. In one of them, she was holding me when I was a toddler. It made me think about what would have happened if she had brought me down here long ago. She probably would've been safe and sound and here with me.

Rusty and I crashed on the couch after everyone had gone to bed, and then next thing I knew, the fake sun was streaming through the windows. And let me tell you, the people of Underfoot weren't quiet in the morning. Someone was yelling something about pastries, and someone else must have been fixing something because the sound of a hammer went on forever.

I slowly got up and stretched my cramped limbs. I made my way into the kitchen and found Tristan there, sitting at a small table and sipping something out of a mug. The kitchen was small but charming. It was covered with wallpaper that had images of centaurs running through a forest. Tristan saw me standing there and put down his mug and went over to the stove. He grabbed the tea kettle that was sitting on a burner and poured the steaming liquid into a ceramic mug on the counter. He then held out the mug toward me.

"What's this?" I asked him.

"Tea."

"Tea? I've never had tea before," I answered him.

"What a sad thing to hear. How are they raising children in America these days?" He shook his head in disapproval. "Well, are you going to try it?"

I didn't want to, but I also didn't want to be rude. And I certainly didn't want him to think I was some lame, unworldly American, even though I totally was. I took the mug from him and chugged a swig of it. Huge mistake. I burned the crap out of my tongue.

Tristan smirked at me and took a sip of his tea. "I think we should head to Sprigs."

"What's that?" I asked him as I opened the freezer to look for an ice cube.

"It's where Vins get their instruments of magic," Tristan explained.

I grabbed an ice cube and put it on my tongue. "Do I need an … instrument?" I asked him, though I'd be shocked if he had understood me with my mouth wide open.

"Sure you do!" Tristan hit my back with his hand, which almost made me swallow the ice cube whole.

"What are you guys talking about?" Rusty entered the kitchen, stumbling around like a zombie. It didn't even look like his eyes were open.

I gagged a little as the ice cube fell out of my mouth and back into my hand. "But what do I need an instrument for?" I asked.

"Instruments are like tools that enhance our skills," Tristan explained. "They'll help you develop your talent. Mine just happen to be my tattoos."

This whole conversation was making me uncomfortable for some reason. "We don't even know what my so-called talent is."

"That's why we go to Sprigs," Tristan continued. "You'll be read there. Either the Crone, Mother, or Maiden will read you. Then they will suggest what instruments you will need to hone your skills."

"Read?" I asked him. "How exactly does that work?"

"Does it hurt?" Rusty was more awake now.

Tristan smirked at us, clearly amused. "Does it hurt for someone to look at you?"

"That's all they do?" I asked.

"That's it. You think you can handle that?" Tristan asked with a bit of sarcasm.

"Yeah, of course."

"Can I come?" Rusty asked.

"Sure," Tristan answered him. "Just try to not draw too much attention to yourself this time. The idea was to keep you under everyone's radar, remember?"

Apparently, Rusty had become the talk of Underfoot after he demonstrated his skills in the Mole's arena. At least, that was what Tristan told us. But as soon as we were back on the streets of Underfoot and heading to Sprigs, I quickly realized Tristan was right. All eyes were on Rusty. Everyone we passed was pointing at him and whispering. A little kid even came up and asked him for his autograph. Some of the girls squealed and freaked out when he walked by.

Naturally, Rusty was soaking it in. This would have never happened back home. Not in a million years. Honestly, I kind of wished my grandfather had made my shoes like his. His were super cool, and mine were completely lame. I could walk to some mythical land. So what? That just sounded like a headache. Why couldn't he have made me something cooler?

Not everyone, though, was treating Rusty like he was a god. There were some who gave us suspicious glares. It was kind of like the permanent scowl on Anik's face, which, of course, we had the pleasure of experiencing again today since he was escorting us to Sprigs.

We walked until Tristan stopped in front of a store that looked like a giant cauldron with circular windows and a rounded, wooden door. The doors and windows reminded me of a hobbit house, minus the green fields in the background. A little bell rang as Tristan opened the door, and we walked into Sprigs. The inside reminded me of an old-fashioned general store from ages ago. Except this store didn't sell buttons and flour. Instead, the shelves were lined with crystal balls, stones, tarot cards, books, and a cauldron in every size imaginable. There were also little, glass containers like the ones Mrs. Tovar kept in her pockets. One side of the store seemed to be devoted to fresh and dried herbs and ingredients. Another section had canes and staffs of every size, material, and color. The room was lit by elaborate, metal lanterns that hung from the ceiling, and somewhere, incense was burning—the scent of frankincense permeated the air. There was a long, wooden counter that continued down the entire length of the store. The surface was scratched and worn, and it looked like there were words carved into it.

Sitting at the counter was a teenage girl with strawberry blond hair and super pale skin, which wasn't surprising for someone who had never seen the sun. The girl looked up at us, and a big smile immediately spread across her face.

"Well, if it isn't the runaway!" The girl flung her hair back and stood up. "Have you brought me anything from up top?"

"My apologies," Tristan replied. "I didn't really have the opportunity to get anything."

"Not even a magazine?" she asked, pouting. "I'm *dying* of boredom down here."

"Well, these two are from up top," Tristan gestured to us. "Do they count?"

The girl's eyes squinted as she looked at us. She leaned over the counter slightly. "Oh yeah, I heard they were down here. And one of them is supposed to be some great warrior."

Rusty preened and shot his hand up into the air. "That would be me."

She nodded. "But of course. I can see a rather powerful aura."

"Sounds about right," Rusty smugly replied.

"Especially around your feet for some reason—"

"Yes, yes, we know all about Rusty. But!" Tristan pushed Rusty out of the way and put his hands on my shoulders, moving me toward the girl. "This fellow is the one we've got to figure out. I'm thinking he's a Crafter."

The girl stared at me intensely. It was awkward as heck. Normally, I would've loved to have a pretty girl staring at me, but this was a little uncomfortable. What was she seeing? I subconsciously began to comb my fingers through my hair.

"Well?" Tristan asked impatiently.

"I don't know." Her voice shook with uncertainty.

"Don't know? What do you mean you don't know?" Tristan moved to the side of me and also stared at me.

"I've never seen such a strange aura before." She was speaking to Tristan, but his eyes never left me. "And his skin—I can see flashes of light. It's almost like he has an electrical storm inside of him."

"What?" I looked at my arm to make sure there wasn't electricity shooting through my veins or something. There was nothing. Just the same old arm. I turned to Tristan. "What is she talking about?"

"I don't know …" Tristan's eyes were scanning my body as if he was trying to see what the girl was seeing.

"Is your mother here?" Tristan asked the girl.

The girl shook her head. "No, but my grandmother is. She's in the greenhouse."

Tristan's eyes darted upward to a second floor. A curved walkway circled the entire building.

Tristan hesitantly grabbed me by the arm like he was afraid I would shock him. "Can we go ask her?"

The girl looked disappointed in herself. "Yeah. That's probably a good idea."

"No worries," Tristan said reassuringly.

The girl nodded once again. "I'm sorry. It's not one I have ever seen before."

"I get it. You're still learning," Tristan responded. "I'll take him up. How about if I leave my friend Rusty here to keep you company."

The girl glanced at Rusty, and a huge smile spread across his face. Oh boy. My guess was she was a few years older than us, so I doubted he had a chance with her. But judging by the idiotic look on his face, he definitely thought he did. All the attention in the last couple of days had really gone to his head.

"Sure," she said with a shrug, but she still seemed troubled by the fact that she couldn't read me.

Rusty leaned over the counter and stuck his hand out. "Hey. I'm Rusty."

She gently placed her hand in his. "Ceridwen."

"Let's go." Tristan took off toward the back of the store, pulling me behind him.

"Do you like music?" I could hear Ceridwen ask Rusty as we walked away.

"Well, yeah," Rusty quickly replied. "Who doesn't like music?"

Tristan and I reached a dark corner in the back of the store, where a very creaky staircase led to the second floor. We began to climb, and there were more than a few times when I feared the stairs were going to give and we were going to be left in a broken heap on the floor. Thankfully, we reached the second floor in one piece. Tristan led me down the narrow elevated walkway that followed the exterior curve of the building. There were several doors along the way. Red ones, gold ones, black ones. Tristan stopped in front of a door with green paint and reached out his fist and knocked.

"Wait a second," I said. "Why couldn't that girl read me?"

"She's relatively new at reading," Tristan answered me. "I'm sure Rose won't have a problem."

"And how can they do this?"

"They are descendants of the Myrddin. It's a very ancient bloodline. The women in their family are exceptionally gifted at reading auras. Historically, there are three. The Maiden, the Mother, and the Crone." Tristan knocked on the door again.

I didn't know why I was so apprehensive about being read. Something about the way Ceridwen looked at me made me feel anxious. I glanced down below while we waited for this Rose woman to answer the door and could see that tables and shelves were magically gliding to the side of the room. A red, velvety chair slid across the floor and stopped abruptly in the center.

"That's for you," Ceridwen said to Rusty, who quickly took his assigned seat. He was probably afraid she was going to move him too. Ceridwen stood up tall, held her hands together in front of her chest, and closed her eyes. Suddenly, her dress changed from a dark, rosy red to a bright turquoise, and her hair transformed into an elaborate updo. She gracefully walked to the center of the room and stood directly in front of Rusty. She cleared her throat like she was getting ready to sing or make a speech.

I was eagerly waiting to see what would happen when Tristan pulled me away from the railing and dragged me past the now-open door into a bright room filled with greenery. An earthy smell immediately struck my nose. I inhaled deeply and was reminded of my greenhouse at home. The one that no longer existed. It dawned on me that this place was a greenhouse too. Only about ten times the size of mine. The magical sun was directly above us, and its warmth seeped through the panes of glass that made up the ceiling. This place truly felt like home.

CHAPTER 27

AMBIGUITY

I could hear footsteps coming toward us. I scanned my surroundings, looking for movement. But the only movement I saw was coming from a group of plants. I walked toward one of the plants to get a better look. The plant had large, velvety, black leaves that swayed up and down even though there was no wind or air circulation in the greenhouse. Also, once I was closer, I could see small bulges on the stalk. I looked at one of them. The waxy surface of the stalk covered it, but occasionally, it opened to reveal a glassy-looking marble. It was like an eyelid, opening and closing over the shiny surface. It was by far the weirdest plant I had ever seen.

Next to it was another strange specimen. This one had tiny, pink tentacles on the interior of the leaves. They swayed in unison back and forth, but when I got closer, the tentacles began to extend toward me. I reached out to the plant with my hand, wondering what it would feel like to touch it.

"I wouldn't do that if I were you."

I looked up—a woman peered through a rather large group of hollyhocks. I jerked my hand back. "Sorry."

"You would've been if those tentacles had wrapped themselves around your hand."

The woman emerged from the plants and was now standing in front of us. She didn't look like a Crone to me, but then again, I didn't exactly know what a Crone should look like. But if I had to guess, I would have thought she would look frailer and be all hunched over, perhaps even walking with a cane. This woman had gray hair tied haphazardly in a knot on top of her head, but except for some wrinkles, she didn't seem that old. She gestured toward the plant that was still trying to attach itself to me.

"We have the hardest time trying to get those things to detach. Last time, it took two days."

"Two days?" I decided to put my hands in my pockets and leave them there.

"Olilock," the woman said. "Sometimes I question whether or not we should even grow them. Sure, they are very helpful for broken bones, but you can't even walk by them without one of those things grabbing at you and trying to attach itself. They are really quite troublesome."

The woman turned her gaze to Tristan. "Kind of like you."

"Now wait a minute—" Tristan began to defend himself, but the Crone—who I assumed was Rose—cut him off.

"Are you really going to challenge me on that?" She cocked her head to one side. "Would you like me to go through the list? How many times you and Bryn have upset the council?"

"Perhaps another time," Tristan relented.

"You sure are lucky that Gwen is so fond of you." Rose wiped her hands on the apron tied around her waist as she spoke.

"Just Gwen?" Tristan asked her. "I haven't burned any bridges with you, have I?"

The woman shook her head back and forth rather quickly. "No, of course not. What is it that you want? I assume it has something to do with this one. One of the strangers from up top, I presume."

The woman turned toward me and looked at me like she was trying to see into my soul.

I nervously looked around the room, trying to find a distraction, but it wasn't what I saw that distracted me, it was what I heard. Unbelievable singing from down below. Ceridwen must have started her performance, and even though it was muffled through the door, I could tell the girl could really sing.

"Oh for Odin's sake, there she goes again." Rose briefly moved her eyes away from me and threw her hands up in the air. "It's always singing with that girl. She never stops."

"She's born to perform," Tristan said.

"She's supposed to have been born the Maiden and then the Mother and then the Crone," Rose answered. "Are we going to have a singing Crone in our future? Is she going to sing out her readings to our clients? I'm beginning to think we got it all wrong. Maybe Saffron would have been a better choice."

"Time will tell, I suppose." Tristan seemed amused by the situation. "My guess is that the Siren blood in her is complicating things. Perhaps that side of her is fighting for dominance."

Rose briefly rubbed her forehead, which left a smudge of dirt. "Please, don't remind me of that, Tristan. I like to think of that as just a little hiccup in our bloodline."

Then she turned her attention back to me. She looked at me for a long time. Her expression turned from irritation to confusion.

"Young man," she addressed me, "what are you drawn to?"

"What do you mean?" I asked, unsure how to answer the question.

"What do you like? What makes you happy?" she clarified.

My mind raced through all the things that I liked—the shoe house, my garden, my greenhouse, the willow tree. Basically, everything that had been blown up. I looked back at the Crone, who was waiting for me to respond.

"This, I suppose," I said, gesturing to our surroundings. "Plants, nature. Things that grow make me happy."

She smiled slightly. "A boy after my own heart. What about his family? What kind of bloodline does he come from?"

Her questions were directed at Tristan, but she was still staring at me.

"As far as I know, his mother's side are primarily Crafters," Tristan answered. "The Needlecoff family."

"Right …" The Crone's eyes never left me as she spoke. "He's Bryn's nephew. The infamous Needlecoff Crafters. The problem is, I'm not getting a Crafter vibe from him."

"What?" Tristan's tone grew louder. "But he should be a strong Crafter. Or maybe even a healer. His mother dabbled in the healing arts."

"What about his father?"

"Nothing. Just a Nullvin," Tristan answered.

"I wouldn't be so sure about that."

"No way," Tristan said firmly. "There is no way his dad is a Vin."

"This kid's aura is very strong. If it was diluted by a Nullvin, it wouldn't be so strong," she answered. "His dad is something for sure."

I wasn't convinced she was reading me correctly.

"That can't be true. My father hates magic." It didn't make any sense.

Rose wasn't backing down. "I'm telling you, he's something, or else he's not really your dad."

"Wait, what?" First, she tells me my dad is really a Vin. Then she suggests he might not even be my real father?

Tristan was clearly bothered by this reading. "Rose, what are you trying to say? If he's not a Crafter, then what the devil is he?"

She didn't answer him. She just kept looking at me with her eyes squinted so tightly, I could barely see her pupils.

"What do you see?" Tristan asked her again impatiently.

"To be honest, it's something I have only seen once in my lifetime," she finally answered. "So … I want to be sure."

She began to walk around me, inspecting me from every angle.

"Tell me about your love of plants. Have you ever felt stronger from touching them?" she asked me from behind. I could feel her eyes on my back. "Have you ever felt any strange sensations?"

What the heck did she mean? Any strange sensations? I pretty much had the same feelings my whole life, so how was I supposed to know if they were strange? The only strange thing that had ever happened to me was when I was holding Maria's hand when she passed out. Or the paralyzed crow back at the shoe house. That was weird, but that didn't have anything to do with plants.

"No, not really," I answered her, unsure whether I should disclose those instances.

"You have to come back when Silvia is here," she said abruptly. "I would like to consult with her before I give you my final recommendation."

"Who's Silvia?" I turned around so I could see her.

"My daughter," she replied. "She's the Mother."

What was up with this lady? I didn't want to wait. I wanted to know what I was. "Is there *anything* you can tell me?"

"I will tell you this: if what I suspect is true, then you do not need an instrument to nurture your powers. Your powers lie within."

"That's it?" I asked her. "That's all you can tell me?"

"For now," she said as she broke eye contact with me. "Wait for Tristan outside. There is something I would like to discuss with him."

I turned toward Tristan, and he nodded that I should do what she had instructed me to do. I walked toward the door, feeling very disappointed and irritated. It seemed like she was hiding something. I knew I shouldn't have been read. I hadn't wanted to do this in the first place. Maybe something wasn't right with me. I looked back at them briefly once I reached the door. It was clear they were waiting for me to leave.

It made me mad. More secrets, just like back in Lewisberry.

When would adults ever be straight with me?

Clearly, not any time soon.

CHAPTER 28
SIREN'S SONG

I opened the door and was hit right away by Ceridwen's singing. It was so powerful, it made me briefly forget how disappointed I was about Rose not wanting to tell me more about my powers. In a way, Ceridwen's voice almost didn't sound human. It was so haunting. I closed the emerald door behind me and was struck by how dark the balcony was after being in the bright greenhouse. I leaned over the railing and looked down.

Surprisingly, it wasn't just Ceridwen and Rusty down there anymore. Rusty was still sitting in the red, velvety chair, but now a bunch of other Vins had come into Sprigs and were watching the performance as well. For some reason, it irritated me that there were so many people down there watching her. When she finished her song, the audience started hollering and clapping. I found myself clapping too. You'd think we had all just witnessed the greatest performance in the world from the way we were acting. Then I recalled that Tristan had said she was half Siren. Weren't they some sort of mythological creature that enchanted and lured people in with their musical voices?

Now that Ceridwen stopped singing, my mind cleared, and I remembered why I was standing outside the door in the first place. Rose and Tristan were still inside, talking about me. What was I doing listening to Ceridwen sing? I should've been trying to listen through the door. I found a small gap in the wood panels of the door and pressed my ear against it.

Tristan asked, "Are you sure?"

"I can't be absolutely sure. I only saw one as a child, a poor fellow who didn't know what he was, and my grandmother had to tell him. Of course, he had to leave immediately. I have never run across one since. If anyone knew one of them was in our settlement, I shudder to think of what the consequences would be."

"But that can't be!" Tristan sounded angry. "I know his family. Bryn would never have kept something like that from me. It's not possible."

My stomach dropped. What had she told him? Was I something terrible, so terrible that I would be kicked out of Underfoot?

"As you know, a Vin will take on either parent's attributes. One will be the dominant force within them. Perhaps his father was one, and he never told anyone. Maybe the Needlecoff family never knew the truth," Rose speculated. "And from the sound of it, neither does he, poor soul."

There was silence for a while, then Tristan asked, "Will you tell the council?"

"I can wait a bit," she said. "But I can't keep it a secret forever. How much time do you need?"

"Enough to figure out what to do," Tristan said. "They're not going to just let him leave now that he knows the location of this place."

"I agree," Rose said. "We may have to do a forgetting spell."

Tristan groaned in frustration. "I just wanted to help an old friend, and now I fear I just made everything worse."

"Let me know what you decide," Rose said. "Soon."

"I will." Tristan's voice sounded as though he was getting closer to the door.

I pushed myself away from the door so he wouldn't suspect I had been listening. I leaned over the railing, pretending I was still watching what was happening below. All the Vins were still crowded around Ceridwen, but I didn't care now. All I could think about was the fact that I was something bad.

Tristan burst through the door. He had a deep scowl on his face, and maybe I was imagining it, but I swore he wouldn't look at me. He turned swiftly and stomped his way down the walkway toward the stairs. Considering the run-down look of the place, I thought he should walk a little less aggressively, or we could end up on the bottom floor sooner than he would like. He was walking so fast, I had to sprint to keep up with him. I followed him down the stairs and into the open area of the store.

"Rusty!" Tristan yelled at the swarm of Vins surrounding Ceridwen.

Rusty peeked his head out and saw us waiting for him.

"Did you guys hear that angel sing?" he asked as he approached us.

"Angel?" I asked him.

Tristan rolled his eyes. "She's got Siren blood. He's been enchanted."

"Enchanted?" Rusty shook his head. "What are you talking about? I'm telling you, that girl has got talent. Let's smuggle her up top so we can all make millions off her. She's amazing!"

"Yes, yes." Tristan grabbed Rusty by the arm and pulled him toward the door. "Your little concert is over. We've got more important things to deal with."

Rusty resisted a bit as Tristan pushed him out the door. "Honestly, I don't know what could be more important than this! I mean, did you *hear* her? You guys must have not heard her or else you would understand."

"I've got protection against such things," Tristan said as he held up his hand. He had a ring on his finger. He turned his hard gaze toward me. "A present from your aunt. Back when I thought I could trust her."

"What?" Even though I had long legs, it was hard to keep up with Tristan's fast pace. "Why would you say that? Why wouldn't you trust my aunt? What did Rose tell you in there?"

"I don't want to talk about it," Tristan grumbled, keeping his back to me.

Anik was standing outside by the door. He pulled earplugs out of his ears when he spotted us. He smirked at Rusty as we passed him.

"How you doing there, hotshot?"

"Thanks for asking, man!" Rusty was talking to him like they were best friends. "I'm doing great, actually. Did you hear her sing? Wasn't it incredible?"

"Oh yeah," Anik said sarcastically. "Very mesmerizing."

"I know, right?" Rusty looked longingly back at Sprigs. "Is she always there? We should stay. Maybe she'll sing again."

Tristan redirected Rusty. It looked as though he was steering a drunk.

"Not going to happen."

I tried to talk to Tristan multiple times as we walked back to his house, but he wouldn't even look at me. Even Anik noticed something was wrong. I could tell because he was watching us extra closely.

Once we were back at the house, Tristan just stomped toward the back and slammed a door before I had a chance to ask him anything. I wondered how long Rusty would be enchanted for. I hoped it wouldn't be too long. I wanted the old Rusty back. I needed to talk to him about what just happened. I needed someone to tell me my imagination was getting the better of me ... and that I wasn't a monster.

Maria peeked her head around the corner of the kitchen.

"What's going on?" she asked, looking concerned. "Is something wrong?"

"Wrong?" Rusty answered her, grinning like an idiot. "More like everything is right. We went to that Sprigs place and heard this angel sing the most beautiful song."

Maria starred at Rusty for a second and then turned toward me. "What in god's name is he talking about?"

I sighed. "There was this girl at the store Tristan took us to. She sang for Rusty, and now he's all ... weird."

"Seriously? All it takes is for a girl to sing to you?" Maria questioned Rusty.

"Tristan said something about her being part Siren," I tried to explain. "I think he's enchanted or something."

"Ah. Figures." Maria rolled her eyes. "Supposed to affect the weak-minded the most."

"Who are you calling weak-minded?" Rusty shot back at her. "Listen, Maria, you don't understand. You had to have been there. It was amazing. She is the most gorgeous thing I have ever seen."

"Wren was there," she said, pointing at me. "He doesn't seem to think she was as great as you do."

Rusty glanced over toward me, and a confused expression washed over his face. "You don't think she's the most beautiful thing you have ever seen?"

"Beautiful?" I pondered. "I mean, she was pretty, but I'm not completely infatuated with her like you are."

"Eyota!" Maria yelled into the kitchen. "We may need your help here. Can you break a Siren's song?"

I recognized that name. It was the girl from the arena.

"This is Eyota, the Eradicator." Maria presented the girl to us when she came out of Tristan's kitchen.

"Her?" Rusty sounded shocked. I was too. I wasn't expecting the Eradicator to be so young. She was basically our age.

"You seem surprised," Eyota said.

Rusty pointed at the girl in amazement. "*She* broke the curse that was on your grandmother?"

Eyota didn't wait for Maria to answer him. "Yes, and now it looks like you need my help to break a stupid Siren's song."

"Siren's song?" Rusty shook his head. "Are you saying that I'm under a spell?"

"That's exactly what I'm saying," Eyota responded.

He shook his head. "No, I don't think so. It's just that you didn't hear her sing. If you had heard it, you would understand."

Eyota let out a heavy sigh. "Oh please. Do you know how many times I have heard Vins down here say the exact same thing? Honestly, someone should tape Ceridwen's mouth shut. It's ridiculous. I can't believe Rose puts up with it. People can't even walk by the place."

"Seriously?" Maria questioned her.

"That's how she lures them in, by her voice," Eyota explained. "They go in normal and come out like idiots. Like your friend here."

Rusty was erupting, clearly not enjoying being treated like a moron. "Hey! Wait just a min—"

"What about me?" I interrupted. "Why didn't her singing affect me like it did him?"

"How close did you get?" Eyota asked me.

I shrugged. "Not very."

"The closer you get, the more of an effect it has on you," Eyota explained. "You must have been far enough away."

"I don't think you guys understand." Geez, Rusty wasn't going to let it go. "Maybe if you had been there—"

"Right, right, if only we had been there." Eyota walked over to him and put her hands over his ears.

"What the heck?" Rusty tried to push her hands away, but then he slowly relaxed and closed his eyes. Eyota's eyes were closed too.

"You sure about this?" I whispered to Maria.

"I don't feel like hearing about this Siren for the rest of the day, do you?" she asked me.

"Not really," I agreed. The sooner Rusty was back to normal, the better. "Listen, Maria, something happened at Sprigs. The woman there told Tristan something about me, and I think Tristan is angry about it."

"Do you know what she said?" Maria asked.

"No. She made me leave the room," I explained. "I think, maybe … I'm something bad."

She gave me an incredulous look. "Bad? Don't be ridiculous."

"What do you mean? I could be something bad," I said softly. "You don't know."

"Wren, you're not bad. Trust me, I'd know." Maria held up her hands.

"Are you talking about how you can see in people's minds when you touch them?" I asked her.

She nodded her head, "Of course."

"But you can only see what I know, not what I am," I argued.

"It's a bit more complicated than that." Maria crossed her arms and leaned in toward me. "Sure, it's kind of a confusing mess right now when I touch people, but I have touched evil, and I can guarantee you, you are *not* evil."

Even though I wasn't sure I believed her, a wave of relief flowed through my body. For now, I would cling to the fact that Maria was convinced I was still one of the good guys.

Eyota removed her hands from Rusty's ears. "Done."

Rusty opened his eyes and looked around at us with a slightly confused look on his face. He took a few steps back. "Why was she touching me?"

"We had to get your mind back to its normal state," Maria answered him. "What, exactly, that entails, I'm not sure."

"What was wrong with my mind?" Rusty asked.

"That girl at Sprigs," I started to explain. "She, like … enchanted you, I guess."

Rusty shook his head. "No, I don't think so. I feel fine."

"Well yeah, *now* you are, thanks to Eyota," Maria said, clearly annoyed with how much of a headache he was being.

"And she's only a half blood," Eyota added. "Can you imagine what he would've been like if she had been a full-blooded Siren?"

Both the girls laughed.

Rusty wasn't going to take being laughed at lightly. "I don't know what you think you saw, but I don't fall in love so easily."

Maria nodded at him, grinning. "All right, sure. Whatever you say. I would just suggest that you stay out of Sprigs in the future."

Rusty scoffed as he plopped himself down on the couch. "You guys are all overreacting."

"Anyways," Maria changed the subject, "after Eyota woke up my grandmother, I told her to stop by and I would tell her what it was like up top."

"That's right," I said to Eyota. "You mentioned you've never been out of Underfoot."

A wave of anger crossed her face. "I'm 'too important' to let out."

I had to stop myself from laughing at her use of air quotes since she seemed genuinely upset at the moment.

"It makes no sense. I mean, I'm Spokane. We're the People of the Sun!"

"Eyota, your mom is coming," an invisible male voice said.

"Whoa!" Rusty shot back up, his weapon in hand. "Who said that?"

The voice had come from the window. At first, it seemed like someone had been standing there. Someone tall with dark hair. But then there was no one.

"Rusty, did you hear that voice too?" I asked him.

"Yeah, it came from over there." He pointed to the window.

"Oh good. So I'm not crazy." Talk about a relief.

Rusty extended his weapon to its full form and began walking toward the window.

"What do you think you're doing?" Eyota grabbed Rusty and pulled him back.

"There's something in here!" Rusty scanned the room.

"Yeah," she said, not letting go of his arm, "it's Pan! He's my friend."

"Her friend is a Tariaksuq," Maria added.

"Am I supposed to know what that is?" Rusty asked, still sounding agitated.

"It means you can't see him if you look directly at him. He kind of hovers between this world and another," Maria tried to explain.

"But that doesn't make any sense," I said.

"Look in the mirror." Maria pointed to the large mirror hanging over the fireplace.

I did what she suggested and saw all our reflections ... and someone else, standing by the window. It was a guy. He was slightly hunched over with long, dark hair and broad features. At first, he looked a bit intimidating, but that went right out the window when he gave us a big, friendly smile and waved at us once he realized we could see him.

"Wait a minute … ." Rusty kept looking at the mirror, then back at the window. "I still don't understand."

"Maybe we can elaborate another time, but right now, we," Eyota gestured between herself and Pan, "need to split." She pointed toward the kitchen. "Pan, back door."

I watched in the mirror as he walked across the room. "Later," he said, giving another small wave as he passed.

"I really don't think this place is ever going to make sense to me," Rusty said as he retracted his weapon and put it back in his coat pocket.

CHAPTER 29
A TERRIFYING VISION

There was suddenly a loud banging on the door. Marcus, the cool guard, walked in. Behind him was an anxious-looking woman. It was the same woman who had been yelling at Eyota back in the arena.

"Is Eyota in here?" Marcus asked. His tone suggested that he was irritated at having to deal with this.

We all shook our heads.

The woman pushed her way farther into the room. "I think we should check!"

Maria followed her into the family room. "Why? You think we're lying?"

The woman swirled back to face Maria.

"No offense," she began, "but I don't know you. You came from up top. I have no reason to believe you are telling the truth."

"You have no reason to believe I'm lying, either," Maria replied quickly.

"I'm sorry, young lady," the woman was scanning the room now as she spoke, "but my daughter is *very* important. She may save us all one day from the darkness that lurks up above."

"Geez," Rusty whispered to me. "Dramatic much?"

I had to agree with Rusty. This woman was super intense.

Now she was looking behind furniture and doors. She gave Marcus a cold glare.

"Well? Are you going to help me?"

Marcus rolled his eyes and began to search the house.

"I'm getting Tristan," Maria huffed and walked to the back of the house.

The woman and Marcus made their way into the kitchen. I followed them and watched as Marcus half-heartedly opened cabinets. He didn't seem to be really examining anything. Honestly, he seemed more interested in his watch. I wondered if he had a date or something. By the look of him, I bet the guy had lots of dates.

"Did you check everything?" The woman was looking under a table as she spoke.

"Yes," Marcus answered her with irritation.

I could hear footsteps approaching, which made me a little anxious. Tristan was already in a crappy mood, and now these people were searching his house. He entered the kitchen, the scowl still firmly planted on his face.

"What's going on?"

The woman stood up and flat-out asked him, "Is Eyota here?"

Tristan rubbed his face, looking tired. "Why would Eyota be here?"

"Because she's obsessed with up top and everything that comes from there, thanks to you and your traitorous wife," the woman said.

Then the room got really small. It was a small kitchen to begin with, but at that moment, with all those people in there and the air being thick with tension, it suddenly felt miniscule. Tristan looked pissed. I expected him to say something, but instead, he silently walked to the center of the room, grabbed the woman by the arm, and pulled her out of the kitchen.

Once Marcus realized what Tristan was doing, he moved quickly to intervene. So quickly that he almost knocked Maria out of the way.

"Sorry." He briefly steadied Maria by grabbing her upper arm, then he moved past her, following Tristan and Eyota's mother into the family room.

Rusty and I ran right behind him.

Tristan opened the door and pointed outside "Get out of my house." The dark tone in his voice scared even me.

"Tristan," Marcus interjected, "she only wanted to see if her daughter was here."

"Listen, Marcus," Tristan snarled, "I may not have a say in anything that goes on in this crazy place, but as far as I know, I still have a say as to what happens in my own home. And if this woman is going to insult my wife, then she isn't welcome here!"

"Let's go. Eyota isn't here anyway," Marcus pleaded with the woman.

"But we haven't checked every room!" The woman peered down the dark hallway that led to the back of the house. "She could be hiding in one of the bedrooms."

"Maybe you should go home and ponder on why your daughter keeps trying to run away from you." Tristan pulled her around and forced her to step onto the porch.

He waited until Marcus followed her, slamming the door closed behind them. He leaned against it and took a deep breath.

"I am so done with this bloody place."

"Man, Eyota's got it bad," Rusty commented. "Not only is she trapped down here, but her mother is seriously insane."

Mrs. Tovar stepped into the room. She must have come to see what all the commotion was about. "Where's Maria?"

I looked around. Maria wasn't in the family room.

"She must still be in the kitchen," I said.

I walked back to the kitchen and found Maria standing against the same wall she had inadvertently been shoved against. She hadn't moved. Something was wrong. She looked scared. Really, *really* scared. I bent down so we were eye level.

"Maria, what is it? What's wrong?"

"I think they're coming," she whispered.

"Who?"

She hesitated before saying, "The Wrathful."

My stomach dropped.

I quickly got her out of the kitchen and into the other room. I forgot all about what had happened at Sprigs. I forgot about my mysterious, and maybe evil, aura. I forgot we were not welcome in Underfoot and that we could be kicked out at any time.

I forgot all of that because of what Maria told us while she was sitting in the middle of Tristan's sofa, her face white as a sheet and her hands folded tightly on her lap. Up until now, she had always seemed fearless to me, ready to take on whatever came her way. But this was uncharted territory. We weren't dealing with crappy teachers like Mad Millie. These guys were real-life monsters, and we were like sitting ducks, trapped in an underground pond.

Apparently, she knew what was coming because when Marcus had almost knocked her over earlier, she saw something when he grabbed her by the arm. She saw the Wrathful through the eyes of Marcus. She heard a plan, a plan to get into Underfoot. At least, that was what she thought she saw. It was murky and dreamlike. That was why she was still standing in the kitchen. She was trying to sort out what she had seen in her mind.

"Are you sure?" Tristan asked as he nervously paced around the room.

"No, of course I'm not sure," Maria said, sounding irritated. "I keep telling you, I have only just started reading people. Half the time, I just see blurry images and muffled sounds. It's like when you wake up from a dream. You think you remember it, but when you try to put it into words, it no longer makes sense."

"You need to try harder!" Tristan stopped pacing and shot her a stern look.

"Tristan," Mrs. Tovar interjected, "give her a break. She is new at this. Don't put so much pressure on her."

"We don't have time for her to get her bloody sea legs!" Tristan was not going to be restrained. "If there is a chance that the Wrathful know about Underfoot and are planning on attacking, we have to get everyone out of here!"

Mrs. Tovar put her arm around her granddaughter. "I agree, but her powers may not always give us the whole story."

"What if you could touch him for a longer period of time? I could knock him out and drag him in here," Tristan suggested.

Rusty seemed to like the idea. "Heck yeah! I'm on board with that."

Mrs. Tovar quickly shot Tristan's idea down. "If he's knocked out, she might not see anything. All she saw was blackness when I was bitten by the trauma hound."

"Then I'll tie him up and drag him in here!" Tristan shot back.

While they argued it out, I went and sat next to Maria on the couch. I felt bad for her. She looked confused and uncertain about how to deal with any of this. I wished there was something I could do to help her with her visions, but there wasn't ... unless ... maybe the shoes my grandfather made for her could help somehow. The label said Clarity of Sight, which was exactly what she needed right now.

"What about the shoes?" I asked.

They all stopped arguing and focused on me.

"Of course, the shoes!" Maria's face lit up. "Yes, I can put on the shoes."

She stood up and began to look around the room. "Where is your bag, Wren?"

I jumped up and went to my backpack. It was on the floor next to one of the couches. I opened the bag and pulled her shoes out and ran back to her.

"Great." She started to remove the shoes she had been wearing and placed the short boots on the ground next to her. She pulled them on and stood back up, staring down at them for a second. "We should test them out. Who wants to be the lucky subject?" She scanned the room, waiting for someone to respond.

Rusty backed up. "Not me. No offense, but I don't want you poking around in my head."

I was just about to volunteer, but then I wondered if she would see something bad in me like the woman at Sprigs did. I wasn't so sure I wanted anyone to read me ever again.

Tristan sighed. "Fine. Let's get this over with." He held out his untattooed arm.

Maria grabbed him around the wrist and closed her eyes. It was only for a few seconds. We all watched intently, waiting for her to say something. When she opened her eyes, her gaze darted from Tristan to me. She was staring at me intensely. Did she know? Could she see what Rose had told Tristan?

My chest suddenly felt tight. "Why are you looking at me?"

Tristan pulled his arm away and rolled down his sleeve. "So did it work? Was it clearer?"

"Crystal," was all she said.

CHAPTER 30
UNDERFOOT UNDER ATTACK

And just like that, Maria walked right out the door.

"What is she doing?" Rusty asked.

"Guess she's going out there to confront the guy," I answered him.

"Is that the best tactic?" Mrs. Tovar asked as she followed her out the door. Of course, the rest of us were right behind her.

But Maria wasn't waiting for us. She walked directly toward Marcus, who was sitting on a stone ledge and eating something wrapped in paper. He briefly looked up as Maria walked toward him intently. He put whatever he was eating down and jumped off the ledge. Anik and a few other guards were with him, but only Anik seemed to sense that something was up. Maria didn't slow down. She made her way to Marcus and reached out and grabbed his wrist. Marcus attempted to pull his hand away, a look of confusion spreading across his face.

Anik stepped in and forcefully removed Maria's hand from Marcus. "What do you think you're doing? Some kind of dark magic?"

"I'm not the one you should be concerned about," Maria responded to Anik, but her eyes never left Marcus.

"What are you talking about?" Marcus backed up slightly until he was stopped by the stone ledge behind him.

"You're going to let them in, aren't you?" she accused him loudly. So loud, the others around us took notice. "They're outside the entrance right now, waiting for you to let them in!"

Marcus looked around nervously. "I don't know what you're talking about."

"You know *exactly* what I'm talking about," Maria said firmly.

Marcus wasn't so cool and calm anymore. Instead of trying to convince the others she was crazy, he just jumped over the ledge and began to run in the opposite direction. Without even thinking, I jumped over the ledge and ran after him. Rusty was right next to me, but not for long. He was way faster than me, and before I knew it, he was ahead of me running with his weapon in his hand, fully extended. He was ready to do battle. Suddenly, the street felt really crowded. We dodged several Vins as we ran through the streets, accidentally knocking a few of them down. I stopped to apologize, but Rusty didn't. He wasn't going to slow down for anything since he was gaining on Marcus. We were now in Crafter Row. I ran by flower stands and kids playing with a ball and shop owners coming out to see what was going on. I had reached the giant fountain in the town square when I realized I could no longer see Rusty. I stopped, trying to determine which way they had gone.

Suddenly, the fountain blew to pieces. I was violently thrown to the ground. I shielded my face from the bits of stone, marble, and water that were raining down on me. Once the pelting stopped, I cautiously opened my eyes. Thick dust filled the air and made it difficult to see, but I could make out shadowy figures running from the chaos, some calling out for their loved ones. I rolled over to my side and realized that the force of the impact had left my body stiff and battered. But as the dust settled and my vision improved, I could see I was lucky compared to some of the others. Many were lying on the ground with bloody injuries.

I had never been in such a terrifying situation before, and I struggled to make sense of my surroundings. As I tried to pull myself into a sitting position, my head began to throb, and my ears started ringing. I ignored the discomfort and somehow managed to stand up. I scanned my surroundings and was shocked by the destruction; even some of the buildings had been damaged. I suddenly felt someone pull at my arm from behind, and the force of the grip almost made me lose my balance. I turned and saw a young woman. Her auburn hair was dripping wet, and the shoulder of her blouse was ripped away, exposing a bloody wound.

"Can you help me? Please!"

She didn't give me a chance to answer and began to drag me toward a large piece of marble. "My daughter is pinned down! You have to help me move it."

There on the ground near the spot where the fountain had once stood was a young girl with a large piece of marble on her leg. The child was crying, but I couldn't tell if it was out of fear or pain.

The woman kneeled next to her child and caressed her cheek. "It's all right. You're going to be all right."

The woman looked up at me with panicked eyes. I nodded and bent down, placing my hands under the piece of marble and bracing my legs. The woman got on the other side, and we both began to lift the stone off the young girl. It was working, but part of me didn't want to see what we would find underneath. Once it was high enough, we threw it to the side, and it hit the ground with a loud *thud*. The woman leaned down and tried to lift her child, but she appeared to be struggling. Her shoulder injury had most likely been further damaged from lifting the marble.

"Let me do it." I reached down and picked up the young girl.

She cried out, definitely in pain this time, which made me feel terrible.

"I'm sorry." I looked down at her tear-streaked face.

"Follow me!" The woman started to make her way through the people.

"My foot?" the girl said weakly. "Is it going to be all right?"

I looked down at it. It was mostly covered in blood, but the foot didn't look like it was pointed in the right direction. What was I supposed to tell the kid? Was I supposed to lie to her like all adults did? The thing was, I wasn't an adult yet. And I really didn't know how to deal with any of this.

"I'm not a doctor, but it doesn't look too bad," I said without looking directly into her eyes.

I turned away from her, but I could hear her cry out in pain every time I took a step. It made me angry. How did this happen? Did Marcus blow up the fountain? Was it the Wrathful? Were they already here? Why should this little girl be harmed in some ridiculous power struggle? I wished more than anything that I could help her.

That was when I started to feel the tingling again. Just like before, it started in my chest and then moved down my arms toward my hands. The tingling was increasing, accelerating. My hands almost felt like they were vibrating.

"Do you feel that?" the girl asked me.

I stopped walking. What if Rose was right? What if I was doing something bad to this child? But there wasn't fear in her eyes—she almost seemed ... comforted.

"What? What are you feeling?" I asked her, nervous about what she would say.

"Hey! What are you doing?" an angry voice yelled.

I turned my head quickly, which was a bad idea. Everything got blurry, and I had to close my eyes for a second to balance myself. I couldn't figure out if it was residual effects of the explosion, or if it was the result of my strange powers again. When I opened my eyes, an unfocused image of Tristan swam before me. He was pulling the girl from my arms.

"Are you trying to drain her?" he spat at me.

"What?" I was confused. "Drain? What are you talking about?"

Maria appeared next to him. "He's an idiot and thinks you're a Drainer."

Tristan was now holding the girl. "You need to face reality, Maria. That's what Rose told me."

"Then this Rose woman doesn't know what she's talking about. Just because he can manipulate energy, that doesn't mean he's a Drainer!" Maria shouted at him.

The girl's mother must have noticed I was no longer behind her and approached us. "Is something wrong? Is my daughter all right?"

"My foot feels better, Mom," the girl answered her. "It doesn't hurt as much."

"What?" The woman nudged Maria out of the way and examined the girl's foot. "Yes, it does look better," she said. "But how is that—"

Before she could finish her sentence, a man ran up and embraced her. "Are you all right?"

He pulled away from her once he realized she was injured.

"I'll be fine," she reassured him. "Jezebel hurt her foot."

The man took the girl from Tristan's arms and thanked us repeatedly for helping his daughter.

"You better get them to safety," Tristan warned him. "We're under attack."

They heeded his warning and ran away from us through the chaotic streets of Underfoot.

"Hey!" I confronted Tristan. "Did you actually think I was draining her?"

His eyes wouldn't meet mine. "Look, we'll discuss this later. We've got to get to the south entrance now!"

And with that, he took off into the crowd, more willing to face the Wrathful than deal with his Drainer nephew.

Maria rolled her eyes and gestured for me to follow her. "Come on."

"You two, stop right there!"

Someone grabbed me from behind, and a forearm pushed against my throat. I tried to pull it away, but I felt weak. Really weak. I came to the conclusion that whatever I had done when that girl was in my arms had caused me to feel all depleted again. I turned my head to see who was restraining me. It was Anik. For God's sake, it was one thing after another.

"Did you do that?" he pointed at the destruction that surrounded us. "Did you blow up the fountain?'

"What?" I asked, my voice weak. "You think *I* did that?" Why did everyone think I was capable of doing such terrible things?

"You or your friend," Anik growled at me. "Where is that little jerk?"

"Wren and Rusty didn't do anything!" Maria yelled at him.

Anik wasn't letting go of me. "I always knew it would come down to this. I knew Tristan would be the one to bring ruin to this place."

"Are you serious?" Maria tried to pull his thick arms off me. "Did you not see your buddy run away like he was guilty of something?"

"What are you saying?" Anik roared.

"Your friend, Marcus, is letting the Wrathful into Underfoot. He's probably doing it as we speak!"

"How do you know that?"

"I saw it!" she answered him with an unwavering voice.

"She's a Cerebral," I tried to say, even though the pressure on my neck made it hard for me to speak.

"Prove it," Anik spat.

Maria was already grasping his arm, so she closed her eyes briefly before opening them to look Anik directly the eye.

"You don't know anything about the Wrathful attack, but you do know an awful lot about the seamstress at the dress shop. Her work hours, her favorite flowers, what nights she has dinner with her girlfriends. In fact, I would say most of your thoughts revolve around her. Gloria is her name, right?"

I couldn't see Anik's face, but I could feel his grip slacken a bit. Maria must've been on the right track.

She continued. "She just broke up with her boyfriend, and you're debating whether or not to make a move—"

"You can stop." Anik pushed me aside and forcibly removed Maria's hand from his arm.

I almost fell to the ground. My legs felt like jelly.

Anik nodded his head in defeat. "Do you know which entrance?"

"South," she answered him.

Anik took something out of his pocket and held it up to his mouth. It looked like a smooth rock, but he spoke into it as if it were a microphone. Somehow, his voice was being blasted from the glowing orb that hovered above us.

"The Guard is to report to the south entrance. Code 11! Again, this is a code 11!"

CHAPTER 31
THE SOUTH ENTRANCE

The streets of Underfoot were chaotic. I didn't know what *code 11* meant, but from the way everyone was freaking out it couldn't be good. Honestly, I was freaking out, too. In the back of my mind, I was trying not to think about the fact that we were running *toward* the bad guys. Kind of seemed like we were running in the wrong direction, but I wasn't about to stop now. We needed to find Rusty and Tristan. For all I knew, they may have succeeded in stopping Marcus from opening the gate.

I was having a hard time keeping up with Maria. I didn't want to admit it, but whatever had happened when I held that girl had resulted in me feeling like crap again. My breath was labored, and I felt like my legs were going to give out from under me. What did it mean? Was I really a Drainer? But wouldn't that mean I would feel stronger, not weaker? I kept telling myself to stop thinking about it and just concentrate on moving one foot in front of the other.

We were now in an area of Underfoot I hadn't been to before. There were no more buildings or shops. All around me were fields that resembled crops of all kinds: soybeans, potatoes, corn. It made sense. Of course they had to grow their own stuff down here, especially since they had closed themselves off from the outside world. I even saw a barnlike structure to the left and some animals hanging out in a field.

I stopped for a second to catch my breath. I was bent over, panting, and when I lifted my head again, my vision was blurry. I could no longer see Maria. Guards were running past me. I could see their blurry images moving toward what looked like a miniature forest up ahead. Besides the clay-colored cave walls and curved ceiling, it could have been the woods behind my house back home. I saw a sign ahead made from wood with the words South Entrance carved into the surface. The sign pointed toward a path that cut through the center of the trees.

I stood back up and pushed myself forward. One step after another. I reached the path and had to focus on keeping my balance due to all the guards bumping into me. As I got closer, the ceiling of the cave curved downward, which made the space feel even more cramped. The greenery on the sides of the path became wilder; tree branches and blades of grass were now pushing inward from the side, narrowing the path. Some of the guards had left the path and were now trekking through the lush, overgrown surroundings.

I decided to leave the path as well after almost getting knocked down multiple times. I stopped for a second and leaned against a tree to catch my breath. But then, something happened that sent a chill down my spine. Up ahead, I could see bodies through the tree branches fly upward, into the air. One after another, the guards were being thrust into the space above and were now plastered against the cave ceiling in contorted positions. Many of them fought against the invisible force that was suspending them from the roof of the cave. As they tried to free themselves, objects fell from the sky. Wallets, coins, and weapons plummeted to the ground. I jumped sideways into the grass before a sword pierced right through me. It hit the ground and was now standing rigid, its blade firmly embedded into the earth. Vials of potions also fell to the ground, releasing swirls of black smoke, bursts of blinding light, and shrieking sounds. The sounds were so disturbing and loud, I had to cup my ears in an effort to stop my eardrums from bursting.

One of the guards near me was yelling to the others still on the ground. He told them to put on their ear protectors. "The shrieks will cause blindness!"

"What?" I grabbed one of the guards by the arm. "Blindness?"

"Move away from the sound," he answered me. "Get as far away as you can!"

I grabbed the sword in the ground and attempted to pull it from the earth. It was harder to get free than I expected, especially since I was feeling so weak, but I eventually managed to pull it out. I tried not to think about the fact that I had never held a weapon before and wouldn't know what to do with it. I just grasped the handle of the weapon and ran away from the shrieking sound.

I stopped and took a breath. There was no denying that the Wrathful had gotten in. I glanced up at the ceiling again. I quickly scanned who was up there, looking for Rusty, Tristan, and Maria. Thankfully, I didn't see any of them. I pushed my way through the wild growth and followed a few guards to the entrance. I could see panic in some of their eyes. That was when it really hit me: this was happening. Underfoot was being attacked, and I was in the middle of it. There was even a possibility that I was their target since they were looking for my shoes.

I peeked through some branches to see what was happening on the path. But once I saw it, I wished I hadn't looked. It was Caterina, the creepy, big-eyed lady from my house. The Mother of the Unbreakable. The one who had cursed Mrs. Tovar. She was walking down the pathway with her fan fully spread. Every so often, she would fling her fan overhead, and another guard would be propelled upward. Behind her were some of the Wrathful, following her as she walked down the path.

I shook my head, trying to recover my nerves, and moved past Caterina, heading toward the entrance. I tried to stay out of sight in the woods. Finally, I could see the entrance up ahead. The door was open, and in front of it were stairs that led to the path Caterina was waltzing down as she wreaked havoc on the guards of Underfoot. Next to the path was a patch of bright green grass, and kneeling on it were Rusty, Tristan, and Anik. All three of them were being restrained by ropes of some kind. The ropes not only wrapped around their hands and ankles but also wound around their bodies multiple times. And they were surrounded by other members of the Wrathful. What really bothered me, though, was that there was blood on Rusty's shirt.

I jumped when someone hugged me from behind and asked, "Where did you go?"

It was Maria.

I attempted to hug her back by putting my free hand on her arm. I was grateful for the momentary support of her body since I still felt a bit unstable.

"Did you see what happened?" I asked Maria. "Is Rusty hurt? He looks all bloody."

"I think Marcus got the worse end of the deal," Maria said as she pointed at a boulder by Rusty and the others. Marcus was sitting on it, and he looked like a mess. His face was all battered, and there was a huge gash on his side that was oozing blood. Someone was trying to dress the wound.

"Rusty did that?" I asked.

"I saw the tail end of it. He was kicking their butts until that creepy woman with the fan showed up." She gestured to other members of the Wrathful who were also sitting nearby. They looked pretty jacked up as well.

"How did they capture Tristan?" I asked her.

She gave me a sad look. "That woman put something over his hand, and I think it's preventing him from casting anything."

I moved my position so I could get a better look at Tristan's hand. Something was covering it. It was a thick, slimy-looking substance.

"He's gotta be so pissed," Maria whispered and then turned to me. "So how are we going to help them?"

I just shook my head, feeling a bit overwhelmed. "I'm not sure what we can do. I mean, you read people, and I'm, supposedly, a threat to society."

Maria looked me dead in the eye. "We can't just leave them there, so we better think of something."

Our conversation stopped abruptly when a couple of tall figures walked through the open door of the south entrance. It was Thomas Ashford, the Drainer who had come to my house. It looked like his son was with him as well. I remembered him from when Rusty and I were hiding up in my willow tree. It all seemed so long ago now, even though it had only been a couple of days.

"What's the status?" Ashford asked.

A broad woman addressed him quickly. "Caterina is taking care of their piddly army," she said as she pointed toward the ceiling. "She is harvesting them as we speak. We have battalions posted outside the other entrances in case the inhabitants try to get away. We will spread out once you give the word and open all the entrances."

Ashford gazed up at the ceiling with a smirk. "What a lovely sight."

Many of the guards were still struggling, moving their bodies back and forth. Seemed kind of crazy to me that they would be wiggling around. If they somehow managed to get loose, they would plummet to the ground.

Ashford was now focused on the group of injured Wrathful that were off to the side. His expression was much sterner now. "What happened to them?"

"Oh ... well ..." The woman stumbled over her words as she looked at Rusty and the others. "Those three put up quite a fight. But, of course, we were able to restrain them with Caterina's help."

Ashford walked over toward them.

"You're kidding me," Ashford said, sounding amused by the situation. He called out to the guy who looked like his son. "Dalton! This is the guy I was telling you about back in Pennsylvania."

Ashford chuckled a bit. "Looks like you weren't able to get away this time."

"The night is young," Tristan growled at him.

"Is it though?" he questioned. "Seems to me your little secret community has been compromised. What is it called again?" he asked the sturdy-looking woman.

"Underfoot, sir," she answered him.

"Underfoot," he echoed. "What a charming name. Unfortunately for the people who live here, their next home may not be quite so charming. But alas, it is in their best interest in the long run. After all, we all want the same things. Respect for our kind. Rightful leadership. To correct the wrongs of the past."

"I have every intention of correcting the wrongs of the past," Tristan responded. "First on the agenda is to finally get rid of your kind once and for all."

Ashford folded his arms across his chest. "My, my. What high aspirations. I have to say that I find you rather amusing. Going on like that when you're all tied up and were defeated so easily. If only we could bottle that optimism."

He turned to walk away but then swiftly spun back around.

"Wait a minute …" His finger was outstretched as if he were making an important connection. "If you're here, then maybe you brought that kid with the Vinland shoes down here as well."

"Vinland shoes?" Tristan was trying to play dumb. "I don't know what you're talking about."

"That kid who flew on that Vess gargoyle." He got closer to Tristan. "The kid you helped escape."

"We parted ways back at Spook Hill. I have no idea where he is," Tristan said smugly. "Sorry I couldn't be *more* helpful."

"I'm sure we can find ways to make you more helpful," he responded.

"Who does this guy think he is?" Dalton contributed to his father's ridiculing. "You must be an idiot if you think you stand a chance against us. And what's with this guy's turban?"

He turned to Anik. "What are you hiding in there?" He grabbed an end of it, acting like he was going to unravel it.

"I would advise you to not touch it." Anik was staring straight ahead, refusing to make eye contact with the arrogant kid.

Dalton bent down so Anik had no choice but to look at him. "You do realize you lost, right?"

Anik didn't answer him.

"Oh, leave the poor guy alone. No need to make him feel even more like a complete failure," Ashford said. "Besides, we have a whole settlement to conquer. Where shall we start?"

He rubbed his hands as though he were getting ready for a delicious dinner.

The woman in charge clasped her hands behind her back. "Now that most of the guard has been dealt with, we can move forward with our plan."

Ashford seemed to have lost interest in my friends.

"What about the fabled girl that guard told us about?" Ashford asked. "The one who can break the unbreakable. Has she been located?"

"One of the Underfoot guards who aided us went to retrieve her." The woman looked down the path as if they would appear on command. "I'm sure he'll be here at any moment."

If what the woman said was true, that would mean there were more guards who had betrayed Underfoot. Marcus hadn't acted alone. That was a chilling thought.

"Very well," Ashford said. "We should proceed rather quickly. Always best to have the element of surprise. Which, I heard, was compromised by the guard who was supposed to let us in. What was his name?"

"Marcus," the woman answered him. "It seems he was read by a Cerebral."

"Really? This place has a Cerebral?" He sounded excited. "Sounds like this was a worthwhile endeavor, after all. A Cerebral, the fabled Eradicator, and, possibly, the boy with the Vinland shoes. Make sure you put the word out that all members need to be on the lookout for a tall, blond boy in his early teens."

"Yes, sir," the woman said, nodding obediently.

"So they're after both of us," I whispered to Maria. "We have to be careful they don't see us."

"What if we run over there and untie them once they start to leave?" Maria asked.

I gave her an exasperated look. "There's no way it's just normal rope."

She bit her lower lip. "Probably not."

"But I do have this killer sword." I tried to lift it in the air. I scanned the area, looking to see if anyone would notice us running out there when I saw something moving in the grass. It was Rusty's retracted weapon. It was slithering through the grass like a snake, making a beeline right for its owner.

I nudged Maria. "Look, Rusty's weapon came back to him."

The small shaft was climbing up Rusty's leg.

Luckily, no one was paying attention because one of the Underfoot guards showed up with Eyota. He was holding her in front of his body as she struggled to break free, her hands behind her back as if they had been tied.

"Here she is. The famous Eradicator." The guard pushed her in front of him. She almost fell to the ground, but she somehow managed to balance herself. "That little brat bit me."

"That's the Eradicator?" Ashford sounded unimpressed. "Are you sure we haven't been deceived?"

"No, that's her," the guard answered him. "The one and only."

"How very interesting." Ashford walked over to her. Eyota stared up at the tall Drainer. "Perhaps we should conduct a little experiment."

"Sir, I believe we should proceed with the invasion as soon as possible," the sturdy woman commented. She didn't make eye contact though, probably nervous about redirecting the guy in charge.

"Yes, yes. Very well. Just secure her," Ashford said. "Or maybe I should drain her so she's too weak to get away."

"If the rumors are true," the woman paused, "your powers may not work on her."

"Really?" Ashford seemed a bit bothered by the idea. "Very well, tie her up and let's move into the settlement. You can bring the rest of the forces through."

Since the Wrathful were all preoccupied with preparing the attack, I decided now was the time to try to get everyone free.

"I'm going in," I whispered to Maria.

I stayed low to the ground and darted behind Rusty and the others. Of course, Maria followed me.

CHAPTER 32
NOW OR NEVER

"Dude," Rusty said as quietly as possible. "Took you long enough."

"At least *I* didn't get captured," I teased.

"Wasn't exactly my fault," Rusty grumbled. "That crazy lady from your house showed up here."

"Yeah," I whispered. "I saw her."

I tried to use the sword to cut through the rope wrapped around his body, but the blade wasn't cutting anything. It seemed impenetrable.

"It's not working," I whispered to him.

"I can't untie it, either," Maria whispered. "It's like it's glued together."

"Use Rusty's weapon," Tristan said under his breath. "Magic rope requires a magic weapon."

The weapon had found its way into Rusty's hand. I took the shaft and extended it. It shot out so fast, it hit the ground and almost knocked me over. Thank goodness it wasn't glowing for me. I figured it must only glow for its supreme master.

"What the heck, man?" Rusty hissed.

I glanced up to see if anyone had noticed what we were trying to do. Luckily, everyone seemed too preoccupied, preparing to march into the streets of Underfoot. I took the spear and went to work. Surprisingly—though nothing should've surprised me by now—the weapon sliced the rope like butter. I cut through his hand and his feet restraints, then moved on to the ropes that were draped around his body.

Maria grabbed the spear once I was done and went to work on Tristan.

"Hurry up," Rusty said impatiently.

Once Tristan was free, Rusty took back his weapon and began to work on Anik. It started to glow again once Rusty was holding it.

"Can't you dim that thing or something?" I asked. "It's going to draw attention to us."

"I have no idea how this thing works," he said as he shrugged. "Guess we're just going to have to hope they don't notice."

"Just hurry up," I urged him.

"So ... you thought we were the bad guys, huh?" Rusty said to Anik.

"I stand corrected," Anik responded.

"Yes, you do." Rusty was just about done freeing Anik when our luck ran out.

Someone must have noticed us because we were suddenly surrounded by the Wrathful. Anik grabbed the sword I had left on the ground, and Rusty was ready to fight with his spear. Unfortunately, the rest of us weren't much help. Maria's Cerebral skills weren't going to do much good, whatever magic goo was draped around Tristan's hand was preventing him from casting anything, and we'd already established that I was pretty much useless.

It was as though time had stopped. Everyone was still, waiting for someone to make the first move. For a moment, all I could hear was the sound of my ragged breathing.

Then one of the Wrathful soldiers stepped forward and all hell broke loose.

If Rusty looked like a ninja warrior back in the arena, he looked like the king of ninja warriors in that moment. He moved in a circle and somehow prevented the multiple soldiers from reaching any of us. Anik was almost as amazing as Rusty. For such a big guy, he moved swiftly and blocked almost everything that came his way.

"Move!" Ashford's voice echoed through the cave.

The Wrathful soldiers began to move away from us. They were backing up because the green grass was turning to ash. Spreading toward us like a plague. We all stepped backward, trying to escape the impending doom that was headed our way, until our backs hit the cave wall. There were a couple of small trees and vines growing there. Tristan quickly lifted Maria toward one of the trees. "Climb the wall!" he told her.

Anik gave Tristan a concerned look. "This may be the end, my friend."

"'Friend?'" Tristan grinned a little and started to whack his hand against the cave wall, trying to release it from whatever was holding it captive. "Glad to know you finally came to your senses."

The rotting earth was getting closer. We all tried to climb upward. My heart stopped when the tree Anik attempted to pull himself up on cracked, and he fell onto the dying earth. Tristan ran to him and tried to drag him to safety, but his strength appeared to be dwindling as well, and he fell to his knees.

Rusty held his weapon out toward Tristan. "Tristan! Grab on to my spear. I'll pull you to the wall."

Tristan tried to reach for the weapon but was coming up short. I measured the distance between me and Tristan. "Maybe I could just run out there and grab them."

"I'm not sure about that, Larkin," Rusty said.

"But he's not like us," Maria said from above. "He might be able to do it."

"What do you mean?" Rusty asked.

"According to everyone around here, I'm a Drainer," I answered.

"What?" Rusty shrieked.

I had no idea if it was true or not, but I wasn't going to stand there and watch Tristan and Anik shrivel up and turn to ash. I jumped into the center of the charred earth and ran toward Tristan. He was hunched over now, clearly having difficulty breathing, and his skin had a gray hue to it. Anik was in worse shape. His skin appeared to be devoid of moisture, and deep cracks spread across his face and hands. His broad form seemed to be reducing before my eyes. But the worst part was that all I saw in his eyes was fear. I grabbed Tristan's arm and began to drag him away from the center of the black circle. Rusty was leaning down from a crevasse in the cave wall, positioning himself so he could grab Tristan from me.

Then I felt weird again. Tingly. I was hoping it didn't mean the circle of death had claimed me as well, but in my heart, I knew that wasn't it. The tingling had become familiar now. I looked down at the shriveled grass under my feet, but it wasn't black anymore. It was green. And the green was spreading outward from underneath my feet.

Tristan looked up at me. "Are you doing this?" Was I? I didn't know.

The grass under Tristan was green as well now and was heading toward Anik, who was dragging himself toward us. But it soon became clear that he didn't need to because the green spread even farther and traveled beyond him. Anik held his hands in front of his face and watched as his skin began to return to its normal state.

"What kind of magic is this?" Ashford roared.

Dalton came charging at me. "I'll take care of him, Father!"

I didn't know what to do, so I just let go of Tristan and prepared myself for his attack.

"You're going to regret playing in the big leagues." He came at me with his face all scrunched up in anger and pushed me hard onto the ground. Then he kneeled down over me and grabbed me by the hair to direct my gaze toward him. "Do you really think some wimpy kid who hides in a cave like a coward can defeat us?"

He took his other hand and planted it firmly on my chest, which really pissed me off. I decided then and there that if I had any power in me, I was going to focus all of it on this guy. I could feel the pressure of his hand on my chest, but more importantly, I could feel something dark trying to invade my body, but something else was pushing back. It was me. Something strong inside me was resisting the darkness. It was like we were battling out where the dark energy was going to go. Then it happened. Instead of feeling weaker, I could feel a tingling at the points where he was touching me. Unlike the other times this had happened, the tingling moved inward toward my heart.

I felt a powerful burst of energy in the center of my chest, then the feeling spread throughout my body. I no longer felt scared or uncertain. Instead, I felt powerful and strong. Dalton fell to his knees, and I pulled myself off the ground and stood over him. I could feel waves of energy coursing through my body, and that was when I realized that the grass at my feet had grown insanely tall. So tall, it almost reached my knees.

Ashford came barreling toward me. He grabbed his son and threw him away from me. Dalton landed on the pathway in a depleted heap. Now I was just standing on an overgrown patch of grass with a tall Drainer glaring at me.

"What did you do to him?" he shouted at me. His arrogant tone was gone. All I could hear was anger.

What could I say? I had no idea what I had done to him. I glanced back at Tristan, who looked fully recovered. He was standing behind me with a confused expression on his face. Anik was the same. He was revived but bewildered.

I suddenly felt guilty, like I had done something wrong. "I don't ..." I couldn't find the words to explain what had happened.

Tristan lifted his goo-covered hand and pointed at Ashford. "Can you do it again? Do the same thing to him!"

I had no idea if I could do it again. It always just happened out of nowhere. I didn't know if I could even control it. Even if I could, this was Ashford. Tristan's best spell couldn't even take him down. I just kept thinking about being chased by him in the woods back in Lewisberry and how terrifying he was. Now this powerful man was standing in front of me, challenging me. He kneeled down and dramatically slammed both of his hands onto the grassy surface in front of him. I watched as the earth began to rot away again as it headed toward me.

I closed my eyes and focused all my energy on stopping the darkness that was headed my way. Strength built within me again.

There was an overpowering feeling building in my chest, then it traveled downward to the soles of my feet and extended outward into the earth. I opened my eyes and saw that I, too, was creating a charred path. But my path was heading toward Ashford. The two dark paths were going to collide.

Once they did, it no longer just looked like burnt earth. It was now a churning life force. A round mass of dirt, rocks, and roots were churning around each other at an alarming speed. But there was something else deep inside the mass. Bursts of blinding light as the mass circulated around itself. Eventually, the light became more prevalent and reached the outer surface of the rotating earth. It looked like an electrical storm was now covering the ball of earth. Thin currents of energy were crashing into each other, creating explosions with purple and blue hues.

Not only did it look like an electrical storm, but it also felt like one. Gusts of wind swirled through the space and pulled branches and leaves from the nearby trees. A loud buzzing filled the space, and every so often, a loud crashing sound echoed loudly throughout the cave. I didn't want to think about the fact that I was partially responsible for whatever this ball of energy was. I just focused on the fact that I wanted it as far away from me as possible. And then it began to move away from me and inched its way toward Ashford. He was still crouched down with his hands firmly planted on the earth. But when he looked up, his eyes widened as the mass began to move in his direction. He stood up, anger replacing his fear. His eyes were fierce, and his body was stoic like a statue. The others behind him began to back up, forcing themselves closer to the south entrance. A couple of the Wrathful had even dragged Dalton up the stairs and were now standing in front of the south entrance.

The ball of energy was moving faster now, gaining speed and strength. The mass was growing and pulling up the earth with it as it moved, leaving behind a deep recess. Ashford remained firm, and at times, I could almost feel his determination. It felt like his energy was trying to invade my body, but I used all my strength to resist it and push it back. Once I did that, the mass moved even faster. Now it was barreling toward him at a rapid pace.

At that moment, I suddenly felt a hunger inside me. The mass of earth and light hit Ashford with a massive explosion that threw him back and left him lying on his back on the broken ground. Most of the mass was now in pieces around him. I could feel a line of energy reach from my body to his. The power I was feeling was so immense, it was terrifying. I could hear screaming. I could see ghostly images of people flash before my eyes. It was like I was trapped inside an endless nightmare.

Someone grabbed my arm. The images vanished in an instant; it was Maria who had grabbed me.

"I think you should stop draining him," she said with urgency as she pulled me backward. "You don't want his energy inside of you."

I looked at her, but, honestly, everything felt like a dream. It took me a second to even understand what she was saying. Draining him? Was that what I was doing?

"Wren," Maria said firmly and grabbed my face, forcing me to look at her. "Just push them out of here. Can you do that? Can you push them back?"

I didn't know. We were on one side, and they were on the other. Most of them had already made their way toward the entrance. Could I do what Ashford had done and make them run in fear? Wait. Eyota was on the other side. "What about Eyota?" I asked Maria.

"Magic doesn't work on her, remember? Besides, I think Pan is working on freeing her."

Maria was right. The ropes around Eyota's wrists were being shifted by some invisible being who had to be Pan. He needed to work faster. Ashford was already pulling himself up from the ground. His expensive clothes were all soiled and ripped, and a rather large gash was under his left eye. He started to slowly walk toward me with a limp, but I wasn't scared this time. I felt even more powerful than before. More powerful than I had ever felt in my entire life. Somehow, I was able to throw him to the ground again before he got too close. I didn't know how long I could hold him there, though. I could feel his resistance. Even though he was injured, he was still very strong.

"Is Eyota free yet?" I asked Maria without looking at her. I was afraid to turn my attention away from Ashford.

"I think he almost has it," Maria said. "Okay, she's free! Do what you gotta do."

I took a deep breath and focused all my energy on pushing every one of the Wrathful out of Underfoot. The blackened earth spread even farther away from me, and they were all pushed back toward the entrance. Eyota jumped over a patch of the charred earth and ran from the Wrathful. I thought I saw a glimpse of Pan. I hoped he was able to avoid the darkness I was creating.

The Wrathful were being forced farther and farther back. A couple of them even tried to help Ashford up, but he pushed them away violently. Then something happened that I wasn't expecting. The earth started to disintegrate into the ground. There was now a huge, vertical crater in the ground between us and them. Their side of the crater began to crumble and fall into the deep recess. Now the Wrathful had no choice but to retreat. They were all running for the south entrance, even Thomas Ashford.

It wasn't until they were all almost at the entrance that I realized my friends were standing by my side, watching as our enemies fled. Once the intruders had all run through the entrance, a large rock flew toward the opening and sealed the bottom half shut. More and more large rocks flew, and before I knew it, the entryway was now filled with rocks. I didn't understand what was happening until I glanced to my side and saw Tristan's hand was now free and pointing in the direction of the south entrance. Eyota was standing next to him, and there was a puddle of goo on the ground. She must have released his arm from whatever had been stuck to it. More and more objects began to fly toward the door—bits of wood, rocks, dirt, twigs, grass. Layer upon layer, thicker and thicker, until I could no longer tell there had ever been a door there. There was a flash of light, and the newly constructed surface was glowing. At first, it was a brilliant yellow, and then the color slightly receded to a soft glow that rivaled the fake sun.

It was over. We were safe ... for now.

CHAPTER 33
ENDGAME

Rusty broke out in applause, and Maria grabbed and hugged me. I could feel someone squeeze my shoulder. When Maria released me, I turned and saw Tristan smiling at me.

"You did well, mate."

"Did he ever!" Anik grabbed me and lifted me in the air, twirling me around.

Honestly, I was in shock. It didn't make a whole lot of sense that I was able to defeat Ashford. The guy pretty much obliterated the entire forest back in Lewisberry. I was just a kid who barely understood how to use my powers. It didn't seem possible … .

More cheers sounded, and I looked up to see that even the guards who were suspended on the cave ceiling above us were cheering. I gave a small, embarrassed wave.

But one of them wasn't celebrating. He was shouting and jerking his head towards the path. looking a bit freaked out.

I turned around to see what he was pointing at.

It was Caterina with her fan. I had mentally renamed her Dead Eyes. As far as I was concerned, villains deserved a fitting name, and she was definitely the villain in my story. Before I knew what was happening, I was slammed up against the cave wall behind me. It literally knocked the air out of my lungs. As I struggled to breathe, I could see Dead Eyes standing in front of us. Her fan was out, partially covering her face, but I could tell by the look in her eyes that she had a smirk on her face. Behind her were a couple of the Wrathful. I had forgotten she had been walking down the path, flinging the guards to the ceiling. Our victory had been very short-lived. We had gotten rid of the others, but she was the most dangerous of all.

I looked around, my breathing more or less back to normal, and could see we were all being pressed up against the cave wall. Tristan was next to me, trying to pull his hand away from the wall. There was nothing I could do. There was nothing living on the rock wall, nothing to drain.

But there was one person who wasn't plastered against the wall: Eyota. She was still standing tall, staring down Dead Eyes. Dead Eyes flung her fan again, expecting to see Eyota fly toward the wall, but she didn't. Instead, Eyota ran over to us and began to climb a tree so she could reach us. Everything was taller now—the grass, trees, bushes—because of me. I had done that, and Eyota had to rapidly climb the tree in order to get to us. It looked like she intended to reach Tristan first. If she was able to release him from the wall, we might have a chance. But then, Dead Eyes did something with her fan, and the tree was ripped from the earth. Eyota screamed as she was thrown to the ground, mostly concealed by branches and leaves.

"Eyota!" Anik called down to her. "You all right?"

There was no movement.

We all waited in suspense until a hand finally emerged with a thumbs-up signal. I let out a sigh of relief. Eyota pulled herself from the tangled debris of the fallen tree, went to the next tree, and began climbing again. I had to hand it to her. The girl was determined.

"Why isn't my magic working on her?" Dead Eyes growled.

That nickname didn't seem to fit her at the moment. She was showing more emotion than I had seen back at my house. There was fierceness in her eyes. Dead Eyes began walking urgently toward the tree Eyota was climbing.

"Don't let her reach him!" she said to the Wrathful on either side of her.

They began to run toward Eyota, but then something really weird happened. A couple of them tripped, and one of them was being dragged backward. I thought I saw someone running toward Dead Eyes. He was there for a second, then he wasn't. Pan.

"It's Pan," I heard Rusty say, voicing my thoughts. "The ghost guy."

Dead Eyes looked concerned and began to thrust her fan upward. I couldn't tell if she was doing anything to Pan, but one of the Wrathful was now being pulled through the air until he joined the Underfoot guards on the ceiling.

"Ha!" Rusty was definitely enjoying the show.

I was more fixated on Eyota reaching Tristan. I glanced over to see if she had made any progress up the tree. She was about as high as she could go. Her hand was outstretched and extended toward Tristan.

"Come on, Eyota," I encouraged her. "Stretch."

The tree began to shake a little. Was Dead Eyes going to yank this tree out of the ground too? Eyota was so close! I turned back toward Dead Eyes. Maybe I could do something. Maybe if I just concentrated. I was about to close my eyes when I saw the coolest thing. Pan must have grabbed the fan out of her hand because it suddenly flew away from her. It landed on the ground and was caving in as if he had thrown it and was now jumping on it. Then a nearby rock levitated off the ground and began to hit the fan repeatedly. The spines of the fan were mangled and destroyed. The fabric was torn and tattered. The dude was really letting off some steam.

Dead Eyes ran over to the fan and tried to pick it up, but I briefly saw Pan push her away because she fell to the ground. At that moment, Tristan had been released and landed with a *thud* on the ground. He held his tattooed hand high up in the sky and beams of light flew out of his fingertips. They dropped like falling stars above Dead Eyes and the remaining Wrathful. Each light divided into eight fragments and moved downward, circling each of the intruders. Vertical lines connected each horizontal one and created an elongated, birdcage-like structure. Finally, they were captured.

CHAPTER 34

AFTERMATH

Pan put Eyota on his shoulders so she could release the rest of us. It wasn't the most graceful descent back to the ground, but we all survived with a few bumps and scratches. Then we had to deal with the real issues. How were we going to get all the members of the guard back to the ground, and what were we going to do with Dead Eyes and her Wrathful companions?

The first part was relatively easy. The Crafters all got together and created the tallest ladder I had ever seen with the longest slide in the world attached to it. The woodworkers and metalsmiths worked through the night, and before I knew it, Eyota was climbing up to the top of the structure and releasing the guards one after the other. Once they were released, they would get to slide down the killer slide. Not gonna lie, Rusty and I snuck up a couple of times and slid down ourselves. How could we not? It was a sweet ride!

As for the prisoners, well, there were endless heated discussions as to how they should be dealt with. It was tragically ironic that the residents of Underfoot's greatest fear was dark magic, and now the person who had given birth to the unbreakable curse was within their settlement walls. Part of me wished she had been with the others when I was able to push them out; then everyone wouldn't have to figure out what to do with her.

Most of the discussion took place at the lagoon so the Scaled could be involved. Some thought we should just release Dead Eyes and the Wrathful guards up top and then reinforce the crap out of all the entrances. Others had more violent suggestions as to how to deal with them. Tristan argued that we should keep Dead Eyes as leverage against Ashford and the Wrathful. His position was that now that the bad guys knew our location, we needed every advantage we could get. Dead Eyes was very valuable to them, after all.

On the flipside, others pointed out that by keeping Dead Eyes, we were basically guaranteeing that the Wrathful would continue to try to get into Underfoot. I could see their logic.

Honestly, we were in a lose-lose situation.

Eventually, we held a vote, and we decided that, for now, we would build a prison and fortify the settlement against the enemy. Everyone knew it was just a temporary solution to an ongoing problem that wasn't going away anytime soon.

Regardless, Tristan worked tirelessly with the other Casters and Crafters to build the most secure prison possible. Everyone got involved with this. The Potion-Smiths were dousing the exterior walls with more vials than I could count; the Moles reinforced the structure with the most impenetrable steel on Earth; and the Nims positioned poisonous arrows around the periphery to ensure that anyone breaking out of the prison would be struck down before they got very far.

After a few weeks, the structure was ready for its prisoners. On that day, everyone crowded around the pathway that led to the newly built prison to witness Dead Eyes and her Wrathful accomplices walk into their new home. Each of the prisoners was wearing a garment that resembled a straightjacket, except they were covered with written spells that glowed in various shades of gold, amber, and violet. It reminded me of Tristan's tattooed hand. Dead Eyes's gaze was fixed on one person as she walked into the prison that day: Tristan. He stood near the entrance and met her stare with an equally intense glare of his own. One thing was for sure: if Dead Eyes ever got out, Tristan would be the first person she would go after.

Once Tristan felt confident that Dead Eyes and the others were securely locked away, he sat us down one night and told us he was going to venture out to find Maria's parents and Bryn. Of course, we all offered to go with him, but Mrs. Tovar and Tristan had decided that we would be safer in Underfoot. Besides, Tristan already had a travel partner lined up. Surprisingly, that person was Anik. Over the last couple weeks, they had gotten pretty close, and it was possible Anik felt super guilty about not seeing what was going on with Marcus and wanted to make up for the fact that he had trusted the wrong person.

On the day they were leaving, Rusty, Maria, and I stood on the pier to see them off. Mrs. Tovar stayed back because she wasn't a fan of goodbyes. Tristan and Anik were there, bags all packed. A canoe had been prepared for them, and many of the Scaled, the ones who had decided to remain in the lagoon, were there to lead them out. A lot of them chose freedom once they were told the lagoon entrance would be closed for good.

"All right," Tristan said as he put both his hands on Maria's shoulders, "try to keep these two out of trouble."

He nodded toward me and Rusty.

Maria laughed. "I can't make any promises." She reached out and hugged him tightly around his waist.

He closed his eyes as he hugged her back. "I'll bring them back," he said softly. "I promise."

They let go of each other, and Tristan turned his attention to me. "Be sure to figure out how to harness your powers while I'm gone."

That made me uncomfortable. Now that we had established I was a Drainer, I didn't know how to come to terms with it. I just kept putting it off, not dealing with the reality of the situation.

He nudged my arm. "Hey, I'm proud of you, Wren. Maria is right. You're not like them. You're different. You're better. Better than most Vins, in fact."

I was struck by his words. I would've been lying if I said it didn't matter what Tristan thought about me. It mattered a lot. I let his words wash over me and allowed myself to enjoy his praise and acceptance.

"Thanks," I finally said. "Be careful out there."

He gave me a firm nod. "Always."

Suddenly, my attention was drawn to someone who called out Anik's name from the beach. A rather petite woman climbed the pier and began to run down it.

"You can't leave yet!"

Anik dropped his bags, slid by us, and ran toward her.

"Gloria!" he called out to her and met her halfway down the pier. The woman was about half his size and could barely be seen once they embraced.

"Is that the lady he has a thing for?" Rusty asked Maria with a smirk.

"I think so." Maria smiled. "I love happy endings."

"Hopefully, we'll have more of them," Tristan commented as we all watched the lovebirds.

There was a glimmer of sadness in his eyes, and I wondered if he was thinking about my aunt.

He blinked quickly and turned to Rusty. "Rus, lie low and don't be a prat. No more showing off and, whatever you do, keep those shoes on as much as possible."

Concern washed over Rusty's face. "Yeah, about that—I'm not so sure I can pull it off." He leaned in and quietly said, "How am I supposed to continue fooling all these people that I'm one of them? I mean, a couple of weeks is one thing, but for a long period of time … I'm not sure I can do that."

Tristan hit him on the back. "It's not too hard. I managed to do it." Then he jumped on the boat and hollered, "Come on, Anik. Time to go!"

"Wait!" Rusty almost jumped in the boat after him. "What are you saying? Are you saying you're like me?"

Anik was sprinting toward the boat. "Seriously, Rusty," he growled at him and physically moved his body aside. "Why are you always in the way?"

"Wait a minute." Rusty refused to back up. "I need to figure out what he meant."

Tristan just put his finger to his lips as if to imply that what he'd said needed to be kept secret for now. It took me a second to process what was happening. I couldn't believe the most powerful caster in Underfoot wasn't a Vin at all. Just an ordinary guy with magic shoes. If the residents of Underfoot knew the truth, it would blow their minds.

They launched off and headed out toward the outside world. I watched them get smaller and smaller in the distance until I heard the grinding of the cave entrance opening. Once they were through the opening, I turned to head back down the pier.

"Dude," Rusty grabbed my arm and yanked me back, "isn't that your freaky, little friend?"

"What?" I followed the direction of his hand and saw a black bird flying toward us. I shook my head. "No way. It can't be. I mean, it's been, like, weeks."

"Well, he seems to be kind of obsessed with you." Rusty was convinced it was Tough Guy. "Probably was out there, trying to find a way in this whole time."

I wasn't so sure, but I watched it approach, and sure enough, it was coming my way. Once it reached us, it swooped down and landed on my shoulder. It really *was* Tough Guy! I couldn't believe it. He nudged at my check, trying to give me something he had in his mouth. I put my hand out, and he dropped it. It was a tiny, gold object. Upon closer examination, I saw a clasp. I pushed it and it opened. It was a small compass.

"Did you put a spell on that bird or something?" Maria asked.

"Like I would know how to do that," I answered her.

Rusty leaned in to see. "Is that a compass?"

"Looks like it." I turned it around in my hand. It looked ancient.

Maria laughed. "That's ironic. Does your bird know about your shoes?"

"Yeah, it's pretty crazy." I marveled at the strangeness of the gift he had brought me. "It's not like I'll need it ... or my shoes. We're basically prisoners down here."

"For now ..." Maria paused and looked out toward where Tristan and Anik had left the settlement, then she turned back to the beach. "Come on. I told Eyota we would meet her and Pan."

I put the old compass in my pocket, and Rusty and I followed Maria down the pier. We passed Gloria, who smiled at us but still had tears streaming down her face. I had no idea what to say to the woman. Mercifully, Maria did.

"They'll be back before you know it," she tried to reassure the weeping woman as we passed.

Gloria nodded to us, but she didn't respond.

Once we went through the tunnel and were on the streets of Underfoot, many of the people we passed greeted us. Things had definitely changed; most of the glances were no longer untrusting and suspicious. They were friendly.

"Where are we meeting Eyota and Pan?" I asked Maria.

"Just up ahead," she said, pointing toward the town square.

"Oh, please no!" I exclaimed once I realized where we were going.

Maria laughed. "I mean, it is the center of town."

I gave her an exasperated look. "Come on. You could have picked *anyplace* else."

In the middle of the street, where the fountain had been before it got blown up, was a statue of me—the Vins had used their fancy magic to build it in just a matter of days. It was beyond embarrassing.

"I don't look like that," I said as we approached Eyota and Pan.

"No, you don't," Rusty said. "You're much dorkier."

"Whatever, Rusty," I said, giving him a little shove. "I mean, why did they do this? It's not like I was the only one responsible for getting rid of Ashford and the Wrathful. We all played a part."

"True that!" Rusty exclaimed. "I couldn't agree with you more. I have a couple of battle scars to prove it."

I ignored Rusty's comment. "As far as I'm concerned, Pan is the real hero. He's the one who stopped Dead Eyes."

"I guess," Pan said. I saw a glimpse of his face and wisps of his dark hair out of the corner of my eye. "But how are you going to make a statue of someone you can't really see? I mean, barely anyone even knows what I look like."

"The sculptors could've used mirrors," Maria commented. "It's not like it would've been impossible to sculpt you."

"Can we all relax about what a hero Pan is?" Rusty was glaring at Maria. I got the impression he didn't like how much praise she was giving Pan. "Now that we have all given homage to the amazing Wren and the extraordinary Pan, can we get something to eat?"

Maria sighed. "Calm down, Rusty. Everyone knows you are a force to be reckoned with."

That shut Rusty up, and his pout instantly turned into a smirk. "Really? Please, go on." Rusty folded his arms across his chest, waiting for her to continue.

I *definitely* didn't need to hear this, so I walked over to Eyota, who was standing in front of the statue.

"I think it's awesome," Eyota said as I approached. She was examining it like she was an art critic. There were words engraved on the bottom of the statue.

"The Replenisher," Eyota read aloud and then turned toward me. "That's a perfect name for you."

"Okay, for once, I agree with Rusty. Time to change the subject and get some food." I repositioned her body so she was facing the opposite direction of the statue.

"More importantly," she continued as she glanced back at me, "why is there a black bird sitting on your shoulder?"

"It's a crow," I answered her. "Let's just say he's an old friend. Now, are there any good places to get something to eat down here?"

And then we were off to find something to eat. All five of us—or six, if you counted Tough Guy. I went from zero to four friends plus a pet bird in a few weeks.

One thing was for sure: never again would I question the absurd. Everything was up for consideration, even going to Vinland. If my grandfather had wanted me to go to the hidden realm, he must've had a reason, and, deep down, I knew the shoes would lead me there. It was just a matter of when.

CPSIA information can be obtained
at www.ICGtesting.com
Printed in the USA
BVHW042339270623
666488BV00006B/49/J

9 781954 614505